THE GIRL YOU THOUGHT I WAS

Also By Rebecca Phillips

These Things I've Done

THE GIRL

YOU

THOUGHT

I WAS

Rebecca Phillips

An Imprint of HarperCollinsPublishers

HarperTeen is an imprint of HarperCollins Publishers.

ISBN 978-0-06-257094-9 (trade bdg.)

Typography by Torborg Davern
18 19 20 21 22   PC/LSCH   10 9 8 7 6 5 4 3 2 1

First Edition

For my parents

Chapter One

THE BIKINI HAS BLACK AND WHITE STRIPES AND
little turquoise beads attached to the ends of the strings. It's
probably expensive, but that doesn't matter because this is it.
The one. I move closer and rub the smooth fabric between my
fingers.

I want it.

No. I *need* it.

Showing up at Jasmine Tully's school's-out-for-summer
pool party in my old, stretched-out one-piece that I've had
since ninth grade isn't an option. Most of the girls will be
wearing cute swimsuits, probably freshly selected at the mall.
Or maybe even from a boutique downtown. But I'm smart

enough to stay away from little shops, where the risk of being noticed is a lot greater. At least this department store has some cute clothes.

With practiced ease, I turn over the price tags. The bikini top alone is thirty dollars, on sale. The bottoms are twenty-two. Over fifty dollars for a few tiny scraps of fabric, which seems silly to me. Like so many other things, the smaller it is, the more you pay.

I think of the two twenties in my wallet—the last of my savings—and turn my back on the swimsuit section. I start browsing through a rack of shirts, my senses on high alert. It's Saturday afternoon, a busy time for big-box stores, and several other shoppers are buzzing around the women's section. Casually, I check them out: an old woman slowly pushing a cart. A skinny blonde picking through activewear. A pretty mom flanked by two small boys fighting over who gets to carry a package of cookies. None of them look even remotely like a loss prevention officer, which is the official job title for those creepy plainclothes people who lurk in the aisles and try to catch people stealing. But that doesn't mean there aren't any around. As usual, the tips I learned from the internet flash through my mind.

Never let your guard down. Stay paranoid, even when you know the store.

I do know this store. I spent weeks studying the layout, locating the cameras, and figuring out all the blind spots. I learned the best times and days to go and what some of the LP officers look like. But no matter how many times I do this, no matter how confident I've become, the paranoia never stops. And it shouldn't. Arrogance can make you sloppy.

I adjust my purse against my shoulder and drift over to a table display of jeans. They're not my style, but it doesn't matter. I take my time digging through the pile and eventually pull out a pair in my size. Draping them over my forearm, I double back to the shirts. That thick blue-and-white flannel one I spotted a few minutes ago will work just fine.

Blend in. Don't give anyone a reason to suspect you.

One good thing about being short—blending in is easy. No one would ever suspect the tiny red-haired girl with the glasses and cute dusting of freckles across her nose. I look like a bouncy student-council-president type, someone who organizes fund-raisers for new gym equipment and paints her face at football games. Not a criminal.

No one looks at me twice.

I pick out a flannel shirt in size small. It's almost summer and getting warm, but a good flannel is always useful. I hold it by its hanger and continue to browse, slowly, picking things up and putting them back, flipping through tops and camis, the metal hangers screeching against the rack. Typical shopper behavior. All the while, I'm listening. Watching. Aware. I know there's a camera above me, but I don't look at it. That's just asking for trouble.

It's time. I make my way over to swimwear again. By now, I have two more shirts hanging from my hand. Cute ones that I'm actually going to buy. Because it's always smart to act normal and go through the checkout.

The bikini is right where I left it. Looking at it again, I see that both pieces have sensor tags. No big deal. I find size smalls in each and hook the hangers over my fingers, positioning them behind the shirts so they're not in full view. Step one—done.

Take advantage of blind spots.

I start walking, making sure my pace isn't stiff or overly fast. In the distance, the housewares section stretches out across several aisles. It's an area, I've discovered, that's not closely monitored. A blind spot. I stroll down an aisle and stop in front of a display of curtains. After double-checking to make sure the aisle is empty, I quickly tuck the bikini into the unbuttoned plaid shirt, then adjust the fabric until it's completely hidden. Step two.

The fitting rooms are across from women's underwear, a short walk away. I continue to browse as I go, head facing forward, pausing every so often to flip through a rack. Cool and casual. No one appears to be following me or paying any attention to me. I'm good to go.

"How many, honey?"

The woman working the fitting rooms barely looks at me.

4

She's busy digging through a messy pile of clothes and putting things back on hangers.

I show her my selections. "Four."

She nods and gets a little plastic hanger with the number four on it, then unlocks a change room. I thank her and slip inside, my heart thumping. The nervous anticipation makes me feel weightless and dizzy, like I'm floating somewhere outside myself. All I can think about is the goal in front of me—doing what I have to do and then getting out as quickly and smoothly as possible.

I drop the jeans on the bench and hang up the three tops. Above the row of hooks, there's a sign: *Shoplifters Will Be Prosecuted*. A scare tactic. Change rooms aren't monitored, and this store doesn't have the extreme types of LP officers who slide mirrors under the doors. No eyes are on me right now, and for the first time in twenty minutes, I take in a full breath.

The bikini is still hidden securely in the flannel shirt. I free it and hang both pieces on a hook of their own. After stripping down to just my underwear, I slide the bottoms up my legs, silently praying that everything fits. Because if it doesn't, I might have to try again tomorrow, when the store isn't quite as busy and the risk of detection is greater. *Please let it fit.*

So far so good. I slip the bikini top on next, tying the strings with slightly shaky fingers. It feels good. Comfortable. I let out a small sigh of relief as I study my reflection. Looks pretty good too. Better than my ratty one-piece, anyway.

As silently as possible, I unlatch my purse and dig out my hook—a small, curved piece of metal that removes several types of security tags—which I ordered online a few months ago. I grip the tag attached to the bikini bottom and work the tip of the hook into the hole on the end. I need to push with enough force to remove the pin, which isn't always easy. But this time the tag pops off right away. I do the same with the one on the top, then stick both tags into the pockets of the jeans I brought in just for this purpose. And that's step three.

Quickly, I get dressed again, arranging my clothes over my new bikini. I twist around, checking to see if anything shows. The ties at the back of my neck stick out a little, but once I put my jacket on, they're no longer noticeable. Satisfied, I stuff the hook in my purse, along with my bra, and grab the rest of the stuff I came in with. In total, I was in here for about ten minutes. Completely respectable.

When I emerge, the woman is still hanging up discarded clothes. I smile at her as I return the number four hanger.

"How'd you do?" she asks, her gaze flicking to the items in my hands. The same number I went in with, as far as she knows.

"This doesn't fit me." I hand over the flannel shirt but keep the jeans. She might feel the security tags in the pockets, and if that happened, it would be all over.

"Have a good day," she tells me, turning back to her work.

"You too."

I head for the checkouts with the jeans and the two shirts I plan to buy. On the way, I furtively dump the jeans on a ransacked table of T-shirts. Thirty or so feet to the checkouts. Twenty feet. Still facing straight ahead, I shift my eyes back and forth. No one is watching me. I strain my ears, listening. No footsteps behind me. No one is trailing. I reach the checkout and stand in line behind a tired-looking man with a baby in a car seat. The baby smiles at me, drool dripping down her chin, but I'm too focused on my pounding heart and the tingling feeling in my limbs to smile back. Just a few more minutes.

You're not free yet. Not until you're leaving the parking lot. Until then, don't assume.

When it's my turn, I set the shirts on the counter.

"Find everything you were looking for today?" the cashier, a girl about my age, asks brightly as she scans my stuff. Each beep echoes through my head, the sound amplified.

"Yes," I say, trying not to fidget. I resist the urge to adjust the collar of my jacket again and dig out my cash instead.

"That'll be thirty-two fifty-nine."

I hand over my twenties, already damp from the sheen of sweat on my palms. The cashier gives me my change and receipt, and I leisurely take my bag, like I'm in no hurry to leave. Next comes the most nerve-racking part. Nothing can be done to you in the store itself—but once you're outside those doors, you're fair game.

"Have a nice afternoon," the cashier says as I walk away.

"You too."

The doors have alarm towers on each side, which I don't need to worry about since I know enough to remove security tags. What I do need to worry about is getting stopped by a perceptive employee or an LP officer outside the doors. I've read stories online about even the smartest lifters getting caught and then taken to a room to be grilled for hours. Obviously, they got sloppy.

I won't let myself get sloppy.

As I approach the exit, I keep my receipt in my hand in case the alarms do go off for some reason and I need proof for my purchases. But nothing happens as I pass through, and just like that, I'm stepping out into the warm, late-May rain.

Don't pause. Don't look around. Just keep walking.

No footsteps. No angry voice yelling for me to stop. No firm hand on my arm. Like always, I walk away free.

My black Honda Civic is parked near the end of the lot. I get in and toss the bag on the passenger seat, automatically glancing in the mirrors for approaching security. All I see is an old lady wearing a plastic rain bonnet, shuffling toward the store.

The adrenaline drains out of my body, and suddenly I'm exhausted. Confident that no one's coming for me, I lean back against the seat and shut my eyes for a moment. As I do, I catch a whiff of my mother's vanilla-scented perfume. This used to be her car, before she left. I've tried everything from air fresheners to leaving the windows open for days to get rid of the smell, the reminder of her. But it still lingers, trapped forever in the seat fabric.

I drive home in the rain with my window open wide, turquoise beads digging into my back the whole way.

Chapter Two

THE MINUTE I GET HOME, I GO STRAIGHT TO MY room and take off the bikini.

It happens like this every time. First, the nervous buildup. Then, the rush of adrenaline in the moment, followed by the crash of calm when it's over. And finally, the hot, prickly guilt, settling like a thorny knot in my stomach. I've never had a hangover, but I imagine this is what people feel like after a weekend of binge drinking, their bodies heavy with exhaustion and shame.

The shame is what lasts the longest. At least until I start the cycle all over again.

I fold the bikini as small as it will go and place it in the corner of my underwear drawer. I don't *need* to hide the things I take—my father never snoops in my room or notices any of the various items I come home with—but I prefer to store my hauls where I don't have to look at them every day.

Fergus, my fat orange tabby, saunters into my room as I'm getting back into my clothes. He sits on the edge of the rug and stares at me with wide eyes.

"Hungry?" I ask.

He lets out a squeaky meow and bolts for the door. I follow him into the kitchen, where I open a can of food and slop it into his bowl. He digs in like he hasn't eaten in weeks. A year ago, when I moved in with my dad permanently, I was so happy when I discovered that Maple View Apartments were cat-friendly. I've had Fergus since I was six; I'm not sure I would have chosen to live here if it meant leaving him with my mother.

As Fergus eats, I go back to my room and open my laptop, thinking I might watch a movie to help calm myself down. My throat tightens when I realize I forgot to shut down the browser this morning after my daily blog check-in.

I found the Tumblr community by accident one day when I Googled "shoplifting tips." For the next two hours, I clicked through dozens of blogs written by people like me—people who take things without paying. Some bloggers post pictures of their hauls, proudly announcing what their stolen objects are worth. Others post tips and tricks, detailing which stores are easy to lift from and which to steer clear of entirely. I've learned everything I know from this community.

Sometimes I think about starting my own blog, but I'm too paranoid. What if it's traced back to me? Besides, I don't want to show off what I've taken and the value of each item. I'm not proud of what I do. Of what I've become. So for now, I just lurk and take it all in.

But I'm not in the mood for lurking right now, not with the guilt still churning in my stomach. A movie doesn't sound appealing anymore either, so I close the laptop and reach for my backpack instead. Finals start in two weeks, and I have a lot to prepare.

I'm still sorting through my notes when I hear Dad come home at six. Ready for a break, I throw down my pen and shuffle out to the kitchen, where he's placing a grease-stained pizza box on the counter. I sniff. Mushrooms and sausage.

"Nazario's tonight," he says when he sees me. "Sausage and mushrooms."

Knew it. My father and I eat a lot of takeout. I've gained about ten pounds since moving here.

"Yum." I open the box and pull out a slice, then slap it on a paper towel. We don't bother with dishes half the time. "How was work?"

Dad picks out his own slice and immediately drops a glob

of sauce on his tie. He looks at it, shrugs, and chomps off a bite of pizza. "It was work."

When I was little and teachers asked me to draw a picture of my family, I always drew my dad in his suit. That's how I knew him—he wore a tie and sold cars to people. He's done both for as long as I can remember.

"Any sales?" I rip off another paper towel and pass it to him.

Instead of answering, he takes another bite, chewing slowly. I study his face. Since Mom left, the lines around his eyes and mouth have been getting deeper by the day. Lately, they seem to be multiplying too. Though he'd never admit it, I know that sales have slowed down at the dealership. Every salesperson has bad months, but usually the good ones make up for it. Since January, it seems like most of his months have been bad. I'm not sure if business has slowed down in general or if he's been off his game since the separation. In any case, it worries me.

"How was your day?" He dabs at his tie, ignoring my question altogether.

I do the same with his. "Dad, I can give up my car. I told you this."

"And I told you no, you are not giving up your car. You need it to get to school."

"School's almost over."

"Okay, then you need it for your summer job."

I lean my hip against the counter. "Royal Smoothie isn't far. I can take the bus."

Dad frowns and puts down his pizza. "Morgan. Your car isn't breaking the bank, okay? Focus on acing your exams and let *me* worry about what we can and can't afford. That's a parent's job. Got it?"

"Fine."

"Good." He picks up his slice again and tears off a piece of crust. "*Breaking Bad* later?"

I nod. Shortly after I moved in, we started binging TV series we'd both managed to miss the first time around. Over the past few months, we've fallen into the habit of watching a couple of episodes a night, usually accompanied by large bowls of ice cream. It's something we both look forward to, a quiet bonding over sugar and addictive TV.

We finish our pizza and I go back to my room, shutting the door behind me. The shame from earlier mixes with a fresh blast of concern for my dad, making me want to scream into my pillow. I know he's right—my car is more than affordable with his discount at the dealership, but still. When I think about all the other bills he has to pay—rent, food, my sister's college tuition, lawyer fees—the last thing I want is to add to it in any way. His bad months weren't so bad when he and Mom were together and contributing equally, but now that it's just us . . .

Eager for a distraction that doesn't involve studying, I grab my phone and send a text to my sister.

Hey, Rach. Call me?

I know from experience that it can take forever to hear back from Rachel, so I crack open my English notebook again. I'm skimming through some *Lord of the Flies* worksheets when my phone buzzes.

"What's up?"

My sister's voice is almost drowned out by what sounds like a dozen barking dogs. Either she's still at work or she adopted a litter of puppies.

"Nothing's up." I lie back on my pillows. "Just wanted to see how you are. I haven't heard from you in days."

"Awww," she coos. "You miss your big sis?"

I snort like this is the silliest thing ever, even though I miss her like crazy. Last year, when she got accepted into her top-choice university, I tried to be happy for her even though it meant she'd be moving a thousand miles away. *She'll be back for holidays*, I reasoned at the time, *and summers*. I was half right. She did come back for Christmas, but she landed a job in the spring and decided to stick around there for the summer, so I haven't seen her since.

"Did I catch you at work?" I ask.

"Yeah. Just finishing up." Another series of barks punctuates her sentence. Rachel works as a veterinarian's assistant at an animal shelter, which she says will help her chances when she applies to veterinarian school. "What have you been up to?"

"Studying."

"How's Dad?"

"He's fine. Working a lot."

The barking ceases as she presumably leaves the shelter. "Well, that's good, right?"

For a second—a very quick second—I have the urge to lay everything out to her. Dad's bad months. The way his shoulders sag, like he's being bowed by an invisible weight. The stolen bikini secreted away in my drawer. But Rachel left partly to get away from all the mess here, so I let it go and change the subject. "So what's new with you?"

"Nothing much. I've been working a lot too. Like six days a week. I haven't had time to do laundry or clean in weeks, and I'm pretty sure my apartment is about to be condemned by the Board of Health."

I laugh, remembering the state of Rachel's bedroom at our old house. Mine was always neat and organized, while hers looked like the aftermath of a tornado. When she lived here with Dad and me last summer and slept on the pull-out couch, her mess spread to every room. "Like you'd clean even if you did have the time," I tease.

"Oh, shush," she says. "Hey, speaking of laundry, you haven't seen my black peasant top around, have you? I could have sworn I had that."

I look down at my torso, clad in her missing shirt. It's one of my favorites. "Um, I think I've seen it."

She snorts. "Mess it up and you're buying me a new one." There's a short pause, and I hear a car door slam. "Anyway, I'm glad you asked me to call, because I have some news," she says, her tone brightening.

"Yeah?"

"I'm coming home for a week at the end of summer! Booked my plane ticket last night."

I sit up, knocking half my notes on the floor. She's coming *home*. My chest suddenly feels a million times lighter. "Really? That's awesome."

"I was going to bring Amir, but he couldn't get the time off work."

"Oh, that's too bad." Amir is her boyfriend. She met him four months ago in microbiology class, and I don't know much about him other than he looks cute in the pictures Rach sends me. I do want to meet him, but I'm also kind of glad I'll have my sister to myself.

She lets out a sigh. "I should probably let you go now. I'm meeting some friends for dinner."

"Okay." Bitterness rises in my throat, but I swallow it back. Rachel turned her life around. She has goals now, a hot boyfriend, a job she loves. I should be happy for her, not resent her for leaving me back here to deal with everything alone.

"Say hi to Dad for me, okay? And Fergus."

"Sure. Bye, Rach."

"Bye, Morgan."

I end the call and lie there, staring at the ceiling. TV voices filter under my closed door, signaling that Dad is waiting for me in the living room, ready to fire up Netflix. Still feeling zapped from earlier, I consider telling him that I want to skip it tonight. But then I think about the lines in his face, the apprehension in his eyes whenever he looks at me. Like he's wondering if I'm going to end up leaving him too.

I get up and make my way to the kitchen, where I dish up two big bowls of double chocolate chunk ice cream.

Chapter Three

"I'M TOTALLY GOING TO FAIL THE EXAM FOR THIS class," Alyssa says as we walk out of English together on Monday. "I *hate* essay questions."

"Same," I say, though neither of us has gotten below a B on a test in our lives, let alone failed. "Luckily it's only worth twenty-five percent of our final grade."

"Remind me again why we took AP English this semester?"

"Because we hate ourselves?"

She flicks her dark hair over her shoulder. "Clearly."

As we shove through the sweaty crowd to our lockers,

Alyssa's phone buzzes in her pocket. She digs it out and looks at the screen. "Sophie texted. Everyone's waiting for us outside."

We drop our books in our lockers and head down the stairs to the north door, the exit closest to the student parking lot. As we step out into the sunshine, we spot Sophie and her boyfriend, Zach, seated close together on a picnic table. Dawson, Zach's best friend, is beside them, sitting on top of the table with his feet on the bench part. Alyssa and I make our way across the lawn.

"Finally," Zach says when we reach them. "What took you so long?"

Alyssa squints through the sun at him. "Class ran a bit late. You know how Blackburn likes to hear himself talk."

Sophie scoots even closer to Zach to make room for me to sit. As I do, Dawson scrambles off the table and brushes away some invisible dirt before offering the spot to Alyssa. She smirks at him and sits on the opposite bench instead, making me laugh.

My friends have definitely been my bright spot this year. Alyssa and I have been tight since middle school, but we didn't start hanging out with Sophie, Zach, and Dawson until last fall, when the five of us were grouped together for a Global History project. After that, we were together all the time. We're what our parents call "good kids," meaning we generally take school seriously and none of us drink, smoke, or do drugs.

We're probably a little geeky, by some people's standards, but we're all fine with that.

None of my friends know about my dirty little habit. They'd never suspect it. I think they'd fall over in shock if they found out about the bikini, or the mascaras and lipsticks, or the dozens of other things I haven't paid for in the past year.

"Are we getting lunch or what?" Sophie says. "I'm going to, like, pass out from hunger."

"Shocking," Zach says, flicking his longish brown hair out of his eyes. Sophie's enormous appetite is well known in my circle of friends. She's five foot one—an inch shorter than me—and weighs about as much as my cat, but she eats like a truck driver. She's an interesting visual contrast to Zach, who's almost six feet tall.

"Beacon Street Diner?" I say as the five of us head for the parking lot. I'm not sure why I bother asking—we always end up there when we leave the school grounds for lunch. The food is plentiful and cheap, and the service is so quick that we've never had any issue making it back for our afternoon classes.

Everyone agrees and we all pile into my car. Since I'm the only one with my own wheels, it's usually me who carts everyone around. I don't mind, but I did give my friends two rules: pay me gas money once in a while, and no fighting over music. They follow the first rule only sporadically, and ignore the second one altogether.

"You are *not* playing that twangy country shit." Dawson

grabs Zach's phone as he's attaching it to the auxiliary cable that's dangling between the front seats.

"Hey," Zach says, lunging over Sophie's lap to snatch it back. "Hands off my phone, asshole."

Sophie squeals and pushes him away. My seat rocks forward as Zach's long legs collide with the back of it.

Alyssa raises her eyebrows at me from the passenger seat, like she's waiting for me to control these animals. I love my friends . . . love them enough to make the long trek into the city every day to Nicholson High, even though I'm in a different school district now. Love them enough to sit in congested lunchtime city traffic for who knows how long just so we can eat together at our favorite diner. But if these boys don't behave, I swear I'm going to make them walk.

I disconnect the aux cord and turn on the radio. A catchy old eighties song comes on and the scuffling stops. For now.

At the diner, we claim our regular booth by the kitchen and take our usual places—Alyssa and Dawson on one side, and me, Sophie, and Zach crowded in on the other. We've tried various other seating combinations over the past few months, but Zach and Sophie always wind up side by side, Dawson gravitates toward Alyssa in most situations, and I'm compact enough to fit pretty much anywhere.

"Are we all going to Jasmine's pool party on the eighteenth?" Sophie asks while we're waiting for our food.

"I am," I say. I think of the bikini, still folded up in my drawer.

Alyssa slaps her hand on the table. "Oh, that reminds me! I need a swimsuit cover."

Dawson's gaze flicks down to her curvy body, like he's wondering why she'd ever want to cover it up. Maybe it's because I'm used to studying surroundings and reading certain vibes, but I seem to be the only one who's picked up on the massive crush Dawson has on Alyssa. Then again, maybe Zach and Sophie *have* noticed, but like me, they've decided not to mention it because they're afraid of messing up the group dynamic.

"I saw cute swimsuit covers at Forever 21," Sophie tells her.

Alyssa bumps my foot under the table. "Maybe Morgan will take us to the mall after school."

"Sure," I mumble around my straw.

"Count me out," Zach says. "Dawson too. We're going to my house to study for physics. And play some *Doom*."

Dawson grins, teeth bright against his dark-brown skin. "First I've heard of this, but okay." The two of them fist-bump over the table.

"You're playing *Doom* without me?" Sophie whines, but then gets distracted when the waitress appears with our food.

As we eat, everyone starts discussing Jasmine's party and who might be there. I focus on the conversation, trying to ignore the way my heart speeds up at the thought of going shopping later. Instead, I let myself imagine the summer ahead and all the fun I plan to have with my friends.

The mall is dead, even for a Monday afternoon. Alyssa, Sophie, and I ride the escalator up to the third floor and go directly to Forever 21. The store is virtually empty.

Sophie leads us to where she saw the cover-ups and immediately pulls one out. "How about this?"

Alyssa and I laugh. She's holding a white crocheted dress that wouldn't cover anything.

"Um, no," Alyssa says, taking the dress from Sophie and putting it back on the rack. "My mother would freak."

I used to tease her regularly about her overprotective mother, but not anymore. Since Alyssa's father died a year and a half ago, her mother's gotten even more clingy and smothering. Alyssa tolerates it because the thought of telling her mom she needs space, after all they've been through, makes her feel like a horrible daughter.

I wonder what it's like, having a mother who values you that much.

"This," Sophie says, pulling out a rose-colored maxidress, "is super cute."

Alyssa frowns. "Don't those usually look better on, um, smaller-chested women?"

"Says who?" I ask. "You can wear whatever you want, Lyss."

"That's right." Sophie holds the dress up to Alyssa's front. "You're gorgeous."

She sighs. "Let's keep looking."

After fifteen minutes of scouring the racks, Alyssa finds a simple black dress with spaghetti straps. She presses it to her body so we can see how it looks with her dark hair and coloring.

"Perfect," I say. Sophie agrees.

Alyssa buys the dress without trying it on and the three of us leave the store. My body tenses as we pass through the door, even though I know we're fine. I'd never take something with my friends around. If I got caught, they'd probably go down with me, and I'd never risk that.

"Let's go get some frozen hot chocolate," Sophie suggests.

"Sure." Luckily, I still have five dollars or so left from the twenty Dad slipped me last night. Chocolate anything sounds good.

We head to the food court, which is located on the bottom floor, two escalator rides down. On the way, we pass a brightly lit electronics store. Just outside the entrance are two wire bins piled high with discounted movies, mostly the straight-to-DVD kind that few people have heard of or ones that were semipopular decades ago. I pause to look through them.

"You and your cheap Blu-ray obsession," Alyssa says as she

and Sophie come to a halt beside me.

I dig around in the pile, moving aside the top layers of cases so I can see what's hiding underneath. "You never know what kind of gems you might find in these clearance bins."

"Yeah, like"—Sophie picks up one of the movies I've discarded and looks at the cover—"*Maximum Punishment Three*. I didn't even know there was a one and two."

"Aren't most of these on Netflix, anyway?" Alyssa asks.

"No." I give up on the first bin and start on the other. "Besides, you know I like to own copies of my favorites." She's probably figured out why too, even though I've never said the reason out loud. But Alyssa knows that watching movies was something I always did with my mother. She's a huge film buff—everything from classics to indie to popular mainstream—and she had me watching things like the *Lord of the Rings* trilogy while other kids my age were watching Disney. My father and sister both have limited attention spans and prefer their entertainment in sixty-minutes-or-less chunks, so movie time with my mom always felt special. Something that just the two of us shared.

But that was before. Now I mostly watch movies alone, in my room. Or with my friends, even though they gravitate toward whatever is current and popular and can't understand my desire to watch stuff that was released before we were even born.

"Yes, we know about your favorites," Sophie says, grabbing

my hand and slowly tugging me away from the bin. No one stands between Sophie and her quest for sustenance. "We've seen your movie collection."

"*And* your penguin collection," Alyssa adds with a grin. They both think it's adorable that I like to collect things. *You don't have a normal amount of anything*, they like to say when they're in my room. It's true. I have stockpiles of stuff all over the place—shoes, scented candles, perfumes, pens. Not to mention the penguin-themed items, which I collect simply because I think penguins are cute.

"Okay, okay," I say, letting them lead me away. There's nothing of interest in the bins anyway, and even if there were, my last five dollars is destined for that frozen hot chocolate.

Arms linked, the three of us continue to the food court. When we reach the bottom of the first escalator, I feel a twinge in my abdomen and realize I haven't peed since the two Cokes I downed at lunch.

"I'll meet you guys there," I tell my friends. "Gotta hit the bathroom."

"Want us to come with?"

I wave them off. "I'll just be a minute."

Alyssa shrugs. "Okay."

We go our separate ways and I make a beeline for the closest bathroom, which is inside Nordstrom. By the time I wash my hands and step out into the store again, I feel a lot better. As I make my way to the exit, the only thought in my head is

getting to the food court, where my friends and cold, choco-
latey goodness await.

Then I walk past the sunglasses section.

Dozens of them sparkle at me from rows of mirrored display cases, each one illuminated by a backdrop of soft, white
light. Normally, I avoid bright, highly visible areas, but for
some reason I'm drawn to that light like a moth.

I pause for a moment, my eyes reflexively scanning the
vicinity for cameras. None that I can see. Maybe this is a blind
spot. My gaze lands on the twenty-something woman behind
a counter nearby, who's ringing up a customer. She doesn't
look up or acknowledge my presence at all. I casually move
toward the sunglasses and immediately spot the perfect pair,
right in front, at my eye level. The frames are the same color
turquoise as the little beads on my new bikini. It's like they're
here just for me.

I risk a glance at the saleswoman. She's still with the customer, talking and laughing. Has she even seen me? Probably, but she's not concerned. She's too busy gabbing about the
vacation she just got back from, how big the waves were on
the beach. Then the customer, an older woman, starts talking
about *her* recent vacation. I'm practically invisible over here.

My movements smooth, I reach up and free the sunglasses. The price tag makes my heart thump. One hundred
and eighty-five dollars. For sun-blocking eyewear. They're
designer, but still.

I go to put them back, then think about how perfectly they'd go with my bikini. How awesome I'd look in them at Jasmine's party. How I really need a decent pair of sunglasses, even though I only wear them when I have contacts in, which isn't often.

I promised myself on the way here that I'd look but not touch, and certainly not take. But I'm alone, at least for the moment, and I've lifted from this store before without getting caught. I can do it again. Plus, I really want these sunglasses.

Aware, always aware, of the two voices behind me, I transfer the sunglasses to my other hand and then lift my right arm, pretending to reach for another pair up top. When my purse gapes open with the movement, I quickly slip the sunglasses inside.

"Thanks! Have a great day."

"You too!"

The two women's voices feel incredibly loud in my ears. My heart's gone from thumping to galloping, and I know I have to get out of here *now*. I wouldn't dare do my go-through-the-checkout trick here. Too brazen. It's best if I leave as quickly as possible.

"Is there something I can help you find?"

I turn around. The saleswoman is smiling at me from behind the counter, like I'm a completely normal customer who doesn't have a pilfered pair of one-hundred-and-eighty-five-dollar sunglasses in her purse.

"No, thanks," I say, and I smile back at her and start walking toward the exit. As usual, I hold my breath as I pass through the door, and when nothing happens, I slowly let it out.

Home free. Again.

Adrenaline still pulsing through my veins, I veer right toward the food court, where my friends are waiting for me. *Breathe, Morgan. Look normal.* I'm so focused on composing myself, it takes me a few seconds to notice the sound of footsteps behind me.

"Excuse me, miss."

I freeze. Everything freezes. *Shit.*

"Miss? I'm with security. Can you come back inside the store with me, please?"

My stomach drops, and I force myself to turn around. A middle-aged man with a beard stands in front of me, dressed in street clothes. Loss prevention officers come in all shapes, ages, and sizes.

"What?" I ask, playing dumb. This can't be happening. I'm too careful. "Why?"

His expression is unmoving. Solemn. "I just watched you steal a pair of sunglasses. That's why. Follow me, please."

I consider running. Can I run faster than this guy? He's not in the best shape. Then again, neither am I. And if I run, he might chase me, and we'd make a scene, and someone I know might see me. One of my *friends* might see me. Oh God. How am I going to explain this to Sophie and Alyssa?

The fight-or-flight instinct in me drains away. I'm not going to do either. The best choice I have right now is to go quietly.

I look at the security guy. He nods at me, like he can sense my decision and approves. I step forward and let him lead me away.

Chapter Four

THE FIRST THING I EVER STOLE WAS A PACKAGE OF purple bubble gum. I was three. As the story goes, I kept it in my pocket until my mom and I got to the car. Then, when she was driving, she heard the crackle of the wrapper and glanced back to see me shoving piece after piece into my mouth. She turned right back around to the store, made me spit out the gum, and marched me inside so I could explain to the cashier what I'd done.

"We can't take things that don't belong to us," she said on the drive home, after giving me a few coins to pay for the gum and making me apologize—through humiliated sobs—for stealing.

I remember none of this, but my mother used to tell the story often, always with a humorous tone. A lot of little kids innocently pocket a treat at the register. Everyone understands. It's almost cute. And, of course, a good opportunity for a lesson.

The second time I stole, it was a lip gloss from Walmart. I was sixteen and fully aware that stealing was wrong, but I did it anyway. I'm not even sure why. All I knew was that I was angry, the kind of angry that fills you and consumes you until you feel like you're going to explode from the force of it. My family had just fallen apart. One minute my world was happy and safe, and the next, my parents were screaming at each other in their bedroom at night. Then my mother was packing her bags, leaving us to be with the man she'd been having a secret affair with for the past two years. A man both my parents had worked with at the car dealership. A man who was married too.

We can't take things that don't belong to us, she'd told me. Apparently this rule doesn't apply to her, so why should it apply to me? And it felt *good*, taking that lip gloss. Like someone had opened a valve in my body and released some of the pressure. So I did it again. And again. I stole whenever I had the chance, moving on from small items like makeup to bigger, harder-to-conceal items, like clothes. Each time I was smarter about it, having armed myself with the secrets and tricks of shoplifting that I'd learned online. Within months, I'd managed to lift hundreds of dollars' worth of stuff without even coming close to getting caught, so I assumed I never would.

Stupid me.

"What's your name?"

I look at the woman behind the desk. She's black, with a round face and very kind eyes. Almost sympathetic. She told me her name when she came in, but I was in too much shock to retain anything.

"Morgan Kemper." My gaze drifts to my purse, open on the desk. The blue-framed sunglasses sit beside it, proof of my crime. I was surprisingly calm when the LP officer led me down a hallway and into this small, windowless room, where he made me sit and wait. I stayed calm when this woman came in and searched my purse, checking each and every pocket until she was sure I hadn't taken anything else.

But now, sitting here with her gentle brown eyes on me, I feel like I'm going to vomit.

"Morgan," she says, "will you please turn the volume down on your phone?"

"Oh." I reach into my purse and bring out my phone, which has been dinging the entire time I've been in here. "Can I just . . . text my friend and let her know where I am?"

When she nods, I quickly type a message to Alyssa: Had to rush home. Everything's okay but I can't come back to mall. Can you guys take the bus? Sorry.

Lies, lies, lies. But I don't have time to dwell on it. There are much bigger things to worry about at the moment.

The woman takes my basic info—address, phone number, birth date—and then asks me if I've done this before.

"No," I say.

She looks at me for a long moment, making me want to squirm. But I force myself to remain still, look her in the face as my lie echoes through the room.

"We're going to have to call your parents," she tells me. Her kind demeanor hasn't wavered once, for which I should probably be grateful. The cops, if they're summoned, won't be nearly as nice. "Are they at work?"

"I live with my dad." I lower my gaze to my hands, picturing my father's face when he gets the call. The lines in his skin burrowing even deeper. "Yes, he's at work." I tell her where and give her the number. Maybe if I cooperate, she'll let me go without involving the police at all.

Dad arrives in under twenty minutes, his face ashen. The sight of him makes my chest ache.

"Morgan, what is going on?" He looks scared and maybe a little desperate, like he's hoping I'll tell him this is all a mistake.

I wish I could. But when I open my mouth, nothing comes out. What can I say to him, this man who's been there my entire life and does so much for me? First he has to deal with a wife who cheated on him and took off, and now this. He deserves better.

A police officer arrives while the woman is explaining

to Dad what happened. Somehow, Dad's face gets even paler when he sees the beefy cop, whose girth seems to fill the tiny room. My urge to upchuck my lunch intensifies. I'm not three years old anymore, and this isn't a pack of gum. A few tears and an apology aren't going to smooth things over this time.

"This way." Dad takes my arm as we exit the mall and starts leading me across the parking lot to his car.

"But I drove here."

"Well, you're driving home with me," he says in a low, even voice that makes my stomach twist. "We'll deal with your car later. You're not going to be using it again for a while, anyway."

He doesn't let go of my arm until I'm sitting in the passenger seat of his CR-Z. He slams my door and circles the car to the driver's side, his jaw set the entire time. I clutch my purse to my chest and shut my eyes, trying to hold back tears. He's *pissed*. And no wonder. He was pulled out of work to deal with his delinquent daughter, then had to sit there while the store pressed charges against me. Being a "first-time offender" doesn't hold many perks. I'm going to have to go to court, maybe even get a record. *This can follow you your whole life*, the cop told me, like I'd just robbed a bank or something.

I might as well have, going by the way my father glares at me when he gets in the car.

"*Why*, Morgan?" he asks. The roughness from a minute

ago is gone. Now he just sounds disappointed. Which is even worse.

I look down at my hands. "I needed sunglasses."

"But why . . ." He turns away and runs a hand through his thinning, rust-colored hair. "Why *steal*? What on earth was going through your head?"

I shrug. He'd never understand. *I* don't even understand. All I know is that shoplifting gives me some kind of strange comfort. It makes me feel powerful, more in control. It centers me when life feels unbalanced. There's no point in trying to explain or make excuses. Clearly, there's something fundamentally wrong with me if I need to steal things to feel normal again.

Dad starts the car. "When you need something, come to *me*. I'll give you the money."

Something inside me breaks free and suddenly I'm pissed. "We don't *have* the money, Dad," I yell, even though it's not really about money at all. But letting him think I stole the sunglasses because we can't afford them seems to make the most sense, so I run with it. "You really think I'd ask you for expensive sunglasses when you've barely been able to keep up with the rent?"

"Then you do without!" he yells back at me.

His words ring in the small space. I turn toward the window, quickly wiping a tear off my cheek. Dad only raises his voice when he's reached the outer limit of his patience, and it takes a lot to get him there. Mom used to push him there sometimes, but today is a first for me.

"I'm sorry," I say after a few moments of silence.

Dad sighs, and I dare a glance at him. His face is flushed and he's gripping the wheel like it's the only thing stopping him from strangling me. Not that he ever would, but the thought has probably crossed his mind in the past hour or so.

"I'm going to have to tell your mother about this."

My body goes cold. Contact with my mother has been sporadic since I chose to stay here with Dad instead of moving away with her. I haven't really spoken to her in months, and I don't want this to be the thing that reopens the lines of communication. Knowing her, she'd use it as proof that Dad's an unfit parent and force me to come live with her.

"No. Please, Dad. There's no reason to tell her. It was my mistake, and I'll deal with it myself. Don't mention it to Rachel either. Please." It's not that I think my sister would judge me— she's not exactly a saint, herself. She spent the summer before college drinking and smoking pot, but she stopped before it got out of hand, unlike me with my stealing. I don't want her to know how out of control I let it get.

"I'm not making any promises." Dad backs out of the parking space a little rougher than usual. "We have no idea what's going to come of this yet. You could be in serious trouble, Morgan. Do you realize that? I need to hire a damn lawyer. Another one."

I face the window again, my cheeks burning. I didn't think of that at the time. More lawyer costs. More time spent in the legal system. First for the divorce, and now for me. When I screw up, I screw up epically.

"I just . . . I don't know what you were thinking. This isn't like you at all. Why would a smart girl like you do something so unbelievably *stupid*?"

All the way home, I sit quietly and let him rant. And I take it. There's nothing I can say to defend myself, because there's no defense. No excuses. Trying would just make things worse.

It's a tense, silent ride in the elevator up to our apartment. When we go inside, Fergus greets us with an excited meow. At least someone's glad to see me.

"I'm going back to work for a couple of hours," Dad says flatly. He fiddles with his keys, unable to look at me. "Don't even think about leaving this apartment. We'll discuss your punishment when I get home." He meets my eyes, finally, and my heart squeezes when I see the hurt and exhaustion in them. "I'm really disappointed in you, Morgan."

He leaves, closing the door softly behind him. Fergus rubs against my leg, his body vibrating with happiness. I scoop him up and let my tears soak into his soft, orange fur.

Chapter Five

MY PUNISHMENT FROM DAD TURNS OUT TO BE A three-week grounding, along with the loss of car privileges except for driving to and from school. All in all, I expected much worse.

For the next two weeks, I'm perfect. I go to school, study, clean up around the apartment, and most important, I stay away from stores. I don't see my friends outside of school, but no one suspects anything's amiss because we're all stuck inside studying for finals anyway. I don't hear anything about my shoplifting charge, and after a while I start to wonder if I ever will. It was a stupid pair of *sunglasses*. Maybe they were just trying to scare me. Maybe they forgot all about it.

I try to forget about it too, and shift my focus to exams. After finishing my last one, English, on Thursday morning, I meet up with Alyssa outside the classroom.

"How'd you do?" she asks.

I make a *don't ask* face. Like we suspected, the exam was mostly essay questions, which hopefully I managed to bullshit my way through. "You?"

She shrugs. "I don't even care. We're *done*. Let summer begin!"

I force a smile. My grounding doesn't end until next week. What am I supposed to tell my friends when they try to make plans? Alyssa and Sophie easily believed my excuse for ditching them at the mall the day I got caught—I told them I came down with a stomach bug and had to go home immediately— but each lie makes me feel like a total jerk. Still, telling them the truth would be so much worse.

Before Alyssa and I head home, we stop in to visit Sophie in the cafeteria, which has been turned into an extra study area for exam week. We find her at a table by the window, surrounded by papers and empty chip bags. Her last exam is this afternoon.

"Hi, guys!" She waves cheerfully as we approach. "I'm so glad you're here to witness the complete meltdown I'm about to have any second now."

I wince in sympathy. "That bad, huh?"

Just as we sit down, Dawson breezes by and taps his

knuckles on the back of my chair. I look up to see his wide smile. "Got the job at Ace Burger," he tells me.

"Awesome! Congrats." I hold out my hand, which he slaps hard before continuing on his way.

"You got him a job?" Sophie asks, momentarily distracted from her breakdown.

"Ace Burger is right across the street from Royal Smoothie," I remind her. "I noticed a Help Wanted sign in the window there when I went for my interview, and I mentioned it to Dawson. That's all."

Alyssa's eyes follow Dawson as he exits the cafeteria. "Huh. He didn't tell me he applied at Ace Burger."

One of Sophie's blond eyebrows shoots up. "Do you guys have a private group chat going on or something?"

We exchange a quick glance. Does Sophie see it too, this quiet connection between Dawson and Alyssa? Maybe his crush is more obvious than I thought.

"We text sometimes," Alyssa says, her tone mildly defensive. "Hello? We're friends."

Now both of Sophie's eyebrows go up, along with one corner of her mouth. "You could do a lot worse, you know."

Alyssa stares at her for a moment and then shifts her gaze to me, as if checking to see if I agree. I give her a slight nod. Dawson is one of the sweetest guys I know, and great boyfriend material.

"Seriously?" She rolls her eyes. "Even if I did have any

interest in dating someone—which I don't—I wouldn't choose Dawson. He's one of my best friends. Besides," she adds, glancing again at the exit, even though he's long gone, "my grandmother would *freak*."

Sophie frowns. "Because he's black?"

"No, because he's not Greek. You know my *yiayia* wants me to settle down with a nice Greek boy. She doesn't listen when I tell her I don't *want* to settle down with anyone right now, Greek or otherwise."

"Um, she knows it's the twenty-first century, right?" Sophie asks.

Alyssa just shrugs and changes the subject, something she does whenever her family is brought up. She and I have that in common. We weren't friends with Sophie, Zach, and Dawson yet when Lyss's father suffered a massive heart attack and never made it out of surgery. Or when my mother shattered our family with her cheating and lies. They're aware of these things, but we've never really discussed it in depth, even though Alyssa and I know our friends would be sympathetic. Still, they didn't live through them with us. Alyssa and I just had each other then, two lost girls stumbling their way around a frightening new reality. The difference is, I *could* see my mom, if I wanted to, but Alyssa will never spend time with her father again. Yet somehow, even in the face of grief, she eventually adapted while I stayed more lost than ever.

"Morgan has zoned out again." Alyssa pokes my shoulder.

"What?" I meet her eyes. I was listening but only caught about every other sentence.

"Do you want to all drive together to Jasmine's pool party on Saturday?"

"Oh." I squirm in my chair, uncomfortable. Again, my mind flashes on the striped bikini, folded among my underwear. All that work and I'll probably never get to wear it. "Um, I'm not going to that."

"What?" Sophie shrieks. A girl studying at the next table over shoots us a dirty look.

"Since when?" Alyssa asks.

Since I got caught stealing at the mall while you guys were waiting for me just a short walk away. I swallow. My throat aches with the effort of keeping the truth from slipping past my tongue. But I can't say anything. My friends are good people, with values and integrity. They're rule followers, and they believe I have all these qualities too. They'd never understand.

"Since I got grounded. Long story." Maybe a half-truth will be enough to dull the ache.

Sophie and Alyssa gape at me, shocked. I can count on one hand the number of times I've been grounded, and this is the first grounding given out by Dad. He's always trusted me, given me lots of freedom. Until now.

"What did you *do*?" Sophie finally asks.

"Nothing horrible." I take off my glasses and pretend to

wipe a smudge off them so I don't have to look at my friends. "I don't really want to get into it. Too embarrassing."

"Well, that . . . sucks," Sophie says.

"Yeah." I put my glasses back on and their faces sharpen into focus. Sophie's bottom lip sticks out in an exaggerated pout while Alyssa regards me thoughtfully, like she's trying to figure out exactly what I'm holding back. She knows as well as I do that my father would only punish me if I did something really, really bad.

When I walk into the apartment an hour later, I startle a little to see Dad sitting on the couch. Sometimes I forget that he's off on Thursdays.

"How was your exam?" he asks dully, like he's not very interested in my answer.

"Fine." I move closer and notice he's just sitting there, not watching TV or on his phone or laptop. A white piece of paper lies faceup on the coffee table in front of him. "What's that?"

He looks down at the paper, then back up at me. "This came in the mail today. Apparently, that nice police officer referred you to a diversion program."

His words make zero sense to me. I sit next to him on the couch and pick up the letter.

"It's for first-time offenders," Dad continues, his voice sticking on the last word. "An alternative to prosecution.

Instead of going to court, you'd need to complete certain requirements, like counseling, for instance. If you do what they ask, the charges will be withdrawn."

"So I *don't* have to go to court?"

He leans back and rubs a hand over his face. "Not if you agree to their requirements."

I scan the letter for this list of available "requirements," one or more of which I will have to complete. Each one sounds more humiliating than the last. Counseling. Restitution. Apology letters. Charitable donations. Community service.

"I spoke with the diversion coordinator this morning," Dad says. "In your case, he'll usually recommend a shoplifting education class, which you can do online, and restitution, meaning you pay the store back for what you took. But since they got the sunglasses back, that doesn't apply to you."

I place the letter on the table and look at my father. His head is tilted away, as if he can't even stand to look at me, and I feel a jolt of self-disgust. All this time, I never once thought about how my getting caught would affect *him*. How it would only add to his stress and burdens, and make him feel like he's failed me somehow. Even though none of this is his fault at all.

"Okay," I say in a steady voice. "I'll do the online course, then. And if it costs money, I'll pay for it myself. I start my job next week and it won't take me long to save up."

He turns his head toward me, meeting my eyes for the first

time since I came in. "Yes, you'll do the course and pay for it, but that's not enough. You need to do something else too . . . something meaningful."

"Meaningful?"

"You need to see how your actions affect other people," he goes on. "You have to learn to give back instead of selfishly taking." He leans forward and points to an item on the list. "The coordinator recommended this."

"Community service? But I'll have work and—"

"Thirty hours' worth," he cuts in. "Thirty hours of being an active, contributing member of the community this summer. *That's* how you're going to make up for what you did."

I open my mouth to protest, to reiterate about my summer job and time constraints and having to explain my sudden burst of "volunteerism" to my friends, but his expression is so stormy that all I can manage is, "So, what, will I have to pick up litter off the side of the highway or something?"

He shakes his head. "Do you remember Rita Sloan? She was a receptionist at the dealership for a couple of years when you were about eight or nine."

I stare at him blankly. No, I don't remember a receptionist from almost ten years ago. There seems to be someone new at the front desk every time I go in.

"Anyway," Dad goes on, "we've kept in touch over the years. She went to business school after she left the dealership, and now she manages a thrift store for a not-for-profit organization. I'm going to get in touch with her and see if she'll give you a job."

A thief. Working in a store filled with potentially steal-worthy items. I stare at him, waiting for the irony to sink in, but he doesn't even blink.

"It's either that or prosecution, Morgan," he says, standing up. "Your choice."

He heads for the kitchen, leaving me alone on the couch. His words linger in my head. *Your choice.* But the more I think about it, the more it seems like I don't have any choice at all.

Chapter Six

RITA'S RERUNS.

I spot the square wooden sign on my left, at the bottom of a long paved driveway. The Rs beginning both words are oversized and curled on the edges, underscoring the rest of the letters. "Guess this is it," I mumble to myself as I turn my car into the driveway. My nonpaying, mandatory second summer job.

I was half hoping this ex-coworker of Dad's would refuse to let me fulfill my community service hours here. But no. After I met with my diversion coordinator and he okayed the idea, Dad called Rita Sloan and set everything up, no problem. I was sure she'd at least ask to meet with me first before trusting me around her cash till, but she must owe my dad a huge favor or something, because she hired me sight unseen.

Not that I'd ever steal from a charity. Even I have my limits.

The thrift store itself is attached to a small community center. I can hear voices echoing from inside as I pull closer to the old building. At least I assume it's old. The red siding is chipped and worn, and most of the buildings in this part of the city have been here for a century or so. The parking lot has been freshly paved, though, and a row of orange flowers near the store's entrance make the place look cute and cheerful.

Thump.

I slam on my brakes. Did I . . . ? Yes, I definitely just ran over something with my car. Heart pounding, I shift into park and get out. At first I don't see anything, but when I circle around to the front of the car, I spot a crumpled cardboard box trapped beneath my right front wheel. Shards of light green glass are scattered across the pavement.

"It wasn't *that* ugly."

I gasp and spin around. Standing a few feet away, next to a pair of donation bins, is a tall, hulking guy with biceps the size of my head. Where the hell did he come from?

"What?" I say, squinting at him through the glare in my glasses. He's about my age, maybe a little older, and he's wearing jeans with rips in the knees, a faded black T-shirt, and work gloves.

"That green vase I just pulled out of the donation bin." He

grins and motions toward the glass, shimmering in the sun. "I mean, it was hideous, but you didn't have to smash it into a million pieces."

Oh Jesus. "I'm so sorry," I say in a rush. "I was looking at the flowers and didn't realize there was a box sitting in the middle of the driveway."

The guy comes closer and bends down to inspect the carnage under my wheel. He shakes his head before straightening back up. "Yeah, those marigolds are pretty distracting."

"Excuse me?"

He runs a large hand through his short, dirty-blond hair. "The flowers out front. They're marigolds. I planted them myself a couple of months ago."

"Oh. Well." I inch toward the car door. "I should probably go inside now."

He nods and backs away, still eyeing what's left of the vase. "Hope that glass didn't get embedded in your tire."

That's all I need. To get a flat and have to stay here for who knows how long while this dude talks to me about gardening.

I wave awkwardly at him and get back into my car. Luckily, nothing happens as I continue on to the parking lot. As I slide my car into a space, I glance in the mirror and see the tall guy hefting another box out of the donation bin. It's clearly heavy, because he loses his grip on it for a moment, the cardboard sliding between his gloved hands. But at the last second he steadies it, avoiding another mess on the pavement.

* * *

When I enter the store, I expect to be greeted by this Rita woman or at least a few customers, but it's completely empty. I glance at my phone. Eight fifty-three. I'm seven minutes early, even after the vase-smashing incident.

I pocket my phone and look around. The place looks like any other thrift store—racks of clothes, sorted by gender and age. Shelves crammed with old dishes and decor. Baby toys and furniture, barely used. Hand-printed signs labeling each rack and section. I notice the *M* in *Men's Tops & Bottoms* is curled at the end, just like the *R*s on the sign outside. Elaborate lettering must be Rita's thing.

A door opens at the far end of the room and a plump, dark-haired woman bustles in.

"Oh!" she says when she sees me. "You're Morgan."

I nod, smiling, and she starts toward me, jingling with each step. It takes me a moment to realize the sound is coming from the half dozen bracelets on her wrist. Her blue eyes scan my features like I'm an interesting relic someone dropped in the donation box. I don't remember her from the dealership at all. Maybe she looked different ten years ago.

"I haven't seen you since you were a little bitty thing. Goodness, you grew up to look like Charles! The red hair. The smile. Except you're a lot prettier, of course." She holds out a hand for me to shake. "I'm Rita Sloan. You probably don't remember me. I was a lot thinner a decade ago, not to mention a blonde. Welcome."

"Thanks." I shake her hand, a little taken aback by her openness and rapid-fire way of speaking. Not to mention her appearance. She looks kind of like an aging movie starlet with her bright red lipstick and blunt, even bangs.

"So today will be mostly training," she says, walking toward the back of the store and motioning for me to follow. "I'll teach you how to use the register—which is old and sometimes sticky—and show you how to sort and tag donations. Have you ever worked in retail before?"

I keep my eyes on her long skirt, which flows out around her as she walks. "Um, I just started working at Royal Smoothie on Gerard Street. But all I do is blend fruit and yogurt all day, so no. No retail. I can use a cash register, though."

She turns to face me, and for a moment I think she's going to ask me if I've ever stolen money. Which I definitely would never do, because it's much too risky. Besides, taking money isn't my thing. *Things* are my thing. Things I can hold and keep and collect.

But all she says is "Your father said you can commit to three hours a week, every Saturday morning. Is that right?"

"Yes." I would have preferred more hours so I can get this over with as quickly as possible, but I work at Royal Smoothie on Saturday afternoons, Rita's is closed on Sundays, and apparently she doesn't need help during the week. But one short shift a week is nothing, and I'll be home free by the end of summer. Hours served. Charges dropped. Like it never even happened.

"I'm very fond of your dad," she tells me, and starts walking again, circling back to the checkout area. "When I worked there, he was the best salesperson on the team. He always went above and beyond to get his customers a low monthly payment. I'm sure he still does. A lot of salespeople are slimy, you know? But Charles isn't."

I nod, even though she's not looking at me. *Slimy* perfectly describes Gary Ellsworth, the guy my mother has been sleeping with for years. The worst thing about him was his ability to hide exactly how slimy he was. He and Dad were good friends at one point, and two of the top salespeople at the dealership. They'd get customers the "best deal possible" and then send them to my mother, who worked in the finance department. Everything was great until last May, when Dad inadvertently saw incriminating texts from Gary on my mom's phone, exposing their affair. No one told me this—I learned it from listening to them argue one night when they thought Rachel and I were asleep. The next day, Mom sat us down to tell us she'd fallen in love with Gary and that she and Dad were getting a divorce. Rachel cried and asked questions, but I said nothing and went to my room. I couldn't even look at her.

A month later, Mom and Gary quit the dealership and moved away together, leaving their jilted spouses in the dust. So, yeah. Apparently, slimy people like to stick together.

"He told me all about your . . . situation," Rita goes on, lowering her voice on *situation* like my shoplifting charge is a terminal disease. She stops at the register and faces me again. "At first I was wary, because, you know . . ." She gestures in the direction of the clothing racks. "But Charles has been good to me, and I trust him. So I decided I'm going to trust you too."

My face warms as a rush of shame washes over me. I clear my throat and force myself to look her in the eye. "Thanks. You definitely can. Trust me, I mean. I—I appreciate you taking a chance on me."

She reaches up to smooth her sleek hair, making the bracelets chime again. "I believe in giving people a fair shot in life. That's why I do this job. Okay," she says brightly, punching a button on the register. "Come over here so I can teach you how to use this monster."

For the next twenty minutes, she goes over how to handle various forms of payment. It's stuff I already learned last week at Royal Smoothie, but I pay attention anyway. Before I left this morning, Dad lectured me about taking this job seriously, even though I'm not getting paid. And how it's a good opportunity for me to learn something about myself. And how

helping out a charity—even if it's to satisfy a community service obligation—will improve my life and make me a better
human being.

I'm not sure how standing behind a cash register for three
hours a week is supposed to turn me into a good person, but
okay.

Next, Rita takes me to a small stockroom where donations
are stored and sorted. The cramped space is overflowing with
boxes and bags of clothing.

"You'll never have to lift any really heavy things," Rita
says as she paws through one of the boxes. "That's what my
nephew, Eli, is for. He helps me out for a few hours on weekends. Did you notice the marigolds out front? He planted those
for me. Eli's a good boy."

Just as I'm about to tell her that her nephew and I met—
sort of—outside earlier, the sound of a door slamming echoes
into the stockroom.

"Speak of the devil." Rita closes the box and stacks it on
top of another one. "Or angel, as it were. Come on, I'll introduce you."

I follow her back into the store area, a knot forming in
my stomach. Only a few people know about my sticky-fingers
habit, and that's the way I'd like to keep it. It's bad enough that
Rita knows; I don't want her nephew to always have to wonder about me too. But there's nothing I can do to stop it. Rita's
doing *me* a favor—she can tell people whatever she wants.

The tall guy—Eli—is standing by the side doors and gulping from a water bottle when we walk in. His work gloves are off, and there's a long streak of dust across the front of his shirt.

"Eli," Rita says with a shake of her head. "The door?"

Eli swallows the water in his mouth. "Oops. Sorry."

"I always know when it's Eli coming in because the entire *floor* shakes," she explains to me. "I told him if he breaks the door, he has to work off the cost of repairs by sorting through the occasional bag of used underwear we find in the donation bins."

I can't tell if she's joking or not, so I just smile thinly. Gross. I hope that won't be one of *my* jobs.

"Eli, this is Morgan," Rita says, gesturing to me. "She'll be doing some volunteering here this summer. Morgan, this is my favorite nephew, Eli."

The knot in my stomach loosens. She's not going to tell him why I'm really here, at least for now.

"Also her only nephew," Eli adds as he walks over to me. I notice he has a slight limp, so slight that I wonder if I'm mistaken. He holds out his hand and we shake, my fingers disappearing completely inside his. "So you're going to be working here, huh?" he says with a smirk. "Better hide the glassware."

My cheeks burn again, this time from embarrassment. I glance at Rita. She's smiling at him like what he said was perfectly normal, even though she couldn't possibly know about

57

the crushed vase. Maybe he says random things all the time and she's used to it.

"Morgan goes to . . ." Rita looks at me. "What high school do you go to? Your dad mentioned it, but I forget."

"Nicholson," I say. "I'll be a senior in the fall."

Eli drains the rest of his water and crushes the bottle in his hand. "Cool. I just graduated from Waverly."

I nod, unsure what to say next. Small talk has never been my strong suit. And all I know about Waverly High is that their football team consistently kicks our football team's ass. I wonder if Eli plays football. He has the build for it.

The door opens then, and all three of us turn toward it. A woman carrying a baby in a car seat walks in. Rita greets her with a smile before returning her gaze to Eli.

"Off you go." She shoos him away. "Morgan's going to take care of her very first customer."

"Sure thing." He smiles at me, his eyes crinkling at the corners. "I still have a *huge* mess to clean up in the driveway, anyway."

I look back at him, keeping my face blank. If he thinks he's going to win me over by mocking me, he's only going to end up disappointed. I'm short with red hair, and I have an older sister—I've been immune to teasing since I was about six.

"Whoa, okay," he says cheerfully when I don't give him the laugh he was probably expecting. Without another word, he heads for the side door and outside. I watch him closely to see if I can pick up on the limp I detected earlier. I was right—he definitely favors his right leg, though it's barely noticeable.

For a moment, I find myself wondering what happened to him, but I shut the thoughts down as quickly as they arrive. I'm not here to make friends. I have enough friends. I'm here to get this punishment over with and move on with my life.

"Let's go see if we can help this lady find what she's looking for," Rita says as she starts in the direction of the clothing racks, where the woman is perusing a collection of baby outfits. I put on a credible smile and follow her lead.

One hour down, twenty-nine more to go.

Chapter Seven

"YOU'RE DOING WHAT?" ALYSSA LOOKS AT ME LIKE she's wondering if she heard me wrong.

"Volunteering," I repeat, leaning back on the couch. The four of us are lounging around in Zach's basement, our second-favorite hangout spot after the diner. There's a giant-screen TV, an abundance of snacks, and his mom is almost never home. "It's no big deal."

Sophie presses pause on her game controller and looks over at me. "You're doing what?"

I sigh. Four days have passed since my first thrift shop shift, and I've only now gotten around to mentioning it to my friends. I wouldn't have even bothered, but I figure they're eventually going to start wondering why I'm never free on Saturday mornings.

"Volunteering," Alyssa says around a mouthful of Doritos.

Dawson pauses his controller too and joins in on the staring. He came here straight from work and is still in his uniform, which consists of a red T-shirt with *Ace Burger* emblazoned across the front and a giant pin that says *Ask Me About Our Bacon Belly Buster Supreme!* "But what about your job?" he asks.

"It won't affect my job," I say as Zach creeps into the room, five glasses balanced precariously in his arms.

"What won't affect your job?" he asks, depositing our drinks on the coffee table.

Sophie unpauses her controller and goes back to shooting things up. "Morgan's gone all altruistic on us."

"I'm working in a thrift shop, guys. Not sewing up wounded soldiers or nursing sick kittens back to health."

Zach starts singing that damn song about thrift shops. Of course. I toss a pillow at him, but my aim is off and it bounces off Dawson's shoulder instead.

"You've never shown any interest in volunteering before," Alyssa points out. "You aren't even on any committees at school."

"I just thought it might look good on my college applications next year." I look her right in the eye as I say it, because that's the type of person I am—the type who lies to her friends because she's too cowardly to tell them the secrets she's hiding and why. A small part of me has always felt separate from the four of them. Like I'm hovering at the edge of our tight circle, not quite worthy enough to truly belong. They're all so intrinsically *good*, so open and honest and kind. I used to think *I* was good too, before Mom left. Then it was like a switch had been thrown, revealing all the damaged parts of me that were probably lurking beneath the surface all along.

"Oh." Alyssa nods, accepting my fib. "That's a smart idea. Maybe I should offer to volunteer there too."

"No," I say, loudly enough that Dawson glances over at us. "Uh, the owner only needs one person, so . . ."

"Oh," she repeats, this time with a slight frown. "Okay. It was just a thought."

I grab my glass of fruit punch and take a gulp, feeling Alyssa's gaze on me. I keep my eyes on the TV, pretending to be riveted by the animated violence on-screen. A few minutes pass before I feel Lyss's hand on my arm.

"Is everything okay?" she asks when I meet her eyes. "I just feel . . . I don't know. Like there's something going on with you that you're not telling us." She laughs a little. "Do you have some sort of secret life we don't know about or something?"

I laugh too, my way of brushing aside the uncomfortable truth in her words. Alyssa used to know everything about me, right down to the smallest detail. Before this year, there was never a time when I felt I couldn't confide in her. But I can't seem to tell her this.

"She's a superhero," Dawson says as he mashes his thumbs into the controller. "Smoothie maker by day, masked vigilante by night."

Alyssa ignores him and smooths her long hair into a ponytail. "Seriously," she says, securing it with her ever-present wrist elastic. "You'd tell us if you weren't okay, right?"

"Of course, Lyss. Everything's fine." I give her a smile to prove it.

"She's fine," Zach bellows over the grunts and gunshots on the screen. "This is Morgan we're talking about. She's tough as nails. Hey, toss those Doritos over here, would you?"

Alyssa ignores him too, keeping her eyes on my face until, finally, I look away. The thing about best friends is that they usually know when you're telling only part of the story.

I'm not grounded anymore, but I do still have a strict nightly curfew of eleven thirty. When I arrive home at eleven twenty-five, I find Dad watching a cooking show in the living room. For someone who survives on takeout and cereal, he's been watching the Food Network a lot lately. Maybe we need to get back to *Breaking Bad*, which sort of fell by the wayside these past couple of weeks.

"Hey," he says as I pass by him on my way to the kitchen. "There's some Thai food in the fridge for you."

I grab a glass from the still-steaming dishwasher and fill it at the sink. "Thanks," I say, raising my voice a little to be heard over the loud chopping on TV. Our apartment is open concept, and pretty small, so we can easily communicate from different rooms. "I'm kind of full, though. Ate a lot of junk at Zach's."

Fergus strides into the kitchen and weaves his body around my legs. I glance at his dish and see that it's empty. Either Dad forgot to feed him or he ate already and wants more. In any case, I dump a scoop of dry food into his bowl for a late-night snack. I leave him there, crunching, and return to the living room.

"Good night," I say, trying to inject some warmth into my voice. Since the Incident, our exchanges have been loaded with awkward tension. It's like we're both trying too hard to be normal again, or whatever passed for normal for us before. Regardless of what happened to get us here, we'd settled into some form of routine over the past year, even if that routine was catching up over slices of pizza, watching Walter White cook meth, and bickering about whose turn it was to scoop the kitty litter. But now, it's like we've regressed to my first few days here, when we circled each other cautiously, unsure how to deal with this new dynamic.

My father acts like he doesn't hear me. "This looks pretty easy."

I follow his gaze to the TV, where a bald guy is pounding

chicken breasts with a mallet. "What?"

"This dish. It doesn't look very hard to make. I bet I could do it."

I look back at him and frown. Mom was the cook in our family; Dad's culinary skills, like mine, are mostly limited to opening cans and ordering in. "Do you even have time to make stuff like that?"

"Maybe I should make time." His voice takes on an edge. "Maybe if we sat down together every night for a healthy, home-cooked meal, you wouldn't have felt compelled to go to the mall and steal a pair of two-hundred-dollar sunglasses."

My throat goes dry. He can't possibly blame *himself* for what I did. My dad does the best he can under the circumstances. So what if he doesn't cook me dinner and spend a lot of time with me? It's always been like that, even before Mom left. There's a reason I used to always draw him in a suit and tie when I was little—because I rarely saw him in anything else. He worked late most nights and didn't get home after bedtime, so to me, he mostly existed as the dad who sat across from me at breakfast each morning before we left for school and work. He made the most of the time he did have with us, but Mom was always the star in our lives while he was more of a supporting character.

I guess that's why he was so surprised when Rachel and I opted to stay with him instead of moving away with our mother, like she wanted. *Are you sure?* he kept asking, like he was afraid we were only choosing him to spite Mom. And maybe that was part of it, at least for me. But after having my life completely upended by the person I trusted most, it was nice to have control over *something*.

So no, Dad didn't have to take me on along with all the debt and devastation my mother's actions caused him. He did it because he loved me and wanted me around. Because he understood why I couldn't live with Mom and her boyfriend, the two people who ripped our lives apart and then left us to clean up the mess.

None of this is even remotely his fault.

"Dad, come on." I sit next to him on the couch and set my water on the end table. "Me stealing sunglasses has nothing to do with you. Okay? It was just . . . I don't know why I did it, but it was *my* fault. Mine. You don't need to rearrange your whole life just because you think it'll make you a better parent or whatever. You're doing fine."

"Am I?" he mutters, as though talking to himself. He lets out a sigh and looks at me, his eyes heavy with doubt and sadness. "I spoke to your sister earlier."

My heart thumps, and my first thought is *He told her.* He told her about the shoplifting and the charges and she's going to hate me for making things more difficult for Dad.

"Did she tell you she's coming home?" he goes on, and my body loosens with relief. He didn't tell her.

"Yeah, at the end of August."

"Right. She said . . ." He pauses to click off the TV, then clears his throat. "She said she plans on visiting your mother while she's here."

Fergus jumps up on the couch between us and proceeds to bathe himself, but his presence barely registers. My head is too busy spinning with the words *your mother* and *visit*.

"What? Why?" I ask. Rachel feels the same way I do about Mom, namely that she's a selfish home wrecker who broke our dad and then left without looking back. Why the hell would she want to go see her?

"Because she's your mother," Dad says simply. "Rachel says she wants to spend the day with her and check out her new house."

New house. My blood boils at that, since I still think about our *old* house, all the time. We used to live right in the city in a cute, modernized duplex near the park. Rachel and I grew up there. But after Mom ran away with Gary, taking her income with her, Dad had no choice but to sell and move here, a new development in the outskirts of town, where each apartment building has a view of another apartment building. And suddenly my childhood home was just a memory, like so many other things.

So no, I don't give a rat's ass about the new house Mom and Gary bought together. It's not like it'll last, anyway. One of them will probably cheat again, or they'll eventually discover that their relationship isn't so exciting when they're not sneaking around behind everyone's backs.

"I think you should go with her, Morgan," my father tells me. "It might be good for you."

I sit up straight, almost displacing Fergus. His ears flatten in annoyance. "You're joking, right? How can seeing her possibly be good for me?"

"Because she's your mother," he says again, like that should be enough. Like I'm supposed to forgive her everything just because she gave birth to me. "And because you haven't seen her since Rachel's graduation last June. You've barely even talked to her."

Rachel's graduation. I remember it well, and not just because it was the last time I laid eyes on my mother. The day was loaded with tension. My mother's affair had been uncovered just three weeks before, and she'd been staying with a friend nearby because Dad didn't want her in the house. But that day, they decided to put aside their differences for a few hours so they could both watch their older daughter graduate. For a moment I considered not joining them, but my love for my sister overrode the still-raw anger I felt for our mom.

My parents didn't speak during the ceremony. I sat between them, my body coiled tight, wishing I were somewhere, anywhere, else. Every so often, Rachel turned to smile at me from her seat up front, reminding me why I was there. She was pissed at Mom too, but like Dad, she was willing to pretend we were a normal family again, just for one day. I wasn't so willing.

Afterward, we went to a restaurant to celebrate with a few of Rachel's friends and their families. It was loud and chaotic enough that I could avoid my mother without everyone noticing. Well, everyone except for her. Shortly after the cake was cut, she started making excuses to duck out. She hugged Rachel first, whose graduation high had softened her enough to hug back. Then my mother turned to me.

"We'll talk soon?" she said, her voice soft and hopeful. I stood perfectly still as she embraced me, then quickly backed out of her arms. Just before turning away, I saw her face sag, like the full magnitude of the damage she'd caused had suddenly hit her.

A week later, she was gone. The day she packed up her things and left, I hid out at Alyssa's house, unwilling to even say good-bye. I haven't seen her since.

"She hasn't talked to me either," I remind my father.

"She tried, at first. Remember? She wanted to apologize to you and explain her side. She called you almost every day. She even came back to see you a couple of weeks after she left, but you refused to even let her in the apartment. You wanted nothing to do with her, so she stopped trying."

"That's right, she stopped trying." My voice breaks and I pause for a moment, collecting myself. "What kind of parent just gives up on her kid like that? *She's* the one who did something wrong, not me. Why should it be me who makes the effort? And why are you defending her?"

"I'm not defending her, Morgan," he says with a tired sigh. "I just think it might help if you put the past behind you and tried building a relationship with her again."

"Help who? Me? Or her?" I cough out a laugh and stand up. "Sorry, but I don't think I owe her a damn thing. And neither do you."

"Morgan—"

"No, Dad. My answer is no."

Before he can say anything else, I gather up Fergus and take us both to my room.

Chapter Eight

*I TEXT RACHEL THREE TIMES OVER THE NEXT COU*ple of days, asking her to call me, but she doesn't get back to me. Finally, as I'm scarfing down some cereal on Saturday morning, my phone beeps with a response.

Sorry, sis. I've been really busy with work.

Right. More like she's been really busy avoiding me because she knows Dad talked to me about this Mom visit and she doesn't want to face my wrath. I put down my spoon and type back, **Call me.**

rebecca phillips

Five minutes pass. Then ten. Finally, thirteen endless minutes later, as I'm rinsing my breakfast dishes, my phone rings. I dry my hands and answer it.

"What the fuck, Rach?"

My sister and I have always been blunt with each other. We unapologetically call each other out on our shit. It's how we operate. Or at least it was.

"What?" she says, playing dumb. "Sorry it took me so long to call. I was just getting in the shower—"

"That's not what I mean." I lean my hip against the counter and pick up a discarded bread tag that's resting near the sink. Dad's always losing these. "Are you seriously going to visit Mom while you're here? Why didn't you tell me?"

"Because I just decided a few days ago. I wanted to tell Dad before I discussed it with you."

"But—"

Now it's her turn to cut *me* off. "Morgan."

I bend the bread tag between my fingers and it snaps in two, the edges digging into my fingertip. "What?"

"It's been a year. I think this silent treatment has gone on long enough." She sighs. "Look, I'm not going to force you to go with me, but I think it would be good. For all of us. I know how hard this has been on you. It's been hard on me too, but I want to at least *try* to work things out. She's our mother. You think losing us hasn't been tough on her too?"

God. She sounds like Dad. "So? That doesn't mean I want

72

to go hang out with her like nothing's happened. Is there a rule that says we *must* have a relationship with every person we're related to, no matter how awful they are?"

"She's still the same mom who raised us, Morgan," she says quietly. "She did an awful thing, but she's not an awful person."

A flash of memory hits me. Rachel and me, ages nine and seven, stretched out on our parents' bed as Mom read us a chapter from a Harry Potter book, which she did almost every night for months. We could both read on our own, but we liked the way she did it, her voice changing for each character. Our favorite was when she did Voldemort. Her tone got deep, almost gravelly, just the way we imagined a guy like him would sound.

"I wish I could live at Hogwarts," Rachel said when the chapter was over. I immediately chimed in with a "Me too," as I often did when Rachel said she wanted something.

"Are you kidding?" Mom closed the book and put it on the nightstand. "I'd never send you to that school. Something terrible happens there every year. Besides," she added, dropping a kiss on each of our foreheads, "I could never be separated from my girls for that long. I'd miss you way too much."

We begged for another chapter, but Mom said it was getting late and tucked us into our own beds. I fell asleep quickly, secure in the knowledge that she'd be there in the morning, standing at the stove in her purple bathrobe and making us heart-shaped pancakes for breakfast.

I push the memory away. Rachel is wrong. If she were still the same mom who raised us, she wouldn't have done what she did. Or maybe she was never the devoted mother I remember. Not really. Maybe she was just pretending, going through the motions, and my warm childhood memories of her are all built on lies.

"I'm just saying . . ." Rachel stops talking, and I hear a man's voice. Then her again, murmuring about needing a second. "I'm just saying," she repeats, with emphasis, "I'd like to try. Besides, I was never really *mad* at her. I mean, I was, but not like you. I was mostly hurt, I think, and in shock. I just couldn't believe she'd do something like that. Not just the cheating, but how she acted after she was caught."

"You mean when she practically abandoned us to start a new life?" I say wryly. "Yeah, so you can see why I might still be angry."

"I know. I am too, a little. But I've been talking to Amir about it, and he's made me realize how unhealthy it is, hanging on to all this resentment. Forgiving her would benefit us as much as her. You know?"

No, I don't know. I don't know why she's taking advice from a guy she's known for only a few months, a guy who doesn't know us or our situation. I don't know why she thinks I'd be on board with this after everything we've gone through together, all the anger and the tears and the uprooted life. I don't know why none of it seems to matter to her anymore.

"I gotta go," I say after a long pause.

"Morgan." She sighs again, this time with an exasperated edge. "Just think about it, okay? If Dad can move past this, then maybe we can too."

Hot anger floods my stomach. Out of all the things she just said, that's the worst. She's been gone all year, living it up on campus and meeting hot guys. She hasn't seen Dad's dark circles, or listened to his weary sighs at night when he gets home from another crappy day at work. He hasn't moved past anything, and it pisses me off when she acts like she knows him better than I do.

"Gotta go," I say again, and hang up the phone. I consider throwing it across the kitchen and then going back to bed, but it's eight thirty. If I don't leave now, I'll be late for my second shift at Rita's Reruns. At least Rachel doesn't know about *that*. She'd never believe that I'd suddenly taken up volunteering.

By the time I get downtown, the anger has subsided somewhat. Now I just feel drained. And sad, when I think about Rachel with our mother, joking around like we all used to. I wish I didn't miss that about my mom, but I do. I miss her dry sense of humor and the uninhibited way she laughed, head thrown back and eyes squeezed shut. Rachel laughs the same way.

I guess it makes sense that she's open to making amends with Mom. My sister is more forgiving than I am; she doesn't hold grudges. That's the biggest difference between the two of us. Still, I can't ignore the sharp sting of betrayal as it works its way through my body.

I'm almost at the thrift store, which is a good thing because my watering eyes have turned the road into a distorted blur. I pull into the long driveway and park in front of the orange marigolds, which for some reason make me feel even worse. I look away, focus on searching through my purse for tissues instead. I hate crying and try to avoid it as much as possible. Crying in front of other people is even worse, so I'm glad for the privacy of the car.

"Hey."

I jump, banging my elbow on the gearshift. I blink through my tears and look to my left. At first, all I see out the open driver's-side window is a wide torso wearing a red T-shirt with a tear in the hem. Suddenly, the T-shirt lowers and two arms and a head appear. Eli.

"Oh," I say, flustered. I turn away and quickly swipe beneath each eye with my thumb. "I was—I was just coming in."

"No rush."

I glance at him. He's crouched down, his forearms resting on the bottom of the window. His skin there is tanned and covered in fine blond hair, lighter than the hair on his head. And he smells like fresh, damp earth, like he's just been digging in soil.

"You're not still upset about the ugly vase, are you?" he asks softly. "Because I'm totally over it, I swear. No hard feelings."

To my surprise and probably his, I snort. "Has anyone ever told you that you're not as amusing as you think you are?"

He bounces a little, adjusting his position. "Yeah, actually. My sister tells me that all the time."

"Your sister?"

"Meredith. She's fourteen and a royal pain in my ass."

I nod and toss my car keys into my purse. "I have a sister too. Rachel. She's nineteen and a royal pain in *my* ass." I put my hand on the door handle, and Eli straightens up and backs away.

"Nineteen," he exclaims as I climb out of the car. "So they don't grow out of it, then?"

"Guess not."

We make our way up to the front entrance together. Eli holds the door open for me, frowning slightly at my swollen eyes as I pass. Our significant height difference makes it possible for me to walk under his arm without even having to duck. I thought Zach was tall, but this guy has a few inches on him. I only come up to the top of his chest.

"There you are." Rita strides toward us, bracelets chiming with each step. Today she's wearing a long gray tunic over black tights and silver gladiator sandals. She has an interesting style, to say the least. "Eli, sweetie, I sent you outside to get those bags ten minutes ago, and now you're standing here with no bags."

Eli looks down as if making sure he is not, indeed, carrying any bags. "Oops, sorry. I found Morgan in the parking lot and she was looking a little lost." He shoots me a grin, unaware of the truth in his words.

"Hmmm." Rita crosses her arms over her ample chest and fixes him with a narrow-eyed look. "Yes, I'm sure you were helping this cute girl find her way inside out of the goodness of your heart." To me, she adds in a low voice, "Quite the charmer, this one."

I don't doubt it. With that smile and those muscles and warm hazel eyes, he probably melts the hearts of a lot of people.

Eli grins at his aunt's description of him. "That's me. Okay, I'll go get those bags you asked for now."

Rita swats him playfully on the arm as he passes her, then turns back to focus on me. Her gaze makes me feel self-conscious. Whenever I cry, my eyes puff up and my fair skin stays blotchy for up to an hour after the tears have stopped. She can obviously tell something's wrong. I wait for her to ask if I'm okay.

"Someone dropped off three bags of women's pants yesterday," she says instead. "They're in the back room, all ready to be sorted. You can spend the morning on that."

I nod, grateful. Sitting in the stockroom, alone, sounds much more appealing than putting on a happy face for customers.

Rita explains exactly what sorting means—checking for

holes and stains, going through pockets, discarding items that aren't fit for sale—and leaves me to my own devices. I sit on a sturdy plastic tote and untie the first bag. Pants of every color, fabric, size, and style stare back at me. This could take a while.

By the time I'm through the first bag, I feel marginally better. There's something soothing about repetitive tasks that don't require any brainpower. The quiet is nice too. It's just me and a room filled with other people's belongings. I wonder about the history of all these unwanted items, what prompted their owners to get rid of them. To make room, probably, for newer and better things.

I'm halfway done with bag number three when the door flies open, smashing against the wall. For the second time today, I jump. And again, it's because of Eli. He squeezes through the doorframe with a huge box in his arms, then sets it on the floor. As he's straightening back up, he notices me.

"Oh, hey. Didn't know you were in here."

I reach into the bag for more pants, bringing out a pair of white skinny jeans. "Do you have something against doors? You're very rough on them."

"No." His mouth twitches. "I find them a*door*able."

I pretend to glare at him. "What's in that box?" I say, nodding toward it. "Looked heavy."

He nudges the box with his foot. "A bunch of toys that look like they're from the Dark Ages. There's probably lead paint on a few of them."

I finish checking over the jeans and put them in the *acceptable* pile. "What happens to the stuff that can't be sold?"

"Trash," he says, then turns away to sneeze. It's pretty dusty in here. "Or recycling."

I nod and start examining a pair of maroon capris. Eli stands there, watching me, for what seems much longer than necessary. Feeling self-conscious again, I lay the capris on my lap and look up at him. "Was there something you needed?"

He shifts his weight to his right leg, the one he favors when he walks, and shakes his head. "I was just wondering how your morning's going."

Oh God. He's going to bring up my crying episode in the car earlier. "Well," I say, going back to the capris, "so far I've found two movie stubs, a paper clip, a fuzzy breath mint, and four dollars and eighty-three cents in change. So, all in all, my morning's been a success."

"Wow," he says, rocking back on his heels. "You have almost everything you need to defuse a bomb."

His comment is so illogical that I can't help but laugh. He smiles at the sound, like it's his goal in life to cheer up sad girls he doesn't even know.

"Seriously, though," he adds. "I just wanted to make sure you were—"

"I'm fine." I fold the capris and reach for the next item. "It's just . . . family stuff. Nothing major."

"Okay." He stuffs his hands into the pockets of his worn

jeans. His clothes, I've decided, would all go in the *unfit* pile. Faded, ripped, frayed . . . nothing he's wearing looks like it was bought in the past five years. It's oddly attractive on him. "So," he says, leaning back against the one bare wall. "Do you volunteer a lot?"

I focus on the pair of jeans in my lap, which appear to have an unfortunate grease stain near the knee. Stain remover might get it out, but I'm sure Rita doesn't have time for that sort of thing. "No," I tell him as I toss the jeans in the *nope* pile. "This is the first time. Something to give me an edge on my college applications," I add, using the same lie I've told my friends.

Eli nods. "Cool. For me it started out as just helping my aunt, but now I think I'd volunteer here anyway. I really like it—except when Aunt Rita's bossing me around—and it's a good cause."

"Yeah, it is," I agree. Rita told me my first day that sales proceeds go to fund group homes for adults with intellectual challenges. I'd like to say I'd volunteer of my own free will too, but I'm not as honorable a person as Eli evidently is.

"I don't like it as much as my regular job, though," he says.

I fish a dime out of the front pocket of a pair of black dress pants. Four dollars and *ninety*-three cents. "What's your regular job?"

He slides down the wall and carefully settles himself on the floor, stretching his legs out in front of him. They almost reach to the opposite wall. "I cut grass for a lawn care company."

My eyes trail over the long lines of his body. *Stop it*, I admonish myself. I'm here to pay my debt to society, not check out cute guys. Especially when the cute guy in question is the nephew of one of the few people who know the truth about me.

"You're into landscaping, then?" I ask, returning my eyes to my pants.

"Yeah. How did you know?"

"Lawn care? The marigolds?"

"Oh. Right." He laughs and crosses his legs at the ankle. "Yep, I'm definitely into landscaping. I'm starting the Environmental Horticulture program at Kinsley in the fall."

"Impressive." I envy people who know exactly what they want to do with their lives. Whenever I think about the coming year and how I'll be expected to decide my entire future, my palms turn sweaty and I forget how to swallow. Normally, I'd discuss stuff like future career plans with my mom—she used to help me decide which courses to take in school and discuss different fields I might excel in—but that was back when I trusted her opinion.

"What about you?" Eli asks, reaching into the box of ancient toys. He pulls out a creepy-looking doll with matted blond hair and a painted-on face. "Any gainful employment?"

"I make smoothies at Royal Smoothie." I glance at the doll and shudder. "Jesus, would you put that thing away? I'm going to have nightmares."

He laughs and tosses the evil doll back in the box. "Royal Smoothie? I love that place. I go there sometimes after the gym for a Booster Berry smoothie."

The gym. Of course. People don't look like him without regular workouts. And high-protein smoothies.

"Well," I say when I realize the last bag is empty. Twenty-four viable pairs of pants are stacked at my feet. Not a bad haul. "I guess I should go see what else Rita has for me to do."

Taking my cue, Eli bends his right leg and uses it and his hands to slowly propel himself to his feet. His left leg seems stiff, like it doesn't want to bend all the way. There's clearly something off about it, but I remind myself it's not my business.

"You just don't want to be in the same room with that doll," he says, gesturing for me to pass through the door ahead of him. "You're scared it might come to life and murder you."

"Nah. I'm a lot tougher than I look, you know."

He gives me an appraising look. "I believe it."

Despite my resolve to see him as a coworker only, I find myself staring at his body again as he walks to the side door and bursts through it, letting it slam shut behind him.

Chapter Nine

WEDNESDAY EVENING AFTER WORK, I WAIT IN MY warm car for Dawson to finish up at Ace Burger. Since our schedules have been in sync for the past week, both us of clocking out at seven, I've been driving him home to give him a break from the bus.

Finally, I see him rounding the corner to where I'm parked along the curb. He gets in and hands me my bag of fries, grabbing his smoothie out of the cup holder with his other hand. This is our little ritual—he brings me fries, I bring him a large Mystic Mango. Employee discounts for the win.

"Why is it so damn hot outside?" he asks, pressing the sweating smoothie cup to his forehead.

I crank up the A/C. "Maybe because it's July."

He grunts around his straw and leans back against the seat, closing his eyes. I rip open the Ace Burger bag and place my fries in the now-empty cup holder. The car fills with the scent of grease, which mingles with the grilled meat smell emanating from Dawson's shirt. Today, his button reads, *Try Our New Heavenly Hawaiian Burger!*

"Bad day at work?" I ask when he doesn't move or open his eyes even after I've started driving.

His eyes pop open. "No. Why?"

"You're just . . . quiet." Usually when I drive him home, he spends the entire time entertaining me with stories about customers and his coworkers and trying to convince me that peanut butter is indeed a delicious topping for a hamburger (I'm still not convinced).

"Oh. Sorry. I'm just . . . Work was fine." He takes a long drink, then grimaces and pinches the bridge of his nose. Ice cream headache, smoothie-style.

I wait until the pain passes and ask, "So what's wrong, then?"

"Nothing. Just, uh, girl problems."

"Alyssa?" I say without thinking. As soon as the word leaves my mouth, I feel like kicking myself in the head. I can't believe that slipped out. When I stop at a red light and look over at Dawson, he's staring back at me with an expression of total panic.

"What?" he asks.

I stuff a few fries in my mouth to cover up my gaffe. And to keep myself from blurting out anything else.

"Aw, man." He groans and runs his palms down his face. "Is it that freaking obvious? Am *I* that freaking obvious?"

I keep driving and chewing. This is fragile territory. Romance within a tight circle of friends can go one of two ways: two people like each other, get together, and the dynamic isn't affected. See Zach and Sophie. Or one person falls in love with another person, that other person doesn't return the feelings, and the circle eventually implodes. The second option, if it ever ends up happening, would absolutely suck.

"Dawson, it's *okay*." I glance between him and the road as we pass into the city's residential area. "I just had a hunch. I'm not going to say anything to anyone. I think Sophie suspects something, though."

He lets out a deep sigh. "I think Alyssa does too."

"What? How?" She hasn't mentioned anything to me.

"I don't know. She's been acting weird lately. We used to text each other and hang out one-on-one sometimes, but now it's like she's avoiding me." He leans forward to adjust the vent, pointing the cold air toward his face. "On my lunch break I texted her and asked if she wanted to go get some ice cream later. You know how much she loves ice cream."

I nod. It's her one true weakness. Well, that and reality TV.

"She said no," he goes on miserably. "Apparently, she's too

tired. Since when is *Alyssa* too tired for ice cream?"

I only vaguely hear him, because I'm remembering that day a few weeks ago in the cafeteria, when Sophie told her she could do much worse than Dawson. Is that what freaked her out? Just the *abstract idea* of dating him?

"I'm sorry." I turn onto his tree-lined street and stop the car in front of his house, a cute red bungalow with white shutters and a neat front garden. The flowers make me think of Eli. Then I wonder why I'm thinking of Eli. "Do you want me to talk to her?"

Dawson makes a *pffft* noise. "Yeah, sure. Maybe you can figure out why she thinks I'm such a loser."

"You're not a loser, and I'm sure she doesn't think that." I offer him a fry. He shakes his head and opens his door. "I'll dig around," I tell him as he gets out. "I mean, in a subtle way. See if I can find out what's up."

"Thanks, pal." He smiles at me and shuts the door.

My father wasn't kidding about the home-cooked meals. When I get home after dropping Dawson off, I find him in the kitchen, pulling a pan out of the oven. The entire apartment smells like garlic and chicken.

"What are you doing?" I ask, looking around. The place is a disaster—open packages everywhere, piles of dirty dishes, and what looks like bread crumbs all over the floor.

"Cooking dinner!" He sets the pan on the stovetop, and I

see four beige lumps that I assume are breaded chicken breasts. "Hope you're hungry."

I'm not, actually, considering I just ate a large order of fries, but Dad went through all this trouble for us. So I gamely dish up a plate, taking the smallest chicken piece and baked potato, plus a teaspoon of corn. Dad fills his plate too and we sit together at our small kitchen table, which normally serves as a resting spot for mail and car keys.

"I totally forgot to get dessert while I was at the store," Dad says as he slices into his potato. "And milk too, for the morning."

"It's okay. I can run out to the store later." I take a bite of chicken. A bit dry, but tasty. And the baked potato looks perfectly done. "This is good."

"Thanks. I know it's not as impressive as the dinners your mom used to make for you, but it's better than pizza, right?"

He looks so proud of himself, I refrain from mentioning that I've never minded pizza, or the fact that he's not an amazing cook. The point is he's trying, which makes me want to try too. "Maybe we can take turns cooking so we don't waste so much money eating out. I think I could make Greek chicken pasta. I've seen Alyssa's mother do it and it doesn't look too hard."

He nods. "Sounds like a plan."

We turn back to our food and eat in silence for a while. Just as I'm starting to think that the tension between us has finally lifted and everything might be okay again, Dad swallows a mouthful of food and meets my eyes across the table.

"Have you given any more thought to visiting your mother?"

There goes what's left of my appetite. I put down my fork with a sigh. "Dad. Can we not do this right now?"

"Do what? Talk? Because we're going to talk about this, Morgan, whether you want to or not."

I stare at him, taken aback. He's never been the demanding, *what I say goes* type of father. Living in the same small space for the past year has been peaceful, for the most part. He generally let me do what I wanted, stayed out of my business, and concentrated on his work. Until the sunglasses incident.

"Last month was a wake-up call," he continues, pushing his plate to the side. "Obviously, you're still having trouble coping with the divorce, or else you wouldn't have done what you did. And I don't think you *will* get past it until you make an effort to forgive your mother."

Having trouble coping with the divorce. Is that why I steal? Or did the trauma of the past year just expose some sort of inner malfunction that was there all along? I grip the edges of my chair, fighting the urge to get up and run. To scream at him, this man who just cooked a nutritious dinner out of love for me. Instead, I take a deep breath and calmly say, "I told you I'm not going to do that. I told Rachel too, so there's no reason for either of you to bring it up again. Okay?"

He glances down at Fergus, who's sitting at our feet and hoping for a dropped piece of chicken. "Rachel thinks you're acting out."

My body goes still and cold. "What do you mean? Wait, did you—did you *tell* her? About the shoplifting?" When he doesn't look at me or answer, a bolt of anger surges through me, warming me up again. "Dad! Why would you do that?"

"I had to talk to *someone* about this, Morgan. Someone else who knows you and loves you. I'm in way over my head here."

I grip my chair even harder, feeling the edges dig into my skin. "Is that all she said? That I'm acting out? She didn't tell you anything else?"

He looks at me, forehead scrunched. "Like what?"

Oh, like that she's far from perfect too. That just a year ago, when you were too heartbroken and distracted to notice, she was spending most of her time in the woods behind her friend Gemma's house, doing vodka shots and bong hits. That she's hardly Miss Innocent.

Of course my sister didn't mention any of *that*. No. She chooses to join Dad's cause and gang up on me instead. Going away to college has clearly changed her. We used to be a solid duo, sisters sticking together no matter what.

"Nothing," I say, and then stand up. "I'll go get that carton of milk now."

There's a grocery store down the street from our apartment complex, but I'm too pissed to face people right away. So I drive fifteen minutes to Birch Grove, a ritzy subdivision a few minutes outside the city. They have their own walking trail and lake, and a pristine commercial area with strip malls, coffee shops, and a big, shiny supermarket. It seems as good a place as any to buy milk.

My body's still vibrating with leftover rage when I enter the store. How dare he tell Rachel? And how dare *she* pretend like she's never been a juvenile delinquent too? Especially after I kept her secret all last summer, covering for her when she came home reeking of smoke and beer at two a.m., or didn't come home at all. It never even occurred to me to tell Dad. I knew Rachel was smart and could handle herself. I knew she wouldn't let one summer of bad decisions snowball into a year's worth of even worse ones. Not like me.

I used to count the days before my sister's visits—now just the thought of seeing her fills me with anxiety. Before, I was just the geeky little sister who looked up to her and missed her and borrowed her favorite clothes. Now I'm the troubled little sister who shoplifts. As annoyed as I am over her concealing her past, I'm also terrified that she'll figure out what kind of person I really am.

I stand on my tiptoes and peer around the store, searching for a sign to point me to the dairy case. I've been in here a few times before with my mom, when she wanted some fancy cake that only this store's bakery carried, but that was years ago. Renovations must have happened since then, because everything seems mixed around.

Finally, I just start walking toward the back of the store, where dairy cases can usually be found. On the way, I pass the pharmacy area, which is vast and well appointed. I pause in the aisle for a moment, remembering what I learned about grocery stores—they are notoriously easy to steal from. And if you do get caught, the staff doesn't usually make a big fuss. I've done it once or twice, at the store near home, with no issues what-soever. It was easy.

Instinctively, I do a camera check. One in the corner, but it appears to monitor only one or two aisles. This place is a cornucopia of blind spots.

I spin on my heel and duck into the makeup aisle. Even though I've just eaten, my stomach feels achy and hollow. Actually, all of me feels achy and hollow, and I know the only thing that will make me feel better—even for a moment—is the exhilarating rush of walking out of here with something I didn't pay for. I know this only confirms Dad's belief that I'm a deviant, but my fear of being seen that way does little to dampen the urge I feel right now.

I zero in on the lipsticks. They're always a safe bet. Small, no bulky packaging, a bar code that's easy to peel off. In fact, they're almost *too* easy for me. I got bored with lifting cheap little items months ago, when they stopped feeling like a challenge. But there's not much time to look around for a better option and I need something, *anything*, to slip into my purse right now.

Randomly, I pluck out a lipstick and pretend to study it. As I'm reading the name of the shade—*Kissable Pink*—a large shadow falls over me.

"I prefer the natural look, myself."

I gasp and whirl around, almost dropping the lipstick. Standing in front of me, grinning from ear to ear, is Eli. Rita's Reruns Eli. *What the hell?*

"What are you doing here?" I ask in a shaky voice. My heart is racing. Five more seconds and he would have seen me steal this lipstick.

"My mom sent me out for dishwasher soap," he says, holding up the green container in his hand. He looks different here, under the bright lights of the pharmacy section. Taller, and better dressed too. His white T-shirt doesn't have even one hole in it. "What are *you* doing here? Do you— I thought you went to Nicholson High."

"I do." The lipstick is still burning through my fingers, so I put it back in its spot. "Oh, I don't live around here, if that's what you're asking. I just stopped in for a carton of milk."

He nods like this makes perfect sense. "I like your shirt."

I glance down at myself and realize I'm still wearing my work shirt, a black polo with the Royal Smoothie logo stitched into the upper left-hand corner. "Thanks. I like yours too. It's so . . . new-looking."

He laughs. "Right, you've only seen me in the old clothes I wear for manual labor. Believe it or not, I don't always dress like I live in a ditch."

"Good to know." I smile back at him. The adrenaline rush of almost getting caught again—even if it's just Eli—has driven away both my anger and the empty, hollow sensation. Now I just feel tired. "You know, for someone so big, you're really good at sneaking up on people and scaring the crap out of them."

"Thanks." He switches the dishwasher soap bottle to his other hand. "No doors, that's why. If I had to go through a door to get to you, you definitely would've heard me coming."

"True."

A woman pushing a cart approaches, and we both move aside to let her pass. In the process, my arm bushes against Eli's. His skin feels warm in the air-conditioned chill of the store.

"Hey," he says, backing up a little, "what are you doing right now?"

"Buying milk, remember?"

"I mean *after* the milk buying. Actually . . ." He scratches the back of his neck and looks away, as if embarrassed. "Do you think you could buy milk later so we can maybe walk over to Starbucks for a coffee or something? I mean, you could buy it now and leave it in your car, but it'll probably be cottage cheese by the time you get home."

"Yuck," I say. When he blinks at me, I add, "The cottage

cheese milk, I mean. Not us going to Starbucks."

He lets out a sigh of relief and then looks at me, waiting for my answer. I'm not sure what to say. A few days ago, I was positive I didn't need any more friends. That I had enough already. But maybe it's exactly what I need. A new friend, someone who doesn't know about my mom or any of the other things about me that I don't like to talk about. Someone fun and funny and simple, a distraction from the overwhelming crapfest this summer has turned out to be.

Also, I really don't want to go home yet.

"Sure," I say with a shrug, like I'm just as carefree as he is. "Let's go."

Chapter Ten

THE BIRCH GROVE STARBUCKS HAS A FLOOR-TO-ceiling fireplace and a cozy-looking nook with two plush sofas. The sofas are both occupied, of course, so Eli and I bring our Frappuccinos to one of the vacant two-person tables.

"What?" he says after we sit down. "Why do you keep checking me out?"

I look away, embarrassed to be caught staring. Though this time, I wasn't checking him out so much as trying to figure him out. First, I run into him at the Birch Grove supermarket, which I assume means he lives around here. Then, on the way over to Starbucks, we stopped for a second at his car so he could drop off the dishwasher soap, and that car turned out to be a shiny new Jeep Wrangler. Having grown up with my parents, I know enough about cars to know that new Jeeps are expensive. At least more expensive than my four-year-old Civic. Which means his parents clearly have money. Which I never would have guessed when I first met him.

"You sure think a lot of yourself," I joke, trying to cover up my embarrassment.

"What's wrong with that? Better than thinking too little of yourself."

I take a sip of my salted caramel Frap because I can't think of anything to say to this. Or anything to say at all. I'm not usually this unsure of myself around guys. I've dated before but have never been in a long-term relationship. Not that this is a relationship. Or a date, for that matter. Just two new friends getting to know each other over Frappuccinos. Never mind the wobbly feeling I get in my stomach every time one of his long legs grazes mine under the table.

"How do you like working at Reruns?" he asks, stabbing his straw into the mound of whipped cream on his drink.

"It's fine." *For community service* . . . "Rita's nice."

"Yeah, she's something." He laughs and leans back in his chair. "When my sister and I were little, she used to take us to plays a couple of times a year. All kinds of plays—we saw some pretty weird shit. And she insisted that we dress up for them. Like, she'd make me wear a jacket and tie, the works. I stopped going when I was twelve or so, but I think Meredith still goes with her sometimes."

"Sounds like fun," I say, smiling at his story. I barely know Rita, but theater definitely seems like something she'd be into. I wonder if she's a movie buff too. "Does she have any kids of her own?"

A weird, undecipherable look crosses his face. "No."

I nod, letting it go. My whipped cream is starting to melt, so I use my straw to stir it into the rest of the liquid. Eli watches me for a moment.

"You remind me of a little fairy," he says randomly. "Or no . . . maybe a sprite."

"Excuse me?"

"Because you're so small," he adds, like I need an explanation.

"Thanks," I say, mildly insulted. There are worse things to be compared to than tiny mythical creatures, but still. "And you remind me of the Jolly Green Giant."

He busts out laughing, causing everyone within earshot to look over at us. I fight the urge to crawl under the table and settle for nudging his foot instead. He moves his leg to the side, evading me, and that's when I see the scars.

The first two times I saw him, he was wearing jeans. But today he's wearing shorts, so his legs are mostly visible. Running horizontally down his left kneecap is a thin, dark line about two or three inches long. Several smaller scars bracket either side of his knee. It looks like something attacked him with tiny knives and he had to be sewn back together.

Eli catches me staring again. "I blew out my knee last fall," he explains, moving his leg under the table again. "Like, completely busted it."

"How? Football injury?"

"No." He gives me a surprised look. "Hockey."

"Oh. Sorry, you just look like you play football." I make a *keep going* motion with my hand. "So what happened?"

"I got checked really hard into the boards. Totally shredded my ligaments and cartilage. I needed ACL reconstruction surgery and—are you sure you want to hear this?"

I realize I'm cringing and force my face to relax. Medical stuff freaks me out. I cover my eyes during the surgery scenes on *Grey's Anatomy*. "Go on," I say, taking a fortifying sip of my drink.

He looks at me closely before proceeding, like he's making sure I can take it. "The surgeon reconstructed my ACL—that's one of the main ligaments in the knee—using a graft taken from my hamstring. She repaired the cartilage tear at the same time. Are you still with me? You're not going to pass out, are you?"

I shake my head. His description is making me feel mildly nauseated, but it's also kind of fascinating how pieces of the body can be rebuilt using other pieces of the body.

"Anyway," he continues, making condensation circles on the table with his cup, "the damage was so severe that it took me ages to recover. Missed the rest of the season, not to mention weeks of school. I was on crutches for months, and spent a lot of time in physical therapy. I'm still not fully recovered, honestly. My knee is still really stiff, and it hurts if I stand too long." He pushes his cup away. "Sorry. That sounded whiny."

"Whiny?" I say, incredulous. "Are you kidding? You must have been in a ridiculous amount of pain."

"Yeah. I actually heard it pop, when it happened. My knee. The pain was unreal."

I shudder. "I can't even imagine. I cry over hangnails."

He flashes me a smile, but it flickers out just as fast. "And then there's, you know, the mental part of it. Months of pain and sitting around the house, missing everything. . . . It takes a toll. Luckily, I found something even better than sports."

"Flowers and grass?"

Eli grins again, and this time it stays. "Flowers and grass. No chance of blowing out a knee while landscaping."

"Unless you get body checked by a garden gnome or something."

Laughter erupts out of him again, this time even louder. "You're a strange girl, Morgan, um— Wait, what's your last name?"

"Kemper. What's yours? Are you a Sloan, like Rita?"

"No, she's my mom's sister. I'm Elias Randall Jamison."

"Morgan Hillary Kemper. Nice to formally meet you."

We shake hands over the table.

✳   ✳   ✳

Dad and I barely speak to each other for the rest of the week. Well, he tries, but every time he asks me a question or comments on the weather or some other banal thing, I answer as briefly as possible. I know I'm acting bratty, but I can't seem to help myself. I'm still pissed at him for telling Rachel about the shoplifting, even though he never promised to keep it a secret and I get why he needed to talk about it with someone. But ever since Mom left, it's like there's anger simmering inside me all the time, just waiting to boil over into a grudge.

The tension in the apartment is unbearable, so I deal with it by staying out as much as I can. On Saturday, after my one-to-seven shift at Royal Smoothie, I pick up Sophie and drive us over to Alyssa's house for a girls' night in.

"Oooh! Little triangles! I love these!" Sophie exclaims. She's standing in front of the open fridge, snooping through leftovers, while Lyss and I microwave popcorn.

"*Tiropitakia,*" Alyssa says, reaching around her for a two-liter of Coke. "And I think they're for brunch tomorrow."

"Just one? Your mother will never know."

Alyssa's eyebrows shoot up. "Have you met my mother?"

Sophie frowns and shuts the fridge. Mrs. Karalis *is* pretty protective over her cooking. One time she scolded me for swiping a tiny piece of baklava off a tray that was meant for someone's sick aunt. The weird thing is, she wasn't even in the room when I did it.

"Tiropitakia," I mumble, trying to recall the taste. "I don't think I've eaten that since—" Suddenly, I remember exactly when I last ate that dish, and I clamp my lips shut before I can finish my sentence. But Alyssa catches on anyway, and a shadow passes over her face.

"My father's funeral," she finishes for me, her eyes on the cupboard as she takes out three glasses. "My aunt Cora brought them to the reception we had here afterward."

"Right," I say quietly, remembering that day and the huge assortment of food that took over every square inch of surface in the kitchen. I'd loaded a plate with a sample of everything and brought it outside to Alyssa, who I'd found huddled against the side of the shed, red-eyed and shivering in her thin black dress. It was November and freezing, but we stayed out there for almost an hour, nibbling flaky pastries and watching the dead leaves skim across the grass.

I shove another popcorn bag into the microwave and try to steer us into less depressing territory. "Your mom doesn't mind us being here while she's at work, does she?"

The shadow lifts from Alyssa's face as she pours our drinks. "No. She'd much rather I stay at home than 'run the streets with my friends,' as she calls it. She worries when I'm out at night."

I used to feel bad for her, dealing with such a clingy mother, but now I feel a stab of envy when she talks about her mom's devotion to her. Mrs. Karalis runs a custom jewelry store downtown—a job she and her husband shared for twenty years before he died—and even with her long hours away from home, she still knows exactly where Alyssa is at all times. My mom was never the overprotective type, but she did use to care about where I was and if I was safe. Now, if I suddenly decided to run away to, say, France, she'd probably just shrug it off.

"What are the guys doing tonight?" I ask once we're all settled on the living room couch with our snacks, ready to watch *Pitch Perfect* for the zillionth time. My friends aren't exactly receptive to my attempts at broadening their movie tastes.

"Video games at someone's house," Alyssa says, flicking on the TV.

Sophie props her feet up on the coffee table. "I thought about going to that, but I decided to hang out with you guys instead because, you know, sistas before mistas."

In an impressive display of timing, my phone dings with a text from Eli. After we left Starbucks the other night, we exchanged numbers in the parking lot before heading to our respective cars. We've been texting sporadically ever since, mostly random stuff about our jobs and other mindless chat. He's the same over text as he is in person—cheerful and open and nice, a fun diversion from all the heavy stuff in my life. I find myself looking forward to his messages, even when he sends me horrible jokes. Like right now.

Have you ever tried to eat a clock?

It's very time-consuming.

I snort quietly and type a quick response: sigh

He responds with a winking emoji, and I set my phone on the arm of the couch, facedown. When I look over at my friends, they're both eyeing me suspiciously.

"Who was that?" Alyssa asks.

I lean forward and grab a handful of popcorn from the bowl on the table. "No one."

"You were smiling," Sophie says with a sly smile of her own.

"Yeah, I do that once in a while."

"No, you were smiling like you were texting with a *guy*."

Alyssa turns to her. "What does a texting-with-a-guy smile look like, exactly?"

Sophie lowers her eyelids and stretches her lips into a wide, dopey grin.

"Like you're on drugs, apparently," I say, then let out a resigned sigh. "It was this guy I met at work. Um, at the thrift shop. Eli."

"Eli," Sophie repeats, drawing out the *E* sound. "Is Thrift Shop Eli hot?"

An image of him from this morning flashes through my mind. Rita sent me outside to ask him if he'd seen the packages of new clothes hangers she'd bought. When I got outside,

I found him in front, digging weeds out of the flower bed. At the sound of my approach, he straightened up and used the bottom of his T-shirt to wipe sweat off his forehead, giving me a glimpse of his defined abs. It took me a several seconds to remember what I was supposed to ask him.

"Maybe," I admit. "In a tall, built jock sort of way."

"Oh, he's a sports guy?"

"Not anymore." I tell them about his knee, and how he took up an interest in horticulture when he realized he wouldn't be able to play for a while.

"That must've sucked for him," Alyssa says as she flips through Netflix. "I mean, having to change the course of his whole life like that."

I shrug and scoop up some more popcorn. "He seems happy. Though I barely know him, so that's just an assumption."

"Do you like him?"

"Well, yeah," I say, chewing. "I mean, he's that type of guy, you know? Impossible not to like."

"I think he sounds cute," Sophie says. "A big muscly guy who likes flowers? That's adorable."

Alyssa rolls her eyes. "You think everyone is adorable."

"That's right." She makes the dopey face again. "Especially Zach."

The mention of Zach makes me think of Dawson, which makes me think of my promise to him—that I'd subtly dig for answers from Alyssa and find out why she's apparently avoid-ing him. Only I have no idea how to go about it.

We're ten minutes into the movie before I gather the nerve to bring it up. "Um, Lyss?"

"Yeah?"

"Oooh!" Sophie gasps, like she just thought of something amazing. She leans over Alyssa's lap to look at me. "If you start dating Thrift Shop Eli, we can double-date. I've never done that with either of you guys." She glances at Alyssa and adds, "And if Alyssa finds someone, we can triple-date. Even better."

I could kiss her. She just gave me the perfect opening with-out even trying. "Or if Dawson finds someone," I put in.

Alyssa nudges Sophie off her lap and stares hard at the TV screen. "Guys, I am *not* dating Dawson."

"Why not?" Sophie asks. She holds up a hand and starts counting off on her fingers. "He's smart. He's cute. He's nice. *And* he likes you."

I keep quiet so Lyss doesn't feel like we're ganging up on her, but in my head I'm thinking *Go, Sophie, go.*

"Are you not attracted to him?" Sophie presses in her curious-but-pushy way. "Is that it? Are you not attracted to *guys*?"

"Can we just watch *Pitch Perfect*?" Alyssa picks up the remote and hits the volume button.

"Or maybe you're bi, like Jasmine?" She raises her voice

to be heard over the movie. "A lot of people are bi, you know. It's a thing."

"You know what else is a thing?" Alyssa says, making her eyes wide like she's about to impart an outrageous truth. "Going through high school without dating. It's not that uncommon. Some people just *don't want to date*."

"And that's fine," I say, though I feel disappointed for Dawson. I'm not surprised, though. Alyssa has never shown any interest in having a relationship, and the few crushes she's had involved fictional people. It never seemed to matter before. But now there's Dawson, who I'd hate to see hurt for loving someone who has him securely placed in the Friend Zone.

Sophie stares at her for a moment, then sighs. "I'm sorry. It's your business, and I shouldn't push you to talk about it if you don't want to."

Alyssa relaxes against the back of the couch. "Thank you."

"What I *should* do is go get one of those yummy triangles. I'll risk your mother's wrath." She jumps up and skips out of the room.

"*Tiropitakia!*" Alyssa yells after her.

I start laughing and, after a moment, Alyssa joins in.

Chapter Eleven

WHENEVER IT'S SLOW AT WORK, SCOTT, MY SUPER-
visor, keeps me busy chopping fruit. That's what I'm doing
Monday afternoon when I hear a familiar deep voice behind
me at the register.

"Can I get a large Booster Berry?"

My knife stills, and I turn away from the counter to see Eli.
His dirty-blond hair is damp and he's wearing a black tank top,
giving me and everyone else an unobstructed view of his mus-
cled arms. He smiles at me and lifts his hand in a small wave.

My coworker Kyle is on cash, and even from a few feet
away, I can tell he's trying hard not to stare. Kyle's nineteen

and skinny with gauges in his ears and tattoos covering both arms, but despite looking like he belongs in a punk band, he's the shyest person I've ever met.

"Sure," I hear him say in an abnormally high voice. A minute later, he's by my side. "Did you see that guy?" he whispers as he reaches into the fridge beside me for the yogurt.

"Yeah." I finish with the pineapple and scoop the chunks into a bag. As I turn to put it in the still-open fridge, I catch Eli's eye and smile. "I know him."

Kyle's eyes get round. "Is he your boyfriend?"

"No."

"Can you put in a good word for me, then?"

I laugh. "Go make the Booster Berry, Kyle."

He heads for the blenders, almost colliding with Scott as he suddenly emerges from the back of the store. "Go ahead and take your break now, Morgan," he says as he breezes by me.

Great timing. I rinse my hands in the industrial sink and untie my apron. By the time I grab my purse and come out from behind the counter, Eli has his smoothie and he's lingering by the door. His size makes the small store seem even smaller, like the walls are shrinking around him.

"You didn't have to stop dicing fruit on my account," he says as I approach him.

"Don't flatter yourself. I'm just on break." I grin at him and step outside into a solid wall of heat. Eli follows me, smoothie straw clamped between his teeth. "Isn't it enough that we work together at the thrift store?" I tease. "You have to show up at this job too? Stalker."

He releases the straw. "Hey, I didn't even know you were working today. For your information."

I give him a mock-suspicious look and gesture to the spacious set of concrete steps leading up to a giant office building across the street. "I usually sit over there on my breaks."

"Mind if I sit quietly beside you and drink my smoothie?"

"If you insist."

We cross the busy street and find a shady spot on the stairs, off to the side so we won't block the general flow of traffic. As usual, Eli lowers himself to sitting slowly and carefully, wincing a little on the way down.

"My knee always aches after the gym," he explains. He told me over text the other day that he went to the gym four or five times a week, both to work out and to build back strength in his knee, using exercises he learned in physical therapy.

"You want some of this?" Eli holds up his perspiring smoothie cup. "More satisfying than boring old water."

Though I've made dozens of Booster Berry smoothies, I've never tasted one. I lean over and take a sip from the straw, acutely aware that his lips were in the same spot just moments ago. The tartness of the berries makes my mouth water. "Pretty good," I say, chasing it with a sip from my water bottle. Sweat beads on the back of my neck. It's much too hot for pants and a polo.

We sit quietly for a few moments, listening to the loud grinding noises coming from a construction site a few blocks away. Pedestrians pass in front of and beside us, but I don't people-watch the way I normally do when I'm sitting here alone or with Dawson. Every bit of my awareness is centered on Eli. The freshly showered scent of him. The way his fingers are wrapped around the cup. The bulging muscles in his calves. The fact that I've been thinking about him all week, hoping I'd get to see him again before my next shift at Rita's. And now here he is, which makes me wonder if he's been thinking about me too.

Okay. It's too damn hot out here. I glance at the time on my phone and stand up. "Break's almost over," I announce, wobbling on my feet a bit. Maybe I'm developing heatstroke.

"I'll walk you back," Eli says, positioning his right leg to take his full weight as he stands. For a second, I consider offering to help him up, but then I realize it would be like a paddleboat pulling a barge. Bad idea.

Neither of us says a word on the short walk back to Royal Smoothie. Then, just as I'm about to tell him goodbye and slip back into the lovely air-conditioning, Eli clears his throat.

"So," he says, scraping his straw against the plastic cup lid.

I've always hated that sound, but I try to ignore it.

"So," I echo.

"So. I was thinking."

I squint up at him, but he's gazing intently at the brick wall beside us. "And . . . ," I say slowly.

"That new Leonardo DiCaprio movie looks pretty good." He looks at me for a second, then back at the wall. "I mean, if you like Leonardo DiCaprio. And movies."

Oh. Okay. I get it now. After all the semiflirtatious banter and the Starbucks nondate and the regular texting, I shouldn't be surprised that he's asking me out. But for some reason I'm a little stunned, even though there's clearly *something* happening between us. Sophie would call it *chemistry.*

"I do," I say over the screeching sound of truck brakes. A sidewalk in the middle of the city isn't the most convenient spot to accept a date. "My friends think I'm kind of obsessed, actually. I have this huge collection of DVDs and Blu-rays. So yeah, I love movies. And Leo."

Eli takes a drink from his cup, which by now is dripping condensation all over his shirt and the pavement. "Awesome. So you want to go see the nine thirty-five show tomorrow night?"

I want to say yes right away, but for some reason I hesitate. How long has it been since I've been on a date? Months. And I don't particularly want to get into a relationship when I have so much going on—the tension with my dad and Rachel, my diversion obligations. Even worse, Eli is *connected* to one of my diversion obligations, and he doesn't even know about it. Or about me. Dating him would mean living a lie.

Then again, I'm already living a lie with most of the people in my life. What's one more? I like Eli, and I want to spend more time with him outside work. Even if it means keeping a few secrets. *Fun and simple*, I remind myself. That's all this has to be.

"Okay," I tell him. He visibly relaxes, his face lighting up in a smile and his shoulders loosening. I like that I can make him nervous. And happy. "You want to pick me up?"

"Sure, if you tell me where you live."

I open the door to Royal Smoothie. Cool air trickles out, making me shiver. "I'll text you my address."

He nods, backing away. "Awesome," he says again. "See you tomorrow."

I wave at him and go inside. Kyle is still by the register, now replenishing the straw dispenser.

"What's going on tomorrow?" he asks when I join him behind the counter. He obviously overheard our last exchange. "Never mind. Don't tell me. I'm not in the mood for raging jealousy."

I smile mysteriously and start chopping into some mangos.

✳   ✳   ✳

Later, after I shower off the day's sweat and fruit slime, I lounge on my bed with Fergus and my laptop.

It's been weeks since I logged on to Tumblr and browsed through the shoplifting blogs. There are dozens of new entries. Lists of tips and tricks I already know about. Personal stories. Most of the entries, though, involve people's hauls. One blogger I follow, a girl called lucylifts, posted a picture of the two hundred dollars' worth of makeup she lifted from Sephora. Impressive, considering how hard it is to steal from there.

Reading these blogs makes me feel both sentimental and angry. I miss taking things, miss the strange, comforting high it gave me. Even the humiliation of getting caught and punished hasn't helped curb the impulse. But at the same time, I know it's wrong to feel this way. I shouldn't *want* to steal. I shouldn't miss doing something that has disappointed my father and caused so much damage. Not to mention the moral and legal issues involved with it. I should want to quit, to reform. And deep down, I do. It's just that I have no idea how to start.

Discouraged, I hit the Facebook button on my task bar, making lucylifts's blog disappear. My little chat icon is alerting me that I have a message. It's from Sophie, sent a half hour ago while I was in the shower.

I want to see a pic of Thrift Shop Eli. Does he have a Facebook page?

I send her a question mark, to let her know that I both saw her message and have no idea. Then I immediately click on the search bar and type in his name.

He's the second person on the list of results. Eli Jamison, Waverly High. When I click on it, his page comes up private. We need to be Facebook friends before I can see his statuses and pictures. Also, his avatar is just a hockey team logo, so Sophie will be disappointed.

I click back into the chat box to tell her what I found. Or didn't find. We message back and forth for a few minutes and then she logs off to go back to whatever she and Zach are doing at his house. I'm still on Eli's page, my cursor hovering over the friend request button. Nah. Too presumptuous. Instead, I head over to Google to see if he has any other social media accounts that I can cyberstalk.

His name brings up hundreds of hits, but none of them are about him, at least on the first few pages. Too broad. I type in his full name—Elias Randall Jamison—plus the name of our city, in hopes that it will narrow down the results.

Nothing again, at least not at first glance. But when I continue to the second page, a line of text catches my eye.

For the past fifteen years, Dr. Randall Jamison and his volunteer surgical team have been providing free cleft lip and cleft palate surgery for children in need.

I click on the corresponding link, which brings me to an article in a small local paper, and read more about this Dr. Jamison. He's an oral maxillofacial surgeon—whatever that means—and every few years he goes on missions to underdeveloped countries, where he fixes children's faces and teaches other surgeons his techniques. He changes lives, basically, and all on his own dime.

Dr. Randall Jamison. Nowhere in the article does it mention his family, but I know, somehow, that he's Eli's father. I lean toward the screen to get a closer look at the head shot that accompanies the article. Dr. Jamison is handsome and beefy looking, with graying blond hair and a wide, slightly mischievous grin. A mirror image of Eli's.

I shut my laptop and flop back on the bed. Fergus, who's wedged himself between my pillow and the wall, glares at me for a second and then rolls over on his back, demanding tummy rubs. But I'm not in the mood to indulge him right now. Eli's father is a big-deal surgeon, not to mention a selfless humanitarian. His aunt runs a not-for-profit thrift shop to raise money for people with intellectual disabilities. His mother and sister are probably saintlike too. And of course, Eli himself is pretty amazing, at least from what I've witnessed so far.

His entire family probably reeks of stability and goodness. I bet his mother never cheated on his father. I bet his sister would never even *consider* shoplifting, let alone do it dozens of times. I bet none of them have ever had the cops called on them or been ordered to do mandatory community service. I bet they'd feel disdain for anyone who has.

Something my father said during our fight last week flits through my mind: *I'm in way over my head here.* I'm starting to understand the feeling.

Chapter Twelve

"MORGAN, I JUST WANT TO TALK."

I should have known, when Dad knocked on the bathroom door a few seconds ago and handed me the house phone, that it was my sister on the other end. I've been ignoring her texts and calls to my cell. I know she'll want to talk about my shoplifting charge, but I don't want to discuss it with anyone, even her. It's bad enough that Dad knows.

"I can't right now," I tell her. "I'm getting ready to go out." It's the truth. Eli is picking me up for the movies in fifteen minutes.

"This won't take long." She pauses to let out a long breath. "Why didn't you tell me about the shoplifting?"

I set the hairbrush I was holding on the counter and shut the bathroom door, in case my father's still lurking nearby. "Because it was a dumb thing to do and it's over now and I don't want to talk about it. The same reasons *you* didn't tell Dad that you spent all last summer drunk and high. We all have our ways of acting out, right?"

"Okay, fine," she says flatly. "I don't have much room to judge. But I stopped doing all that shit ages ago, once I realized how stupid I was being. So why would I bring it up to Dad now? And why are you mad at *me*?"

"I'm not mad at you, it's just . . ." Sighing, I plop down on the edge of the tub and check the time on my phone. Twelve minutes. "Don't pretend to be the perfect daughter when you're not much better than me."

Rachel sighs too, causing the line to crackle with static. "Okay. I'm sorry. I'll tell Dad everything, if that's what you want."

"No," I say, straightening the hem of my sundress. "You're right. There's no point it bringing it up now. I don't think Dad can take much more, anyway."

"Yeah." Her voice is softer now. Sad. "I just wish you would've told me that you were struggling."

Tears sting my eyes, but I blink them away fast. I don't want to have to redo my makeup.

"I'm fine," I say. I'm sick of talking about myself. "So what's new? How are things going with Amir and work?"

"Work is great. I helped neuter a Yorkie today."

I wince. "Rach."

"What? You asked." She laughs. "Amir's good too. He's taking me out for a late dinner after he gets off work. What are you up to tonight?"

"I'm going to the movies with this guy from work." She doesn't have to know which work.

"Really." She draws out the word, a smile in her voice. "A date? I need details."

"Later. I have to finish getting ready."

"Okay, just let me say one more thing." Rachel clears her throat. "I talked to Mom on Sunday."

Just like that, the lightened atmosphere disappears. "And?"

"I told her I was coming to visit at the end of summer. She was thrilled. We talked for like an hour about school and her new house and stuff. She sounded . . . I don't know. Like the same old Mom." She pauses for a moment. "She asked about you. I told her you weren't ready to see her yet. She understood, though she really wishes you'd come. She misses us, Morgan."

Pain flares through my chest, swift and unexpected, and I grip the edge of the sink. Grip it hard, until more pain shoots through my hand, overriding the throbbing behind my eyes and in my throat. I will not cry. I will not feel bad about her missing me. It's her fault she's gone, not mine. She caused this.

"I really have to go, Rach," I say once I'm sure I can speak without my voice cracking. "Or I'm gonna be late."

"Oh, sure." If she hears the slight tremor in my words, she doesn't let on. "Talk to you later."

I hang up and take a few deep breaths, waiting for the pressure to ease and the pain to fade. Finally, after I've exiled my mother to the far corner of my mind again—the only place it doesn't hurt to have her—I pick up the brush and finish fixing my hair.

Five minutes later I'm in the elevator, debating whether I should hit L for Lobby or just walk right back out and go home. Ever since yesterday, when I found out about Eli's dad, a banner with the words *Out of Your League* keeps blinking in my head. In eye-scorching neon. We clearly have very different family lives, and I'm not sure if I could ever fit into his.

It's a just a movie, I repeat to myself. *No one's saying we have to trade life stories.*

I smooth my hair off my face and press the L button.

Eli is here and waiting for me when I step outside into the humidity. He's standing next to his black Jeep, gazing up at the apartment building like he's expecting me to rappel down the side of it any minute. At the sound of my footsteps, he looks toward me and smiles.

"There you are," he says, sounding relieved. "For a second, I thought I went to the wrong building."

Not surprising, considering there are six of them on this

street alone and they all look basically the same. "Sorry for keeping you waiting," I say once I reach him. "I was . . . on the phone."

"No worries. I just got here myself."

Silence falls between us and we smile at each other awkwardly. His eyes stayed glued to my face, and for a moment I wonder if my skin is blotchy from holding back tears earlier. Then I catch his gaze pinging downward and I realize he's trying very hard not to stare at my exposed skin on display in a short, strapless sundress. Just like I'm trying very hard not to stare at his biceps straining against the sleeves of his dark blue crewneck.

A car horn honks somewhere in the distance, popping the bubble of awkwardness surrounding us, and we turn to climb into his Jeep. Literally climb, in my case. I have to hold on to the door handle and pull like I'm scaling up the side of a cliff. If Eli notices, he doesn't let on. He probably senses that I wouldn't be very receptive to a boost.

"We still have about an hour before the movie starts," he says after I'm settled in the seat. The interior of the Jeep is roomy and neat. I wonder if it's usually like this or if he cleaned it just for me. "You want to walk around the mall or something while we wait?"

"Sure. Maybe we could pick up some snacks to smuggle into the theater." I smile and hold up my purse, which is big enough to store multiple drinks and several boxes of candy.

"Lawbreaker," he teases.

I shift uneasily in my seat. If he only knew. Sneaking outside food into the movies is frowned upon, but it's not an actual crime like, say, shoplifting. And unlike shoplifting, a lot of people do it. "Yep," I say, trying to laugh it off. "I'm a total rebel."

The movie theater we're going to is downtown in the South End Mall. I spend the entire drive there trying to force myself to relax and stay present in the moment. I really have to tell Rachel to stop mentioning Mom during our conversations. No matter how hard I try to stifle it, what she said tonight loops endlessly in my head. *She misses us, Morgan.*

My mother said she misses me.

"You okay?"

I snap to attention and realize we're in a parking garage, the car is off, and Eli is looking at me. *Oops.* "Yeah. I'm fine."

And I *am* fine as we walk through the musty garage toward the exit. It's just beginning to get dark as we step out onto the sidewalk. The night air smells like a mix of food and beer and warm, damp pavement. As Eli and I hike the short distance to the mall, I do my best to put aside whatever thoughts are plaguing me and act like someone he won't regret asking out. I think I'm doing a fairly decent job until we arrive at the mall.

Shortly after we step inside, my body starts to tense and then the hyperawareness kicks in like it always does when I'm in or near stores. My paranoia was bad enough *before* I got caught; now it's ten times worse. Of course I'm not going to shoplift—not with Eli right here—but my intentions don't seem to matter. Every person I see is a potential LP officer, watching me and lying in wait for the right moment to strike.

"Is someone chasing us?"

"What?" I look over at Eli and realize he's several inches behind me. Embarrassed, I slow my pace to match his. Even though his legs are way longer than mine, his knee prevents him from traveling at warp speed, like I was obviously doing. "Sorry."

He grins and reaches for my hand, threading his fingers though mine. "There. This'll help keep us in sync."

His hand is surprisingly soft, and holding it heightens my awareness in a different way. Suddenly, all I can notice is the warmth of his skin and the way his thumb brushes against my palm. Our fingers stay linked as we stroll down the mall to the drugstore, one of the only places to get chips and candy. We don't let go until we need both hands for loading up on snacks.

By the time we get to the theater, I have to switch my purse to my left shoulder because my right one is aching from the weight of all the junk food crammed inside. Eli and I find this highly amusing and start laughing right there in the ticket line.

"It's a good thing they don't randomly search bags here, like at the airport," he says, taking my hand again. "Or else you'd be arrested for sure."

Again, I feel a twinge of unease. The purse I'm carrying is the same one I slipped those expensive sunglasses into at Nordstrom. The same one mall security searched through while I sat there watching, my face hot with shame. It happened at a different mall from the one we're in now, but still, being here makes me feel like I have *Shoplifter* branded on my forehead. Every time I manage to relax even a little bit tonight, something happens to remind me what a mess I've made of things.

To get my mind off it, I try to focus on Eli instead and how much I like having him beside me. He keeps his fingers wrapped around mine until he has to let go to pay for the tickets, then immediately reaches for me again. Even with the waves of anxiety rippling through me, holding his hand feels natural, comfortable, like we're characters in a movie and this has been in the script all along.

"Are you sure you're okay?" Eli asks after we're settled into our seats in a middle row.

"Yeah, why?" I dig into my purse and hand him a bottle of water and a package of Twizzlers.

"I don't know. You just seem a little off."

I lean over to place my bag on the floor so I don't have to look at him. He's right. I *am* off, and it's not just because of my conversation with Rachel or my paranoia over being at the mall. This date, sitting here with him, doesn't feel as easy and straightforward as I'd expected. It feels like the beginning of something more, and I'm not sure I'm in a good enough place for something more right now. Maybe this was a bad idea.

"I don't think we know each other well enough yet for you to determine whether I'm on or off." I say it in a light, teasing tone, even though I really mean it. He *doesn't* know me. All he's seen so far is the sarcastic, cries-alone-in-her-car-and-hates-creepy-dolls Morgan.

"True." He opens his water and takes a drink, keeping his gaze on the preshow commercials. "I do know you well enough to determine that you intimidate the hell out of me, though."

I almost choke on a sip of iced tea. "What? Why on earth would *you* be intimidated by *me*? I'm five foot two and you're like, what, six three?"

"Six three and a quarter," he corrects, like this is a significant distinction. "And I'm not talking about size."

"What *are* you talking about, then?"

He puts his water in the cup holder and angles his upper body toward me, resting his arm on the back of my chair. A nice piney scent rises up between us, and I lose my focus for a second.

"Well, let me see if I can explain it without sounding like a total knob." He takes a deep breath. "Okay, not only are you smart and funny and obnoxiously cute—"

"Obnoxiously?"

"—but you're also this, like, really decent person. Most of my friends spend their Saturday mornings nursing hangovers, and you spend yours volunteering at a charity."

"So do you," I point out.

"Yeah, but Rita's my aunt. And to be honest, it was my parents who suggested that I help her out. But you're doing it because you're thinking about the future and getting into a good college. So yeah, putting all that together, I find you very intimidating." The lights go down and the previews start playing. Eli faces forward again, his arm sliding off the back of my chair. "Okay, I'm done complimenting you for now."

I give him the smile he's looking for, even though it feels plastic and strained. Everything he just said is wrong. All of it. If I were thinking about my future, I wouldn't have risked it by doing something stupid that could follow me forever. It's appalling, when I really stop to think about it, how horribly I've misrepresented myself to almost everyone in my life, even my own father.

I'm not a decent person.

The movie is one long, disjointed blur. I spend the majority of it forcing myself not to jump up and run from the theater like it's on fire. I shouldn't have agreed to this. I should've backed out while I had the chance. I shouldn't have been so stupid as to think I had anything in common with a guy who plants flowers and does his aunt's heavy lifting and was raised by a parent who devotes his life to improving the lives of needy children.

This was definitely a mistake.

"What did you think?" Eli asks after the lights come up. We stay in our seats while everyone around us files toward the exit, murmuring about the movie and where they're going next.

"I liked it," I say, because I probably would have, if I'd paid attention for longer than two minutes.

"Me too." He stretches his legs as far as they'll go in the cramped theater seating and glances at his phone. "It's twenty to midnight. Do you want to walk around the city for a bit?"

"Sorry, I can't. My dad wants me home by twelve." For once I'm not lying. Dad recently relaxed my strict eleven thirty curfew, with the condition that he knows exactly where I am at all times. I'm kind of grateful for the excuse to leave, because I'm not sure I can walk in the dark with Eli without wanting to kiss him. And kissing him would just make it harder to shut down whatever this is between us, which is really what *should* happen.

Eli's cheerful expression falters a bit, but he rallies quickly and nods. "Sure thing. No problem."

We don't speak much on the way back to Maple View Apartments. I can tell Eli is confused by my sudden mood change, but neither of us mentions it. He probably thinks he did something wrong, but for some reason I can't seem to find the words to set him straight.

"Thanks for tonight," I say as we pull into the parking lot of my building. "You can just drop me off here."

He doesn't argue or make any comment at all, even though he's probably baffled by my desire to get away from him as fast as possible. He just stops in front of the main doors like I asked him to.

"So . . . we should do this again sometime," he says. His tone is sincere, but I can hear the uncertainty and hurt layered underneath.

I nod vaguely and get out of the Jeep, careful not to fall on my face as I hop down. Because a broken neck would be the perfect topper for tonight. "See you Saturday," I say as I shut the door behind me.

He waves at me through the window and then sits there, idling, waiting until I'm safe inside. Even though the building is lit up like Vegas at night and no one has ever gotten mugged in the parking lot, as far as I know. Still, I appreciate the gesture, especially after I basically just blew him off. The same guilt that coils in my stomach whenever my father blames himself for my actions starts doing the same thing now. It's not Eli's fault that I'm a two-faced mess.

He waits until I've passed through both sets of glass doors before he hits the gas and drives away.

Chapter Thirteen

USUALLY, I DREAD THE SEVEN-TO-ONE SHIFT AT work, but this morning it feels like a blessing. The early bedtime plus the scrambling to get ready at dawn gives me an excuse not to answer the series of late-night texts from Sophie and Alyssa, asking me how my date went. It's hard to discuss something when you still haven't fully processed it yourself.

There are no texts from Eli, which doesn't surprise me. He'd have to be stupid not to feel the weird vibes I was throwing out last night, and despite looking like the stereotypical clueless jock, he's clearly got a lot more going for him than muscles and charm.

I try not to think about him as I make smoothie after

smoothie for morning runners and groups of stroller-pushing moms. But even the constant whir of the blenders doesn't drown out my memories of last night. The warmth of his fingers as he held my hand. The sincerity in his voice when he called me a decent person, like he truly believed it. I'm thinking of nothing *but* him by the time my shift ends and I'm able to get back to my phone. Even though I know it shouldn't bother me, my heart still sinks when I see that he hasn't texted.

"I'm pathetic," I mumble to myself as I pocket my phone and shove through the door.

The sky opened up about an hour ago, unleashing fat rain-drops and rumbles of thunder, and it hasn't let up since. In my haste to get to the dryness of my car, I almost miss hearing my name being called as I'm zipping down the sidewalk. I turn to see Sophie's mom's blue minivan and Sophie sitting in the driver's seat, Zach beside her.

"Get in, loser," she bellows, borrowing a line from one of our favorite movies. "We're going to the diner."

I grin and slide open the door to the back, startling a little when I see Alyssa and Dawson sharing the two-person seat. I hadn't noticed them through the rain-smeared window. I greet everyone and move to the way back, which always smells like Sophie's little brothers' sweaty soccer gear. But the van is so warm and dry that I don't complain.

"Why is no one at work?" I ask my friends. Out of all of

us, Zach is the only unemployed one. He's been unsuccessfully looking for work since May, but to be fair, he hasn't tried very hard. Dawson has Ace Burger, Lyss helps out her mom at the jewelry store, and Soph lifeguards at the beach.

"Day off," Dawson says.

"Same," Zach adds with a snort.

Sophie eases the van into a gap in traffic. "Boss sent me home after it started pouring, so I figured, why not pick up the squad and get food?"

"They practically kidnapped me from the store," Alyssa says, tossing an annoyed glance over her shoulder. "Ma was not impressed."

I expect Dawson to come back with some good-natured remark about how her mother can't ban her from eating, but he just sits there, staring straight ahead. He's directly in front of me, so I can easily see the tension in his shoulders. Whatever's going on between him and Alyssa is obviously still unresolved.

The first *e* in the Beacon Street Diner sign is burned out, making it the *Bacon* Street Diner. Dawson's mood lifts at the sight, and he wonders aloud if they did it on purpose because BLTs are on special today. But his smile droops again when Alyssa squeezes in next to Sophie and Zach instead of sitting on the opposite side of the booth with him. Feeling awkward, I take her usual spot beside him.

"So, Morgan," Sophie begins after we order our drinks.

"You can ignore our texts, but you can't ignore us in person. Tell us about last night."

I lower my head and run my finger over a scratch in the table. "There's nothing to tell. We went to a movie and then he drove me home afterward."

Zach folds his hands under his chin and leans in like we're having a secret gab session. "Did you guys make out?"

"Zach." Sophie elbows him in the side and he jerks away, bumping into the wall. "Don't be rude."

"Making out is *rude*? I'll remember that next time we're in my basement."

Alyssa rolls her eyes and looks at me. "So you didn't have a good time?"

"It's not that, it's just . . ." *He thinks I'm a wonderful, selfless person and I'm not.* "We don't have much in common, that's all."

Sophie frowns. "But you seem really into this guy. Why just give up after one date?"

I shrug, at a loss to explain. What can I tell them? That I'm wary of adding yet another name to the long list of people who I've fooled into believing I'm honest and good? Luckily, the waiter arrives with the drinks then, distracting everyone. After he takes our orders and disappears again, Alyssa excuses herself to use the bathroom. Sophie watches her go and then quickly switches from her side of the booth to mine, forcing me to scooch closer to Dawson. He's arguing with Zach about the best headphones for gaming and barely notices.

"What are you doing?" I ask Sophie, who's looking at me with a fiery-eyed intensity that reminds me of Fergus when he sees a fly on the window.

"No," she says firmly.

"What?"

"Thrift Shop Eli. You like him. I *know* you like him. And now you say your date was fine but you have nothing in common? No. I don't accept that." She glances past me to Dawson and lowers her voice to a whisper. "We get enough of this from Lyss. I don't need it from you too. Do you want to be like her? Afraid to date, afraid to *live*? No."

She bounces out of the booth and returns to Zach's side like nothing happened. I'm still digesting her words when Alyssa comes back from the bathroom.

"What did I miss?" She sits down, studying our faces with narrowed eyes. Suddenly, I realize I'm still squished into Dawson and quickly slide back to my spot.

"Nothing," Sophie says, taking a sip of water. "Just badgering Morgan about her date some more."

"Do you ever stop and think, *Hey, perhaps this is none of my business?*"

Sophie furrows her brow like the idea had never occurred to her. Which it probably hasn't. She's never had any qualms about inserting herself into someone else's personal life. She's lucky we love her. "No," she replies.

I laugh, but I can't stop thinking about what she said. No, I *don't* want to be like Alyssa, who I'm almost positive avoids dating because she's afraid of getting hurt. I'm not afraid. No guy could ever hurt me as much as my mom has. It's more that I'm afraid of hurting *him*.

But maybe I don't have to. I dated two guys over the past year and managed to keep my dirty little secret intact around both of them. The trick is to only show people the good parts. To keep to the edges of the circle, making sure no one gets close enough to see the ugliness underneath.

The first thing I do when Sophie drops me off at my car is pull out my phone and text Eli. She's right. I really like him, and I don't want to shut down whatever it is that's building between us, even if it's partially built on lies.

Hey, what are you up to?

I turn on the car and wait, my palm slick against the back of my phone. I don't know why I'm so nervous. Maybe because there's a really good chance he'll reject me right now, tell me to get lost. Or maybe he'll choose to ignore me, which would honestly feel even worse.

My phone chimes.

Just hanging with my friend Matt. How are you?

I shut my eyes for a second and sigh. For once, I didn't ruin everything.

> Feeling bad about last night. Sorry if I was being weird after the movie.
> Consider it forgotten.

I'm not sure if he means the weirdness or the entire date, and I don't dare ask. Instead, I type, Talk to you later? It's vague and kind of impersonal, but also a promise of more to come. I hit send and tip my head back on the seat as I wait for his response. My full belly and the rhythmic tap of raindrops on my windshield lull me into believing that everything might actually turn out okay.

My phone chirps again. I peer down at it, fully expecting to see Eli's answer waiting for me on the screen. Instead, I see another name, one that's been buried in my contacts, unseen and unused, for almost a year.

Mom.

I blink once, twice, before what I'm seeing sinks in. What the hell? My thumb hovers over the text alert, hesitating. Why is she texting me? My brain starts tossing out all these horrible scenarios: She's terminally ill. She left Gary and is moving back home. Dad is sick/injured/dead and she's still his emergency contact. It's the thought about Dad that finally convinces me to open the text.

Your sister suggested you'd be more comfortable
with a text than a phone call. I just wanted to say
that I hope you'll reconsider coming to visit next
month. There are some things I'd like to discuss
with you and I think it should be in person. I miss
you to the moon, Morgan. Congrats on the job, by
the way. Rachel keeps me updated.

The car and rain and everything else around me disappears
as I read her words to me. *I miss you to the moon.* When I was
little, the first thing I'd do when she picked me up at the baby-
sitter's after work was ask her, "Did you miss me today?" And
she'd answer back, every time, "I missed you to the moon."
I never knew exactly what she meant, but hearing it always
made me feel safe. Treasured.

That was years ago, though. It's been a long time since my
mother has made me feel safe and treasured, and one stupid
text isn't going to fix that.

I reread her words, sparks of fury quickly burning through
the nostalgia. She knows about my job? Rachel keeps her
updated? Exactly how long has my sister been in contact with
her? Maybe she knows about the shoplifting too. I get a jolt of
satisfaction, imagining her guilt when she realizes the effect
her actions have had on me, how all the bitterness and pain she
caused drove me to a life of petty crime.

I dump my phone in the cup holder and take a few deep

breaths, trying to pull myself together enough to safely operate a motor vehicle. As I'm drying my eyes with a crumpled
napkin I found in the dash, my phone dings with another text.
Shit. After a long pause, I reach for it. My heart slows when I
see it's from Eli, a belated response.

Sure thing.

I stare at the words for a moment, imprinting them in my
brain for the drive home. At least something in my life at the
moment is guaranteed.

Chapter Fourteen

I CONSIDER NOT TELLING ANYONE ABOUT THE
text from my mom, but two days later I find myself blurting it
out to Alyssa while the two of us are hanging out in my room.

"Wow," she says, her eyes wide. She's lying on her back
beside me, her dark hair spilling across my light blue comforter. "What are you gonna do?"

I lean back against the headboard, legs stretched out in
front of me. "Ignore it? I have nothing to say to her."

Alyssa frowns. Like Rachel, she's a big advocate of forgiveness and second chances. Ordinarily I am too, but not when it
comes to my mother.

"I wonder why she decided to get in touch with you now."

She rolls toward me and props her head up with her hand. "What if she wants you to live with her in her new house? Would you ever consider it? Leaving here?"

I glance around my small room, decorated and organized just the way I like it. When I first moved in I hated it, mostly because it didn't feel like mine. Not like the bedroom I'd just left. Packing up my childhood room was one of the worst days of my life. Alyssa came over to help me, and together we sorted through my possessions, tossing all the unused and worn-out items and boxing up everything else. When the room was finally empty, save for a desk that would never fit into my new room, I leaned into Alyssa and cried.

"It'll be okay," she said, patting my back in a smooth, comforting rhythm. "Life always works itself out eventually."

I believed her—and still do, I guess, even though my life clearly hasn't finished working itself out. But it helps to know she thinks it will someday.

Packing up this bedroom wouldn't make me quite as sentimental, but I'd live in a closet before I'd ever move in with Mom again. Besides, I could never leave my friends.

"No way," I tell Alyssa. "Not even for a second."

Hearing the firm certainty in my voice, she lets out a breath and smiles.

The next morning, as I drive past the Rita's Reruns sign, it hits me that after today I'll have completed twelve hours. Which means I'm almost halfway there, and right on target for finishing my requirements with a week or so of summer left over. It'll be nice to get all this diversion stuff behind me.

"Morgan!" Rita exclaims when I walk into the store. She's at the back of the room, fanatically dusting a shelving unit I've never seen before. "Come see my new addition."

I obediently make my way toward her. The new shelves are made of dark brown wood and just narrow enough to fit between the "miscellaneous kitchen supplies" shelf and a window. "Nice," I say politely.

She runs the dust cloth over the wood one more time and then stands back to admire her work. Today she's wearing a black shift dress and the brightest orange lipstick I've ever seen. It's hard to look anywhere else. "Eli and his dad put it together for me yesterday," she tells me. "Well, mostly Randy, because he's a surgeon and good with hand tools. Eli's more suited to gardening than carpentry, poor boy."

Aha. Internet findings confirmed. Eli's dad is Dr. Randall Jamison, oral maxillofacial surgeon and healer of underprivileged children.

"What's it for?" I tilt my head, examining the limited space between the shelves. "Little knickknack-type things?"

She beams at me. "Books! Someone dropped off scads of them the other day. Boxes and boxes of books. They're stacked in the back room. I had nowhere to display them until now."

I know without her telling me what my job will be

today—affixing price stickers to books. Rita doesn't spend much time on the inventory, at least not while I'm here. She likes to be out front, straightening things up, chatting with customers, helping them find things they didn't know they needed, like a candy dish shaped like a boat or a gently worn Christmas sweater. She's definitely not a behind-the-scenes kind of person. Which works out well, because I am.

"Some of the books look almost brand-new," she continues as she turns and walks toward the front. At the door, she flips the sign on the window to *Open*. "Mark those two dollars. The rest can be a dollar or fifty cents, depending on their condition. Use your judgment."

I nod and head to the back, leaving her to her tidying. The moment I open the door, I realize what Rita meant by "scads." Six large boxes are haphazardly stacked into two groups of three and pushed against the wall. I try to lift one, but it's not happening. My arms are too short and the boxes are too heavy. Eventually, I settle for opening the top box and hauling out books an armful at a time. Soon, the room smells like an old library.

It's not until I sit down with my price stickers that I realize most of these paperbacks are of the romance variety. Shirtless cowboys and tattooed bad boys smoulder at me from the covers like they're beckoning me into the pages. I stare for a moment at one guy's perfect denim-covered butt and feel my cheeks go red. Maybe I'm missing out by limiting my reading to fantasy and sci-fi novels. I stop ogling the cover model's tight behind and open the book to page one.

I'm two chapters in when a large shadow appears in the open doorway, blocking my natural light.

"Slacking off on the job?"

I stick a pen between the pages to mark my place and squint up at Eli. He's back to his living-in-a-ditch wardrobe today—a dark gray T-shirt with a tear in the neck and grass-stained cargo shorts. It may be the sexy book getting to me, but I find his scruffy look almost as attractive as his well-groomed one.

"Just taking a little break," I say, which is an obvious lie because my price sticker sheet is still full and so are all the boxes. "What are you doing?"

He smiles and inches into the room. "Just taking a little break."

I give him a cautious smile back. We haven't seen each other since Tuesday night, after our date ended on a sour note, but we've been texting every day. He seemed to accept the excuse I gave him for why I'd acted a little off the other night. I said it was because I hadn't been on a date in so long, which is partially true. Still, there's been no mention of going out a second time, so I'm not sure how to act around him right now.

"What are you reading?"

"Oh, um . . ." I slide the pen out and rest the book cover side down on the floor beside me. I know he'll tease me if he sees it, especially considering the buff cover model looks vaguely like him. Or at least how I imagine he'd look if he wasn't wearing a shirt. Not that I ever picture Eli without a shirt. Not often, anyway. "It's nothing. Just a book."

He peers inside the open box. "Just a book, huh. You mean *erotica*."

"They're not *erotica*. They're romance."

"*Erotic* romance."

"Shut up." I grab the price stickers and start attaching them to the paperbacks at my feet. Well, except for the one I was reading, because I plan to buy that one for myself. "Can you lift those boxes down for me? The ones on top?"

"Sure thing." He lifts the open box like it's filled with cotton balls and sets it on the floor in front of me, then does the same with the others. Soon there's no room for him to walk, so he sits on one of the closed boxes and massages the back of his knee. I've seen him do this before, after he's been standing for a while. Sometimes I wonder if he downplays his pain around me.

"Need some help?" he asks, lifting the flaps on the box beside him.

I shrug as I put a dollar sticker on a book with a slightly ripped cover. "If you're not busy."

"I'm free for a few minutes."

Rita's strident voice filters in from the front. She's gabbing away to what sounds like a woman and her army of kids. Usually, she has Eli running around doing everything from lugging donations to finding the pair of scissors she swore she just had in her hand two seconds ago. But she can spend ages chatting with customers, so it's safe to assume that it'll be several minutes before she calls for him again.

"Whoa." His eyes widen as he pulls out a small, thin paperback. "You can't tell me *this* isn't erotica."

I lean over to look at the cover, which features a busty brunette wearing a few tiny scraps of lace and clinging to the bare chest of a faceless man. In her right hand is a long, black whip. "Okay," I say slowly. "*That* might be erotica. Rita won't actually put that out for sale, will she? I mean, kids shop here."

He snorts and starts thumbing through the pages.

"Hoping for diagrams?" I ask, going back to my price sheet.

"Hey, I wasn't the one sitting in here all by myself reading filthy literature while I was supposed to be working."

"I wasn't . . . ." I shake my head and sigh. "What I was reading had, like, a story. It wasn't just sex scenes."

"Mm-hmm." He pauses on a page in the book and clears his throat. "'She runs her trembling fingers over his granite abs—'"

I reach over and try to grab the book from him, but he keeps a tight grip on it.

"'—and then shivers in pleasure when he moans her name—'" He dodges my hand again, holding the book out of my reach. "Hey, this is pretty hot."

"Eli," I say in a warning tone, but I'm laughing now, partly out of relief that he's still treating me the same as he did before Tuesday. "You're, like, *obnoxiously* irritating."

He cracks a grin at the borrowed adjective, the same one he used to measure my cuteness the other night at the movies. "Okay, okay." He closes the book and dumps it back in the box. "I would've liked to read the scenes with the whip, though."

"Take it home with you." I stand up and stretch my back muscles, cramped from being hunched over on the floor for so long. "Hide it under your mattress so your mom won't find it."

"Wow," he says, rubbing his knee again. "You really know how to kill a mood."

I laugh and sit down on the box next to him, not bothering to close it first. A book corner digs into my thigh, but I don't care. I think about Sophie's response the other day when I said Eli and I had nothing in common: *No. I don't accept that.* Right now, I don't either. No, we don't have much in common. No, I'm not who he thinks I am. But at moments like this, when he's mere inches from me and I'm feeling the heat from his skin and breathing in the piney scent that turns the rational parts of my brain to oatmeal, all those hesitations seem to take a flying leap out the nearest window.

"Is your knee bothering you?" I ask, then bite my lip when I realize how husky my voice sounds.

"A little." He stops rubbing it and leans back, pressing his palm against the pile of books behind me. His biceps grazes the back of my shoulder and all the nerve endings in my body ignite at once. "I think I tweaked it when we were putting the bookshelf together yesterday."

I look down at my hands, folded tightly in my lap. "Rita mentioned that your dad's a surgeon. Did he operate on your knee?" As I say this, I hear how stupid I sound, but my brain doesn't seem to want to cooperate with my words.

Thankfully, Eli just laughs. "No. One, surgeons aren't allowed to operate on their family members, and two, he's not an orthopedic surgeon. He specializes in oral maxillo-facial surgery, which means he mostly fixes people's mouths, faces, and jaws. And as you can plainly see, my face is already perfect."

I smirk at him. "How about your mom? What does she do?"

"Besides nag at me to take out the garbage? She's the principal at Haven Elementary."

Wow. Two impressively successful parents. His house must be huge.

Eli shifts his weight on the box, which only succeeds in sliding the box closer to mine. "Okay, tell me about your parents now, since we're on the subject."

Talk about a loaded question. "Um, my dad sells cars for Honda."

"And your mom?"

"She works for Honda too, in the finance department."

"So they work together?"

I brush some dust off my jeans. "Not anymore. She moved to another dealership." *In another town, with another man, to live another life* . . .

"Oh."

I don't look at him, but I can sense his brain working, gearing up to ask more questions. But he doesn't, and I'm glad. There are other things I'd rather do right now than talk.

We're sitting very close, but I move over a few inches more, pretending to search for a comfortable spot on this mountain of books. I'm on his left, which means his damaged knee is right there, almost-but-not-quite touching mine. After a moment or two of hesitation, I reach over and trace his biggest scar with my fingertip. He keeps stock-still, barely breathing as I skim my fingers from one scar to the next, connecting them with invisible lines across his skin. Once I've touched every millimeter of fibrous tissue, I lay my palm gently over his kneecap. Eli lets out a breath and looks at me, his eyes suddenly as dark as his shirt.

"I'm healed," he whispers.

The way he's gazing at me makes my stomach flip-flop. I hold my breath as our faces edge closer and closer, until finally, our lips meet somewhere in the middle. Then, barely five seconds in, I almost take out his eye with the corner of my glasses. We back away from each other, laughing.

"Sorry," I say, quickly removing them and placing them on one of the boxes.

When I turn back to him, he puts his hand on the side of my face and pulls me in again. This time, there's nothing in the way. I try to divide my attention between kissing him and listening for footsteps heading this way, but it's hopeless. Soon I'm lost in the feel of his hands tangled in my hair, then gripping my waist, drawing me against him. The boxes strain against our weight as the scents of cardboard and musty books rise up between us.

"Eli! Eli, darling, where did you run off to? I can't find the Scotch tape."

We jerk away from each other, and I almost tumble off the edge of the box. Eli takes hold of my arm, righting me, and glances over his shoulder at the still-open door. "Damn it, Aunt Rita," he mumbles. "You and your Scotch tape have the worst fucking timing ever."

I snort and then burst into giggles. Eli sighs dramatically and reaches for my glasses, which he polishes on his shirt before handing to me. He gives me another quick kiss before standing up. "I should walk in on you reading smut more often."

"It wasn't—"

"Eli!" Rita calls again, this time with more force. She must really need that tape.

"Be right there!" Eli calls back to her, then faces me again.

"To be continued later? I mean, somewhere that isn't the back of my aunt's store?"

I put my glasses on and the room slides into sharp focus. The stacks of bags and boxes. The piles of books still needing price stickers. Eli's red, slightly swollen lips. Do mine look the same? They feel like they do.

"Sure thing," I say, borrowing another one of his phrases.

He backs out of the room, grinning. "Maybe next time I'll let you feel my granite abs."

I snatch a random ball of newspaper off the floor and chuck it at him. He ducks behind the door before it can make contact, snickering the whole time. I ignore him and get back to work.

Chapter Fifteen

THE IDEA OF DAD AND ME SHARING COOKING responsibilities didn't exactly pan out like we'd hoped. After one mediocre dinner from me and two from him—one of which ended in a small grease fire—we resigned ourselves to the fact that we aren't the culinary type and went back to pizza and Chinese. I don't mind. Greasy fast food is better than having a mountain of dishes to wash after these cooking experiments.

At least that's what I tell myself when my father starts coming home later and later at night, shoulders sagging under the weight of stress and takeout bags. After yet another expensive meeting with his lawyer to go over divorce details, he's been working extra hours, taking on more sales, and generally dedicating his life to the dealership. It's giving me flashbacks to when I was little and mostly saw him at breakfast.

He's even at work on Thursday afternoon, one of his supposed days off, when I bring in my car for its semiannual maintenance appointment.

"What are you doing here?" I ask when I walk out to the sales floor after dropping off my keys at service and find him sitting at his desk. He was still sleeping when I left for my early shift this morning.

"Oh. Morgan. I forgot you were coming in today." He glances back at his computer screen and types in a few numbers. "Just catching up on a few things. Is your car with Wayne?"

Wayne, a heavyset bald guy with a gravelly voice and a permanent pack of smokes in his pocket, is Dad's favorite mechanic in the service department. He's usually the one who takes care of my car.

"I guess so." I sit in the padded chair across from him, as I've done so many times throughout my life. I used to spend quite a bit of time in this building when I was younger and both my parents worked here. The clean white floors, the shiny display models, and the selection of Top 40 hits running on a loop over the sound system feels as familiar to me as home.

Dad stops typing and looks at his watch. "How did it get to be two o'clock? I haven't even eaten lunch yet."

"Me either." I came here straight from work, grabbing a

strawberry banana smoothie for the road. But that wore off about fifteen minutes ago and now my stomach is rumbling for something substantial.

"Let's go get something, then." He loosens his tie and wheels away from the desk. "I've been meaning to try the new café that just opened across the street."

I quickly agree. My car will be here for at least another hour, anyway, and I haven't spent more than ten minutes with my father all week. Residual tension aside, I do miss him when he's not around much.

We're almost out the door when a woman suddenly appears and intercepts us. "Charlie," she says, gripping my father's forearm with her manicured hand. "Debra Faraday called and said she wants the Odyssey after all."

"Really? Which trim level?"

"Touring. Can you believe it?"

Dad smiles and congratulates her, this woman I've never seen before in my life, and several things hit me at once. One, she called my father "Charlie." No one calls him that because he hates it, but he didn't even blink when this woman did it. Second, she's obviously a new salesperson here, and a young one at that. Pretty too, with her long dark hair and even longer legs, showcased to their best advantage in high heels and a short black skirt. Third, she's gazing at my father with something more than professional courtesy, which is kind of strange seeing as she can't be older than thirty and looks like *that* while

Dad's a forty-eight-year-old divorcé with thinning hair and an increasingly flabby middle from too much fried food. He still has a nice smile, though, and this woman seems to be basking in the glow of it.

"And who's this?" she asks, finally noticing my presence. She flicks her hair over her shoulder, and I catch sight of her name tag—*Kristi*. Of course. Of course it's spelled with an *i*. She probably dots it with a heart whenever she signs her name.

Dad rests his hand on my shoulder. I suppress the urge to shrug it off. "This is my daughter Morgan."

Kristi with an *i* beams at me. "I should've *known*. Gosh, Charlie, she looks just like you." She holds out a hand for me to shake. "Hi, Morgan, I'm Kristi McGrath. Can I interest you in a new vehicle?"

She and Dad laugh like this is the funniest joke ever, while I stare blankly at the floor. God, this is all I need. I don't mind the idea of my father moving on, but not with someone like *her*. Being in a relationship with someone he works with didn't turn out so well for him last time. Also, she's like ten years older than me. This can't be happening.

Finally, we say good-bye to Kristi and walk across the street to the café, which is virtually empty after the lunch-hour rush. Or maybe it's always empty. In any case, we're sitting at a table with our paninis in less than ten minutes.

"Are you okay?" Dad asks as he uncaps his bottle of water. "You haven't said a word since we left the dealership."

I open my mouth to tell him I'm fine, but different words gush out instead. "She's kind of young for you, don't you think?"

He takes a drink, his forehead creasing in confusion. Then, a beat later, the light comes on and his eyes widen. "You mean Kristi? It's not—" He lets out a cough. "It's not like that. Kristi's one of the top salespeople on the team. She's me ten years ago. Driven, competitive—"

"Into you," I finish for him. My chicken avocado panini is sitting in front of me, slowly growing cold, but I can't eat until I know what the hell is going on.

"Morgan, it is *not* like that," he repeats, red creeping up his neck. Like me, his fair skin shows everything. "She's young and energetic and bright and I'm . . . Anyway, a work relationship, or any relationship for that matter, is the last thing I need right now. Okay? And besides," he adds, picking up his sandwich, "even if she was *into me* or whatever, it wouldn't be any of your business. I haven't grilled *you* about the boy you've been out with almost every night this week, have I?"

I blink at him. How does he know about Eli? I haven't brought him up at all, and Dad has barely been home all week. It's not like I'm coming home with giant hickeys or something. He must've seen Eli pick me up at some point. He's hard to miss.

"Touché," I say, and bite into my lukewarm sandwich. I take my time chewing, letting my thoughts organize themselves before I add, "You *could* move on, though, you know. I mean, with someone you're not in competition with, who's closer to your age than mine. I mean, Mom moved on a long time ago. Obviously."

Dad swipes a napkin across his mouth, avoiding my gaze. "Maybe once you're in college. There's no rush."

The chicken in my mouth turns to paste, bland and rubbery. I hate the thought that I'm holding him back from living just because he has me to take care of for another year or so.

"Oh, Miss Morgan," Dad says with a sigh as he finishes his panini. "I'm glad you're here with me."

My anxiety fades into warmth. I'm not sure if he means *here* as in the café, or *here* as in with him instead of Mom, but it feels good to know he still wants me around after all the shit I've put him through so far this summer.

This renewed connection between us prompts me to dig out my phone and bring up the text Mom sent me last week. I slide my phone across the table and watch his face as he reads her words. But his expression doesn't change, even after he slides the phone back to me.

"I knew she texted you," he says, pushing his plate away. "She mentioned it to me last Thursday when we met with the lawyers."

I drop the piece of crust I'm holding. "You—you've seen her? She was—was she here? In the city?"

He gives me a weird look, like I've suddenly begun

speaking Latin. "We have to see each other sometimes, Morgan. It's not like you can get a divorce over email."

He's right, of course, but I've never thought about them still occupying the same space before. When Mom moved away, it felt like forever. Like she not only left everything behind but threw a lit match on it as she went, torching it to the foundation. The thought of her being here, in the city, so close to me, makes my chest throb with . . . something. Resentment? Longing? Both? Did she even consider trying to see me while she was here? I have no clue how I'd react if she did try. If she walked into Royal Smoothie tomorrow, what would I do? Say?

"At least she's doing something, I guess," Dad says, crumpling his napkin and tossing it on the plate. "Trying to make things right."

She'll have to try harder than that, I think, but to my father I say, "My car will probably be ready soon."

Dad smiles sadly and nods and then does something he hasn't done in at least five years—he reaches across the table and ruffles my hair.

When I leave work the next evening, I'm surprised to see Eli's Jeep—with him in it—parked in front of my car. When he sees me, he powers down the passenger-side window, letting out a gust of AC. I pause and duck my head in.

"What are you doing here?" I ask him. We'd made

tentative plans to hang out at nine, but it's only ten after seven.

Instead of answering, he gives me that dark, scorching look, the one that makes my brain dissolve. "Get in for a sec."

"Eli. I'm, like, covered in yogurt and pineapple guts. I need to go home and get a shower before we go out."

"That's fine, because I just finished a landscaping job and I'm covered in dirt and grass clippings. Hop in for a minute. Please," he tacks on, flashing me his usual mischievous smile.

I add *irresistible* to his list of attractive qualities and climb into the Jeep. Before I can do or say anything else, he leans across the gearshift and kisses me full on the mouth. I kiss him back without hesitation, raking my fingers through the damp hair at the back of his neck. He smells like a blend of sunscreen and cut grass and fresh, clean earth. All the best parts of summer. It's more appealing than any cologne, and I have to force myself to pull away.

"Okay, let's hear it," I say, pressing my palm against his chest. "What do you want? I mean, besides . . . more of this."

He rears back in mock horror. "Whatever do you mean?"

I narrow my eyes at him. He's acting even more affectionate than usual. I get the sense that he's trying to disarm me with his lips so he can soften me up for something.

"Okay, okay." He rubs at a smudge of dirt on his forearm. "This dude I'm sort of friends with, Zander, is having a party at his house tomorrow night, and he asked me if I wanted to drop by. A lot of people I graduated with are going to be there, including the ones who forgot I existed after my knee injury, so I just . . . I don't know. When I was recovering, I realized who my real friends were, and I can literally count them on one hand. The thought of socializing with people I don't like just to hang out with the few I *do* want to see makes me kind of not want to go. At least not by myself. You know?"

I think back to last Saturday, when I decided it was finally time to add him on Facebook. After he accepted my friend request, I spent the next few minutes creeping around his page, looking through pictures. Most of the ones I found were from last year, before his injury. In each shot he was surrounded by smiling groups of people—friends, family, hockey teammates. But the pictures I paused on the longest were the ones of him and a beautiful, dark-haired Asian girl. Ruby Liao, according to the corresponding tags.

I can't help wondering what happened to her. If she was one of the ex-friends who dumped him when his obviously shiny life was disrupted by months of painful recuperation.

I refocus on Eli. He's given up on the dirt splotch and is now gazing at the steering wheel. "Are you asking me to go with you so you can use me as a scapegoat when we cut out early?"

He lets out a breath. "Yeah, if you wouldn't mind."

"Of course I don't mind. But you could've asked me when you saw me later tonight, you know. You didn't have to come here straight from work."

"I know, but I just found out about it, and also I didn't really want to wait until nine to see you."

I smile and he leans over to kiss me again, skillfully avoiding the edges of my glasses. I'm just getting into it when he suddenly pulls back, his gaze fixed on something over my shoulder.

"Um, do you know that guy?"

I spin around to see Dawson standing on the sidewalk a few feet from the Jeep. He's peering into the passenger-side window with a vague expression of alarm, like he's wondering if I'm in the middle of being kidnapped. Damn it. I forgot that I'm driving him home.

"Oh. Yeah, that's Dawson."

Cheeks blazing, I get out of the Jeep and shoot Dawson a *be nice* look. His crosses his arms, affecting a slightly threatening vibe as he eyes up Eli. But it's hard to look threatening when you're clutching a grease-stained bag of fries in your hand and sporting a giant red button that says *We Put the SWEET! in Sweet Chili Burger!*

"Dawson, this is Eli," I say.

Dawson's wary expression clears and they shake hands through the open window.

"I've heard a lot about you," Eli tells him, which isn't really true seeing as I've only mentioned my friends to him maybe three times total.

"Same here," Dawson says. Also not really true. I've talked

about Eli to Alyssa and Sophie, snippets of which he may have overheard, but generally he and Zach don't concern themselves with my dating habits.

Eli nods at Dawson's shirt. "The NuttyButter Burger is *awesome.*"

Dawson grins, pleased to have finally found someone who thinks peanut butter on a hamburger is a sound idea, and I could kiss Eli for bringing it up. But there's no way I'm doing that in front of Dawson again.

"See you later," Eli says to me, then waves to us both before pulling away from the curb and driving off. Once he's no longer in sight, I turn to scowl at Dawson.

"How long were you standing there?"

"Too long." He shudders and then looks me up and down, frowning. "Hey, where's my smoothie?"

"You don't get one today." I snatch the bag out of his hand and start walking toward my car, my face still prickling. Naturally, he's going to tell all our friends that he caught me making out on a public street and they'll never let me live it down.

"Damn." Dawson laughs as we climb into my sweltering car. "Get any redder and your head might pop off."

"Shut up." I shove a handful of fries into my mouth to hide my embarrassment.

Chapter Sixteen

ELI'S SORT-OF FRIEND ZANDER ALSO LIVES IN Birch Grove, in a large two-level house situated on an expansive, landscaped lawn. On the way to the front door, Eli pauses at one of the fat shrubs planted along the pebble pathway.

"Hydrangeas," he exclaims happily, and I can't believe I'm dating a guy who gets *that* excited about flowers. Still, I let him tug me along as he moves in for a closer look. "Smell," he tells me.

I lean in and sniff one of the round white blossoms, hoping I'm not about to be attacked by jumping spiders. The subtle floral fragrance makes my nose itch, but that's okay. I'm nervous about going inside, where I won't know a soul except for Eli, so I'd willingly smell every flower in the yard if it meant postponing the inevitable.

"Nice," I state.

Eli nods approvingly and we continue up to the door. He mentioned last night that he's not close with Zander and has never been to his house before, so he rings the doorbell instead of barging right in, like I do at my friends' houses. When no one answers after a minute or so, he opens the door and we step into the airy, high-ceilinged entryway.

The handful of small, quiet, alcohol-free parties I've been to over the years has not prepared me for the chaotic scene inside. The main floor is crammed with people—circled together in groups, spilling over onto the living room furniture, sitting on the stairs leading to the top floor, dancing to the loud, thumping music. Red cups and beer cans occupy every available surface, including the small table in the entryway that we still haven't left.

Eli takes my hand and gives me a small, fleeting smile. "Ready?" he asks, and it hits me then that he's nervous and unsure too.

I nod, and before I can even brace myself, we're sucked into a whirlwind of heat, cologne, and sweat. Eli squeezes my hand as we shoulder our way through the massive crowd. Every few seconds, someone says hi to him or slaps his back, but we manage to make it to the kitchen without being intercepted.

We find a vacant pocket of space in front of what I assume is the door to a pantry. This room is no better. People file like ants toward a tapped keg in the corner, and every inch of counter space is covered with empty bottles and packages and another dozen or so red cups.

"You want a drink?" Eli says in my ear. He has to bend to reach me. Even though the shoes I'm wearing tonight give me an extra two inches, I still barely clear the top of his shoulder.

"Oh, I don't drink," I tell him. I tried wine a couple of years ago, at the wedding of one of Alyssa's cousins, but all it did was make me nauseated and headachy.

"Me either. Not anymore, anyway. I might be able to find us something nonalcoholic."

As I'm contemplating this, Eli is accosted by a guy with shaggy brown hair and a stubbly beard. They do that one-armed, back-thumping guy hug thing and then Eli turns to me. "My friend Matt," he says, gesturing to the guy. "And this is Morgan."

We nod to each other in greeting. Eli's mentioned Matt a few times. His best friend since elementary school and one of the handful who stuck with him during the slow, boring process of recuperation. Matt is to Eli what Alyssa is to me—someone who's been there through the worst.

"So you're Morgan," Matt says, grinning. He's not as tall

as Eli, or as cute, but he's appealing in a different kind of way. "The girl who sneaks a bagful of food into the movies."

I shoot Eli a glare, and they both crack up. I can tell just by the way they interact with each other that they've probably gotten into some trouble together over the years.

Matt gazes into his red cup. "Gotta get in line for more beer. I'll catch up with you guys later." He claps Eli on the shoulder and, with a quick glance at me, leans in to him and says, "You weren't kidding."

He smiles at me again and then turns away, immediately getting swallowed up by the crowd. I raise one eyebrow at Eli, who's looking at me with wide, innocent eyes. I take advantage of the lack of space around us and step closer to him, stopping an inch or two from his chest. My heels make me about eye level with his neck.

"You weren't kidding about what?" I ask, blinking up at him.

"Oh . . ." He shrugs and places his hands on my hips. "I might've told him that you were the perfect combination of cute and sexy."

"Really."

"That's the PG-rated version, yeah."

I laugh and twist out of his grasp. "I'm gonna go hunt for a bathroom. Don't go too far, okay? I'll never find you in this mob."

"I'll stay here and try to dig us up some bottles of water or something."

I nod and head right, past the kitchen. A house this size must have at least one bathroom per floor. I weave between bodies until I reach the hallway, where there's a line so long that I'm not sure where it begins or ends. My bladder aching, I stand on my tiptoes and peer between limbs. There are people coming and going from a doorway next to the living room. I'm guessing it leads to a basement, and where there's a finished basement, there's likely a bathroom. I start in that direction.

As I pass the kitchen again, the crowd clears for a moment and I spot Eli, standing right where I left him a few minutes ago. And he's not alone. I catch a glimpse of shiny black hair and smooth, tan arms. The girl turns her head and my suspicions are confirmed. Ruby Liao, the star of many of Eli's Facebook pictures. She's even more beautiful in real life.

I swallow back the sourness in my mouth and keep moving, slowly this time, my gaze pinging from them to the sunburned neck of the guy in front of me. Just like when I'm scoping out shoppers in a store, my eyes catalogue every detail, from facial expression to posture to body language. The girl—Ruby—is talking to him, and every few seconds she reaches down to straighten her already straight skirt. She's nervous . . . or maybe contrite. As for Eli, his stance screams *defensive*—arms crossed, shoulders tensed, expression flat and closed off.

Still, even though he clearly doesn't want to be talking to

her, I can't help wondering if he knew she was going to be here tonight. If that's the reason he invited me. Not as an excuse to cut out early, but to parade me in front of his ex so she'll know that he's completely over her.

Or maybe he *does* want to be talking to her, and he's just tense because he knows I might come back any minute. Well, I'm not about to interrupt them, *or* act as some kind of prop to make his gorgeous ex-girlfriend jealous. I have *some* dignity.

I turn away and continue to the doorway, which, as it turns out, does indeed lead to a basement. Several people clog the stairs, and I hang on to the railing to avoid being trampled. Finally, the congestion clears and I pop out into a large living area with leather furniture, a giant-screen TV, and a foosball table. It's not as crowded down here—probably because there's no keg—and I have a straight shot to the bathroom door.

But when I flick on the light, I realize I'm not in a bathroom at all. I'm in some sort of office, with a dark wood desk and built-in shelves to match. Jesus. Why are there so many rooms in this house? As I reach up to flick the light off, something on one of the shelves catches my eye. A tiny metal statue of a penguin, no bigger than a tube of lipstick.

I love penguins.

After a quick glance behind me, I step farther into the room. Sometimes I'm able to forget about my hunger to steal, or at least stifle it. But other times, when I'm stressed or mad or even mildly hurt—like now—all I want is to feel that rush, that calming sense of balance and control.

Without pausing to think, I scoop the penguin off the shelf and tuck it into my purse.

The effect is immediate. Something inside me shifts, falling into place. I feel my heartbeat in my ears, strong and rhythmic and overriding everything else. Well, everything except my need to pee.

I flick the light off as I leave the room, then try the door opposite. This time it's a bathroom. When I'm done, I head back upstairs to find Eli, my emotions and face and every other part of me back in total control.

I find him standing outside the kitchen, leaning against a wall with two cans in his hand. Ruby is nowhere to be seen.

"Oh, good, you survived," he says when I finally get to him. He hands me one of the cans. "A Sprite for my sprite. Sorry, it was either this or tomato juice."

"This is fine." I pop it open, my stomach fluttering over the fact that he just called me *his*. A good sign. Maybe beautiful Ruby is ancient history, after all.

"Want to go outside? I need some air."

I nod and he takes my hand, veering into the dining room area. I stick close to him, dodging elbows and spills until we reach the glass doors to the deck. We step out into a haze of damp night air and cigarette smoke.

"Eli! Hey, man."

We turn toward the right side of the deck, where a half dozen people are sitting around a stone fire pit, roasting marshmallows. As we approach, a wiry guy with a buzz cut—the one who called out a second ago, I assume—stands up and thwacks Eli on the shoulder. His skin must be red from all the greeting slaps he's gotten tonight.

The buzz-cut guy turns out to be Zander, the host of the party. He invites us to grab a seat and a marshmallow, both of which are in short supply. Eli waves me toward the one vacant patio chair and sits next to me on a closed cooler. I'm introduced to the rest of the circle, but I'm bad with retaining a bunch of names at once and forget most of them a minute later.

"Dude, you're getting fucking huge." Zander gestures with his cup toward Eli's arms, which are slightly flexed and resting on his knees. "You training to play this season?"

The entire group focuses on Eli, who drops his gaze and stares intently into the fire. "Uh, nope. Not this season. Still waiting to be cleared by the doctor."

"Sucks, man," says the guy across from us—Brendon? Brandon?—as he skewers a marshmallow and holds it above the flame. "You heard about Colton Latimer, right?"

The girl on my other side offers me the last marshmallow in the bag. "No, thanks," I tell her, distracted by the weird look on Eli's face.

"No," he says flatly.

Brendon/Brandon lifts up his partially charred marsh-mallow and blows on it. "He'll be playing for the Bobcats in the fall."

"Full athletic scholarship," Zander adds with a smirk. "Coach Rudd must have an in or something at Burleson, because Latimer isn't even that fucking talented. Not like you were, man."

Eli's jaw twitches, a movement so subtle that only someone sitting close to him would probably catch it.

"Well," he says with a smile that even I can't tell is real or fake. "Good for him. Burleson's a great school."

Zander opens his mouth like he's about to say something but is interrupted by a girl who needs to get something out of the cooler. Eli stands up and moves behind my chair, out of her way. As the girl fishes a vodka cooler out of the ice, he bends down close to my ear and says, "Do you want to get out of here?"

"Oh, um, sure," I say, flustered. Last night, we'd joked about devising a signal, something one of us could do or say to alert the other that it was time to go. Every idea we came up with was ridiculous, of course—"pretend to fall down the stairs" is one example—but I was kind of expecting something more than *Do you want to get out of here?*

We say our good-byes to everyone, ignoring protests that it's too early to leave and the party's just getting started. Instead of going back inside the house and leaving through the same door we arrived at, Eli leads me down the deck stairs to the yard. We loop around the side of the house and come out on the pebble pathway again. This time, he doesn't pause at the hydrangeas.

"What now?" I ask as we walk down the long driveway. I met him here earlier, so we both have our cars.

Eli looks at me, and the rigid set of his jaw makes my stomach tighten. Usually, he's either smiling or on the verge of smiling. Cheerful and joking and light. I don't know what to do with dark, broody Eli.

"We could go to my house," he suggests, his first words since we left the deck. "It's just a few streets away."

I slow my pace. "Your house?"

"Yeah. My parents are out and my sister's away at camp, so you won't have to go through the third degree tonight."

His house. His *empty* house. It hits me then how little I actually know him. A few kisses and hundreds of texts don't mean we're soul mates, or even boyfriend and girlfriend. Oh God. Does he think we've moved on to serious-relationship territory already? Does he expect me to sleep with him? I'm not sure how I feel about that.

He seems to sense my hesitation. "I thought we could watch a movie or something. That's all. Jeez," he adds, his features lightening. "I love how your mind goes straight to the gutter. Must be all that erotica."

Relieved to see him smiling again, I sock him playfully in

the arm. We're almost to my car, parked in a line with several others across the street. I reach into my purse for my keys, and my fingers brush against the metal penguin. I yank my hand out like I touched something hot.

"Fine," I say, covering up with a smile. "Lead the way."

Chapter Seventeen

IT'S HARD NOT TO BE IMPRESSED BY ELI'S HOUSE, a sprawling slate-gray bungalow with a two-car garage. As he unlocks the front door, I breathe in the sharp scent of the trees that surround the entire property. Birch Grove is so different from the city, and my cluttered apartment building community, that it might as well be in another country.

"How long have you lived here?" I ask when we step into the cool, quiet house.

"Since I was four or five." Eli leads me past the foyer and into the kitchen, flicking on lights as he goes. "Meredith was just a baby, I remember that."

I look around. The kitchen is all shiny white cupboards

and dark granite and stainless steel. Directly across from it is a cozy-looking living room with light gray furniture and a flat-screen TV mounted above a stone fireplace. Like my apartment, the layout is open concept, but that's where the similarities end. My apartment could fit three times over into this place.

"Do you want a drink or a snack or something?" Eli asks, yanking open the fridge door and then slamming it closed again. He's still acting off.

"No, thanks." I'm too keyed up to eat or drink anything. The realization that I stole something out of a stranger's house has finally caught up with me, and I feel like my purse is made of glass, the contents inside on full display for anyone who cares to look. What the hell is wrong with me? Why didn't I just leave the damn penguin where it was and walk out of the room? Why can't I deal with negative feelings like a normal person?

We sit on the living room couch, which is velvety and plush, and Eli turns on the TV. I double-check that my purse is securely closed and then place it on the floor by my feet. When I straighten back up, I notice a framed family picture on the end table, taken on a white sand beach. Dr. Randall Jamison looks more relaxed here than he did in the head shot I saw when I Googled him. Eli's mom is tall and pretty, with chestnut-brown hair and an infectious smile. His sister is a younger version of her, but with longer, wavier hair and a mouthful of braces. Eli looks the same as he does now, only more tanned. They're like a postcard version of a family, exuding health and good fortune.

I look away, forcing down an unexpected surge of envy. It's been a long time since my family went on vacation, or posed for a picture together. It's been a long time since we did *anything* together, including existing in the same room.

I shift my focus back to Eli. "So your sister's away at camp?"

"Performing arts camp." He settles back on the couch with the remote, stretching his left leg out in front of him. "Acting is her thing. Aunt Rita's influence, I think, from taking us to all those plays."

I nod, then fall silent again. It feels weird being here, in this cavernous house, with Eli acting like he's only semiaware of my presence. He flips through channels aimlessly, pausing on each show for only a second or two before switching to the next one.

"Should I leave?" I ask bluntly. He seems miles away. Why did he even ask me to come over if he's not in the mood for company?

He looks at me, surprised. "What? No. Of course not." Sighing, he sets the remote on the arm of the couch and takes my hand. "Sorry. I'm just . . . We never should have gone to that stupid party."

"What do you—"

His phone vibrates in his pocket, interrupting me. Mumbling another apology, he digs it out and looks at the screen.

rebecca phillips

"Matt," he tells me, one corner of his mouth quirking up. "Wondering where we ran off to." He thumbs in a quick response and then places his phone next to the remote.

I try again. "What do you mean, we shouldn't have gone?"

He stares ahead at the TV, which is showing one of those house reno shows. "I don't really fit in with them anymore. That whole crowd. They try to act like nothing's changed, but I can tell some people feel sorry for me. Ever since I got hurt, they look at me like I'm . . . I don't know, tragic or something because I'm not that big-deal hockey guy anymore."

Just from watching people's reactions to him tonight, and seeing his hot ex in the flesh, I'd already gathered that he was once a member of the popular crowd in high school. "Who was it the guys were talking about at the fire pit? Connor something? Who's that?"

"Colton Latimer," he corrects me. "He's the one who checked me into the boards last fall."

My breath catches when I realize what he means. "He's the one who caused your injury?"

"Yep." He laughs, but there's no joy to it. Just raw bitterness. "And as we found out tonight, he also got onto the college team I always dreamed about playing for. So, you know, there's that too."

I stare at him, horrified, remembering what Alyssa said when I mentioned Eli's suspended hockey career: *That must have sucked for him . . . having to change the course of his whole*

176

life like that. Until right this second, I've never really seen the impact it made on him. He's never talked about it, or indicated that it bothered him, though I've always known it must have.

"God, Eli," I say, squeezing his hand. "That really sucks. I'm sorry."

He shrugs and turns my hand over, running his thumb along my wrist. "I hate the saying 'It is what it is,' but in this case it really *is* what it is. Dwelling on it isn't going to make my knee heal any faster."

"Did he at least apologize for hurting you?"

"Sort of. He showed up at the hospital the day after my surgery and dropped off a card for me. Didn't even step into my room. To be fair, though, we barely knew each other. Since we went to different high schools, the only time I saw him was on the ice."

"Still. A *card*?"

"A get-well card," he confirms. "I guess the *Sorry I smashed your knee and ruined your future plans* cards hadn't been invented yet."

I shake my head. It baffles me, how some people can shatter lives and then just walk away like it's nothing.

Figuring it's time to get off the subject of Colton, I ask, "Will you go back to playing when you're healed?"

He's silent for a moment, gazing ahead at nothing like he's lost in his head. "I don't know," he says, surprising me. "I mean, I loved the three years I played for the Warriors in high school. Being a part of the team. That rush you get when you first skate out onto the ice and hear the crowd. When I found out I was done for the season after only three games, it almost killed me. I thought nothing would ever come close to that rush again." He glances at me and smiles a little. "Then one day last April, Aunt Rita handed me a tray of seedlings and told me to plant them in front of her shop. I didn't know the first thing about flowers, and it hurt like a bitch to kneel on the ground for so long, but I sucked it up and did it. And when the marigolds actually took root and started growing, I felt this weird sense of accomplishment. There was something so satisfying about watching them thrive. It was like a different kind of rush." He huffs out a laugh. "I know that sounds stupid."

"It doesn't," I tell him. His words make me wonder if it's possible for me too, to trade one rush for another. I don't think flowers would cure me of my shoplifting problem, but maybe there's something else out there. Something I just haven't found yet.

Eli slides his hand out of mine and rests it on my waist, pulling me closer. I wrap my arms around his neck and lean in to kiss him, the party and Ruby and the stolen penguin in my purse all fading away as his lips move against mine. But after only a minute or so, he stops and pulls me in for a hug, like that's all he has the energy to do. I hug him back, letting him know I understand.

"Do you mind if we stretch out?" he asks into my hair.

"My knee is really aching tonight."

Instead of responding, I pile the throw cushions against the arm of the couch and then gently push him on top of them. Once he's settled, he reaches for me and I nestle in between him and the back of the couch, carefully avoiding his sore knee.

"Sorry about tonight," he says, brushing his cheek against the top of my head. "We should've just come here and cuddled instead."

I smile into his chest. His body is somehow both firm and soft at the same time, and my head fits in the slope between his shoulder and neck like it belongs there. "You don't need to apologize. It was . . . interesting."

His laugh rumbles against my ear. "That's one word for it."

An image of him talking to his ex-girlfriend flashes through my mind in vivid detail. I shut my eyes, not wanting to see him when I ask my next question. "Did the reason you invited me to that party have anything to do with your ex?"

He tenses beneath me. "My—what? You mean Ruby? How do you know about her?"

"Facebook."

"Oh." His chest falls as he slowly releases a breath. "You saw us talking tonight."

I don't answer. It wasn't a question. Obviously, I'd seen them, or I wouldn't have asked.

"No," he says after a pause. "The reason I invited you had nothing to do with her. I haven't even spoken to her for longer than two minutes since, I don't know, February? That was when she dumped me."

I lift my head to look at him, but he's staring up at the ceiling with the same vacant expression that was on his face when I saw them talking earlier. "She dumped you? Why?"

"I was kind of an asshole to her after I blew out my knee. I was an asshole to everyone, actually. I guess I can't really blame most of my friends for keeping their distance. I was in excruciating pain all the time and I couldn't play hockey anymore—couldn't even leave the damn *house* sometimes—and I felt so fucking sorry for myself that I took it out on whoever happened to be near me."

He sighs and tilts his head to the side, and I can almost see that version of him, the one whose anger and pain made him lash out until everyone around him felt it too. Sometimes the only way to cope with the unfairness of life is to spread it around.

"Anyway," he continues, facing the ceiling again, "I understand now why Ruby broke up with me, but at the time it really sucked. We were together for two and a half years. Since the end of ninth grade. One day she came over and told me that she was sick of seeing me in pain every day. 'It's too depressing,' she said. That's a direct quote, by the way."

"Ouch," I mumble, letting my head drop to his chest again.

"Yeah. So that was that. She stopped texting and coming over, avoided me at school. After I got my shit together I called her to apologize, but not because I was trying to get back with her. About a week after she dumped me, she started dating one of my so-called friends. Another guy on the team."

I wince. "Yikes."

"Right?" He smooths a strand of my hair between his fingers. "So yeah, I can safely say I didn't take you to that party to make her jealous or whatever. I don't want to be with her anymore. I want to be with someone else." He turns toward me, causing my head to slide off him and onto the pillows. "Someone who's short and wears glasses," he goes on, lowering his face to my neck. "Someone who runs over ugly vases with her car and hides my Twizzlers in her purse."

My breath hitches when he finds the sensitive spot near my collarbone. "I'm never going to live that down, am I?"

"Nope."

He rolls over onto his back again, taking me with him, and the conversation stops there.

Chapter Eighteen

"HAVE YOU STARTED YOUR THEFT EDUCATION class yet?"

I pick a piece of onion off my pizza and meet my dad's eyes across the living room. "Not yet."

"Morgan." He sighs and lowers the volume on the TV, which is showing the evening news. "The court gave you a deadline of August twelfth, remember? And it's already the end of July."

"It's a four-hour online course, Dad. I think I can get it done in the next two weeks."

"Well, don't put it off too long," he says, scooping up another slice from the open box on the coffee table. Sausage and mushroom from Nazario's, as usual. "It's part of your diversion requirement, and the court needs to see proof that you completed it."

"I know." I guess I *have* been putting off doing it, mostly because I assume the entire course will just be a four-hour lecture on how shoplifting is wrong and hurts society, which I already know. I'm not sure how watching videos and doing quizzes is supposed to deter me from stealing, but since the alternative is court and possible prosecution, theft education class it is.

Dad finishes his pizza and reaches for the remote. "Ready to watch?"

I swallow the food in my mouth and frown. "Sorry, but I have plans to hang out with Alyssa tonight."

He frowns back at me for a moment, his finger poised on the remote, before breaking into a too-wide smile. "Oh. Well, that's nice."

I nod, trying to ignore a stab of guilt. My friends haven't been around all week—Dawson and Alyssa had work, Sophie's on vacation with her family, Zach's been doing whatever it is he does when Sophie's not around, and Eli left on Sunday for a spontaneous five-day camping trip with his father—so I've spent the past few nights marathoning *Breaking Bad* with Dad. Not that I mind spending time with him, but I'm excited about getting out tonight with my best friend, who I feel like I haven't seen in weeks. Her mother's been keeping her pretty busy at the store lately.

"Maybe tomorrow, okay?" I say without thinking. Tomorrow's Friday, the day Eli comes back. Or so he said before he left. He hasn't been able to text me all week, seeing as he's out in the wilderness. I can't imagine camping with *my* dad, unless it was in a well-equipped cabin with a Pizza Hut nearby.

"Oh, don't worry about me," Dad says, firing up Netflix. "There are plenty of other shows I've been meaning to binge-watch."

I leave him to it and take the leftover pizza out to the kitchen. Fergus is sitting by his dish, staring into it like he's trying to make Fancy Feast magically appear. I open a can for him before heading to hang out with Alyssa.

When I pick her up at Karalis Custom Jewelry, Alyssa collapses into the passenger seat and sighs wearily, like my father does after a bad day at work.

"My mother," she says, eyes shut tight. "Is driving me. Crazy."

I pat her shoulder and pull away from the curb, merging with the late-evening traffic.

"She got it into her head that she needs to advertise on social media." She opens her eyes and leans over to turn up the stereo. Beyoncé almost drowns out her next words. "You know, to drum up business, which hasn't been the greatest. But she barely knows how to do more than email, so guess who had to teach her how to make a business page on Facebook today? Yeah. Me. *That* was fun. By the time we got it set up, I felt like going to the bar next door and ordering a beer."

"You don't drink," I remind her with a smile.

"Well, maybe I should start, because she also wants to 'learn how to Twitter.'" She makes quotation marks around the words with her fingers. "That's how she said it. So I have to give her a tutorial tomorrow. If I make it through that, I think I'll definitely deserve one of those big slushy cocktails, at least."

I laugh. "Hey, maybe I'll join you. My dad's been kind of clingy lately too. He was disappointed when I told him I couldn't hang out with him again tonight."

"Clingy? *Your* dad? But he's usually so chill. I'm totally jealous of all the freedom he gives you and how much he trusts your judgment."

My hands tighten on the wheel, and for a moment, I consider telling her everything. The shoplifting. Theft education class. How I ruined Dad's trust in me so completely that I'm afraid I'll never gain it back. But the words stay lodged in my throat. She'd never understand, and there's no way she could keep it from the rest of our friends, even if I begged. Unlike me, she's a horrible liar.

After driving around and singing along with the stereo for an hour, we stop off for some frozen yogurt. We get our usuals—chocolate topped with mini M&M's and Nutella sauce for me, strawberry and vanilla topped with gummy worms for her—and sit at a table by the window.

"So," she says, chopping the head off a gummy worm with the edge of her spoon, "Dawson asked me out the other day."

I almost choke on an M&M. "What?"

"He asked me if I wanted to go to the Lighthouse on Friday night. Just the two of us."

Wow. The Lighthouse is a very trendy, very pricey restaurant on the south end of town. None of us have ever been there, because none of us can afford it. *Dawson* can't afford it, not on minimum-wage pay. He must've really wanted to impress her and make their potential first date extra special.

"And you said no," I guess. I don't even have to ask. Alyssa rarely changes her mind once it's set. She's the most stubborn person I know.

"Of *course* I said no. You know I don't like him that way, and I didn't want to give him the wrong idea." She bites her lip. "*Do* I give him the wrong idea? Oh, crap, do I flirt with him without realizing it?"

I shrug. She treats Dawson the same way she treats Sophie and me, with innocent, maternal-like affection. But to a guy who's been in love with her for months, a simple smile or hug might carry a much different meaning. "I think you're pretty clear about where you stand."

"I try to be." She sighs and takes a large bite of strawberry. "He probably hates me now. He hasn't texted me since I turned him down."

That explains his recent absence from the group chat we have going on Messenger, and why, when I drove him home from work yesterday, he talked about everything *but* Alyssa. I feel a twinge of sadness. Hopefully their friendship can survive this.

"He doesn't hate you, Lyss."

She ignores me and pushes away her fro-yo cup. "What is wrong with me? Am I defective? It seems like everyone wants to be in a relationship but me. It's just . . . I have so much going on with my mother and the store and senior year coming up, dating is the *last* thing on my mind. And what's the point of relationships at our age, anyway? They're only going to end."

I think of last Friday night, Eli and I stretched out on his living room couch, his warm hands on the back of my shorts, pressing me tight against him. There are definitely some benefits to dating.

"Oh God," Alyssa says, snapping me back to the present. "You're thinking about Eli, aren't you? I can tell, because your freckles look like they're all melding together. When are we going to meet him?"

"Soon." My friends have been so busy lately, it's hard to pin them all down at once. "He gets back from camping tomorrow. I'll ask him. Maybe Saturday night?"

She nods and slides her yogurt cup back in front of her, then spoons a half-melted bite into her mouth. "Soph is back tomorrow too, and Zach is always free. Dawson might even put aside his hatred for me long enough to join us, if it means getting to know your new boyfriend."

Boyfriend. Considering how much I've missed him this week, I guess the term fits.

Chapter Nineteen

ELI IS TOO TIRED TO GO OUT ON FRIDAY NIGHT, SO
I don't see him until Saturday morning. When I pull into
Rita's Reruns, I spot him by the drop-off bins, knee-deep in
donations. Rita must have left last week's offerings for him to
sort through.

He looks up at the sound of my car and smiles. My heart
does this weird fluttering thing, and I have to stop myself from
jumping out of the car while it's still running. I park and get out
slowly, then walk over to him at normal speed. As I get closer, I
see that he's even more tanned than before, and his jaw is shadowed with light brown stubble. My mouth goes dry.

"Hey." He steps over a torn plastic bag filled with old shoes and hugs me, lifting me up off the ground.

"Hi," I reply, and wrap my arms around his neck, holding on. When he pulls back to kiss me, his cheek scrapes against mine, making me yelp.

"Sorry." He gives me a quick peck and sets me down on the pavement. "Didn't get a chance to shave yet."

"I like it," I say truthfully. Facial hair looks incredibly sexy on him. "So you had a good trip?" He texted me for a few minutes last night, talking about foreign-to-me things like fishing, sleeping in tents, and cooking over fires, but he fell asleep before he could go into much detail.

"Yeah." He shoves aside a beat-up cardboard box with his foot. The contents make a clinking sound. "On the way back, we picked up Mere at camp and stopped at Vickers Beach for the day. It was great."

"Oh, I love Vickers Beach. I haven't been there since I was little."

He scratches his jaw, smiling. "You should go before the summer's over. You and your dad or whoever. Stay in one of those little cottages near the beach."

I nod like it's a possibility, even though it's not. Dad already has a week booked off for Rachel's visit, even though time off work means losing sales commissions. He can't afford to take another vacation right now. But our money troubles are definitely not something I want to discuss with Eli. Just like I don't want to discuss my family. He knows my parents aren't together and that I live with my dad and haven't seen my mother in months, but he's never pressed me for details. It's one of the things I like most about him. It's like he senses that the topic of my mother is painful for me, so he's waiting until I'm ready to bring it up myself.

"I guess I'd better get inside," I say grudgingly, like I'd like nothing better than to stand out here with him in a sea of dusty castoffs. Which is true.

After one last hug, I head toward the side doors. Then, remembering something, I walk toward him again.

"Are you doing anything tonight?"

His eyebrows shoot up. "Hanging out with you?"

"My friends want to meet you. Would you mind if we hung out with them instead? No pressure. I mean, we'll probably just sit around and play video games in my friend Zach's basement. His mom is always with her boyfriend, so he practically lives by himself."

"I like video games. And sitting around in basements." He takes my hands and draws me closer, grinning down at me. "How about this. I'll hang out with your friends tonight if you come to my house tomorrow for dinner."

I stare at a tiny hole in his T-shirt, unsure how to respond. Introducing someone to friends is one thing, but bringing them home to meet the family is something else altogether. Are we really at that stage?

Eli sees my hesitation. "Aunt Rita will be there too. She

comes for dinner every Sunday. So you'll know someone besides me."

That doesn't make me feel any better. Having Rita there will make me even more nervous, because unlike Eli and his family, she knows why I'm really working at the thrift store. I don't think she'd reveal my secret over dinner, but still. What if she drinks too much wine or something and lets it slip accidentally?

Screw it. I'll have to take the risk. Eli will start wondering about me if I avoid his family. And I do want to meet them, even though it's a big step on the relationship meter. Considering how adamant I was at first about keeping things casual, I'm surprised at how much I like the idea of us getting more serious. Still, it's scary to think about all the things I'm still hiding from him, even as our relationship advances.

"Okay," I say after a pause.

He grips my shoulders and leans down to kiss me, then turns me in the direction of the door. "Now get moving. Slacker."

I stick my tongue out at him and go, skirting past the minefield of boxes and bags on the way to the side door. Inside, I find Rita polishing the counter, her bracelets clanging together with each swipe of the cloth.

"Sorry I'm a little late," I say.

She squints at me over her glasses, which are perched on the end of her nose. All of a sudden I feel self-conscious, wondering if my face is red from Eli's stubble. But she just nods and goes back to her polishing.

I stand there awkwardly in front of her, waiting for her to tell me where she wants me today. When she doesn't speak or even look at me, I turn toward the rear of the store. Surely, there's something that needs sorting back there. Just as I'm about to move, Rita speaks.

"You're a good girl," she says, her eyes on her cloth.

"Sorry?"

She suddenly stops cleaning and picks up her bottle of Windex, bringing it and the cloth over to the main door. "You're a good girl," she repeats, spritzing down the square of window. "I know that in my heart. But I also know my nephew, and that boy can't handle getting hurt again."

I stare at her. How does she know we've moved on from just friends? She was bound to find out eventually, of course—like when I show up for dinner tomorrow—but Eli hasn't told her about us, and I certainly haven't. We thought if she knew, she wouldn't leave us alone in the stockroom anymore. What, can she see through *walls* with those bifocals?

And what does she mean, Eli can't handle being hurt again? Does she think *I'm* going to hurt him? Why would she think that?

An ice-cold tremor creeps down my spine. Of course. Rita knows the other version of me—the lawbreaker, the liar. Good deep down, maybe, but not quite good enough for Eli. I've earned her trust around the thrift shop, but not around her family. Not yet.

She finishes with the window and turns to face me, pushing her glasses up high on her nose. "That's all I wanted to say. You can work the cash today, okay? Not much to do in back until Eli brings that newest load in."

I swallow the annoying lump in my throat and do what I'm told. For the next three hours, I stand behind the counter and try my best not to smudge the shiny clean surface.

After the thrift store, I go straight to Royal Smoothie, where I spend the next six hours blending fruit and wondering if Rita will eventually tell Eli the truth about me. Why hasn't she? When she hired me, she said she believed in giving people a fair shot in life. Maybe that's why she's kept my secret. Or maybe she's waiting for *me* to tell him.

Thinking about coming clean to Eli and my friends rattles me so much that I screw up making a Pineapple Punch smoothie and have to start over. I try to picture how they'd react to finding out what I'm really like. Shock, definitely. Anger. Disgust. Or maybe they'd feel sorry for me. Poor Morgan resorts to committing petty larceny to make herself feel better after her mom's betrayal. Sad, misguided girl.

No. I won't be the one everyone pities. The one who can't handle life's infinite crap. Alyssa's father died. Zach's parents are divorced and his mother leaves him home alone all the time. Eli lost a possible hockey career and the ability to walk for long periods without pain. Dawson and Sophie each have their own troubles. They've all experienced pain, anger, and injustice, and not one of them uses a vice like mine—one that causes personal *and* public harm—to ease the sting.

I need them all in my life too much to risk driving them away with the truth.

After work, I go home to shower. My cell rings as I'm standing in front of the bathroom mirror, twisting my damp hair into French braids. When I see Eli's name on the screen, my heart leaps into my throat and all I can think is, *This is it. She told him. He knows.* But when I pick up, all he says is, "Hey, do you think your friends would mind if Matt tagged along with me tonight? He's looking for something to do."

My relief is so strong, I need to grip the edge of the counter. "Oh. Sure, he can come. The more the merrier."

He doesn't seem to notice any weirdness in my voice. "Great. See you later."

I finish braiding my hair with slightly shaking fingers and leave for Zach's house. I'm the last one to arrive, with the exception of Eli and Matt, who will be coming later. When I walk into the basement, I immediately sense a hint of tension crackling through the room. It takes me a moment to figure out what's off. Instead of sharing the love seat like they often do, Alyssa is sitting with Sophie and Zach on the couch as they pummel each other in a game of *Street Fighter*, and Dawson is sprawled in the chair a few feet away, watching. Just like at the diner, our regular seating arrangements have evolved. It makes me uneasy.

I sit by myself on the love seat just as Sophie releases an outraged yell and tosses her controller down.

"Serves you right after coming at me with those fireballs," Zach crows.

They start squabbling back and forth over game-play tactics while the rest of us sit in a triangle of edgy silence. When the doorbell rings a few minutes later, I've never been so glad for a distraction in my life.

Eli and Matt's presence lightens the atmosphere immediately. After I go through the introductions, Sophie relinquishes her controller and comes over to join me on the love seat. Alyssa does the same, leaving the four guys to take turns beating the hell out of each other on-screen.

"You didn't tell me you were dating Captain America," Sophie says in my ear. She gives me a discreet high five. "Nice job."

I laugh and turn to Alyssa. She's watching the guys too, but her gaze keeps flicking to Dawson. Whenever she looks at him, a slight frown appears on her lips.

"Is he still ignoring you?" I ask. I'm not used to seeing them this way. Usually, Dawson can't pry his eyes from her. Now he doesn't even glance in this direction.

"He barely even said hi to me," Alyssa replies, her frown deepening.

Sophie jumps up. "Chips! There are chips in the kitchen. Let's go get them."

I look at Eli. He's playing a round against Dawson, his brow knit in concentration as he taps on the controller. It's cute. Zach and Matt are chatting like they've known each other forever. My two worlds have merged seamlessly in less than ten minutes. I feel myself relax.

Up in the kitchen, Alyssa refuses to talk anymore about Dawson and the romance that will never be. Instead, she busies herself dumping chips into bowls like her life depends on it while Soph and I gather drinks, keeping our questions to ourselves.

We head back downstairs, balancing everything in our arms. Zach's now playing against Eli, and Dawson's back in the chair, deliberately focused on the sparring figures on TV. He doesn't even look up when Sophie and I deposit the drinks on the coffee table. Alyssa is right behind us, and just as she reaches the table, one of the bowls she's carrying tilts sideways, spilling a handful of Doritos. Matt jumps up quickly and grabs it before the rest of them hit the floor too.

"Close call," he says, grinning at her.

She smiles back, her cheeks slightly pink, and then crouches down to pick up the fallen Doritos. Matt immediately crouches beside her, sweeping up the crumbs with his hands. Sophie and I exchange a quick look before both our gazes shift to Dawson. Just as I figured, he's watching them like he's trying *not* to watch them, his face falling more with each moment the two of them stay huddled together on the floor. I feel a pang of sympathy for him. A few days ago, Alyssa turned him down flat, and now here she is laughing with the charming new guy.

Not that I think Alyssa is interested, even though Matt is cute and nice. She means it when she says she doesn't want to date. But in Dawson's case, even the most basic interaction is probably hurtful when witnessed through a haze of rejection and unrequited love.

"Thanks," Alyssa says to Matt once the chips are cleaned up. He stands and nods at her, his gaze lingering a little longer this time. Oblivious, Alyssa rejoins Soph and me on the love seat, taking one of the bowls with her.

Across the room, Dawson quietly seethes, his jaw twitching as he glares at the TV. Tension rises from him like steam. The guys are going to think he's sullen and unfriendly, even though he's neither. I resolve to explain the situation to Eli later.

"Later" comes sooner than I thought. Dawson ducks out early, claiming he has something to do at home, and the party breaks up shortly after that. I'm mostly glad. My friends are great, but I've been waiting all night to spend some time alone with Eli.

"You'll give me a lift home, right?" he asks as we leave the house. "Matt drove me here."

"You should've asked me before you let him leave," I say teasingly, then pretend to think it over. "Okay, I guess so. Do you want me to take you home now?"

He grins slyly. "Well, not home exactly, but maybe to my neighborhood. I know of a good deserted spot."

I raise my eyebrows, intrigued. When we get into my car, Eli has to put the seat back all the way to accommodate his legs, and even then he has to scrunch. His head almost touches the ceiling. His size and height make my car feel as tiny as a Hot Wheels.

"It smells like vanilla in here," he says.

I don't want to think about my mom's scent locked forever in the seats, so I lean over and kiss him. He kisses me back, and all the weirdness from earlier fades away. Until we stop kissing and he says, "That was fun. Your friends are cool."

I almost laugh, because in most worlds, *he'd* be considered the cool one. Mr. Popular, with his athleticism and magnetism and smoking-hot ex. *Cool* isn't a word that's often used to describe my friend group, but I'm relieved he thinks so. After going to Zander's party, I was afraid he'd think our get-togethers were hideously dull.

I start the car and back out of the driveway. "I hope Matt had fun too."

"Matt has fun everywhere."

No kidding. I remember the way he smiled at Alyssa, how he jumped to help her before anyone else had the chance. "Is he always like that? So flirty?"

His head snaps toward me. "Did he flirt with you? I'll kill him."

"No. *No.*" We reach an intersection and I flick on my right blinker. "With Alyssa."

"Oh." He relaxes against the seat. "Figures. She's exactly his type. Do you think they'd . . . ?"

"No," I say again, firmly. "She doesn't date, and Dawson's in love with her."

I see him wince out of the corner of my eye. "Man, that sucks. I'll make sure Matt backs off, then."

"Probably a good idea." I start to say something else when the flash of lights ahead distracts me. Several police cars are parked along the road leading into Birch Grove. My heart thumps. I've been wary of cops ever since I faced one down at the mall security office. "What's going on over there?"

Eli leans closer to the windshield and surveys the scene. "Spot check," he announces. "They set up there every few months. Trying to catch drunk drivers, I think."

I'm definitely not drunk, and I haven't done anything wrong tonight, but still. My palms break out into a sweat as I stop the car beside an officer standing on the road. She motions for me to roll down my window, which I do with a shaking hand.

"Where you heading?" she asks, pointing her heavy-duty flashlight into the car.

She's tall with a firm, no-nonsense air and I resist the urge to cower. Instead, I nod toward Eli and say, "His house." Not a total lie, since I'll eventually drop him off there.

"Have you guys had anything to drink tonight?"

"No, Officer." I squint up at her, debating on whether to smile. She must notice how jumpy I am, because she asks to see my license and registration.

Eli grabs the registration out of the glove compartment for me while I dig out my wallet. After she's studied everything under her flashlight beam, her stoic expression relaxes and she waves us on. I'm so freaked out that it takes me a second to remember how to drive.

"Are you okay?" Eli asks as we move past the red-and-blue glare.

I let out a jagged breath. "Yeah, I'm fine."

"Were you worried that she'd confiscate your penguin?"

My leg jerks, and I almost smash into the car in front of us. I hit the brake and glance over to see him holding the tiny penguin statue I stole from Zander's house last weekend. I tossed it in the glove compartment after it fell out of my purse during my drive to work the other day, and I'd totally forgotten it was still there.

"Um, can you put that back?" I ask. I don't like seeing it in his hand. What if he recognizes it? But no, Eli has never even been in that room. He'd never figure out where it came from. There are probably a million things in that giant house that no one would ever miss. Eli's house too, though I refuse to let my mind go *there*.

"Sure thing." He puts the penguin back without comment and shuts the compartment door behind it. I start breathing normally again, until I catch him watching me like he's wondering about my sanity. "Are you sure you're okay? If I didn't know any better, I'd think you were a wanted criminal, on the run from the law."

My body goes cold. One of those things is right, at least. I force myself to smile at him. "Do I look like a criminal?"

"Oh, yeah, totally," he says, then laughs like the idea is too ridiculous to even joke about.

I don't laugh with him. *If I didn't know any better*, he said. The thing is, he *doesn't* know any better. In fact, when it comes down to it, he doesn't really know me very well at all.

Chapter Twenty

"WHAT TIME DID YOU SAY THIS LEVI KID WAS PICK-ing you up?"

I shake my head. My father is even worse with names than I am. "It's Eli, and he said four o'clock."

Dad places his empty bottle of beer on the coffee table and rises from the couch with a groan. "I guess I should get dressed, then."

I examine his outfit of baggy pajama pants and wrinkled T-shirt and agree that he probably should. Sunday is the one day of the week that Dad allows himself to laze around and drink beer. He never has more than three, and he spaces them out throughout the day, a routine he's been following for as long as I can remember.

While he's getting dressed, I rinse the beer bottle and put it in the recycling bin. Then I walk around the apartment for the tenth time in the past hour, making sure everything is tidy. When Eli insisted on picking me up for dinner at his house, I was hesitant. For one, I always like the idea of having my car in case I need to take off for whatever reason. Two, I figured Eli would want to pick me up at my actual door like a nice, polite date, which meant he'd see where I live. Not that I'm ashamed of it, but my tiny apartment is downright drab compared to his beautiful, ginormous house.

"Don't expect anything special," I told him last night when I finally agreed to him coming over. "It's just me and my dad, so we don't need anything big or fancy."

"Morgan," he replied with a tinge of exasperation, "do you honestly think I give a crap about what your apartment looks like? You could live in a cardboard box under an overpass and I'd still want to visit you."

I didn't have any snappy comebacks for that.

Dad emerges from his room wearing old shorts and a slightly less wrinkled T-shirt. Fergus darts ahead of him, his fur ruffled from sleeping in the laundry hamper for the past few hours. I have the urge to groom them both, but Eli will be here any minute.

"You said this kid was Rita Sloan's nephew?" Dad confirms,

scratching his day-old beard growth. He doesn't shave on his days off. "So does he know about why you're working there?"

"No, not yet." Or possibly ever. "So please don't say anything."

"But don't you think you should—"

The buzzer rings then, cutting him off, and I send up a quick thank-you to the timing gods. Dad would definitely not approve of me misrepresenting myself as a selfless do-gooder to Eli, especially since Rita knows the truth. Luckily, he seems to forget what he was going to ask and looks at me with a wistful expression instead.

"When did you get old enough to date?" he says, shaking his head. "Actually, when did *Rachel* get old enough to date? Where did the time go?"

I give him an indulgent smile and smooth down my skirt. Rachel has definitely gone beyond simply dating Amir. Her Instagram lately has consisted of mostly selfies of them together, taken in what appears to be his apartment or house or wherever he lives. It's not *her* apartment, which she shares with two other girls. I think she would have told me if they'd moved in together, but maybe she's keeping it a secret for now. I'll have to grill her about it in person when she comes home in three weeks.

Three weeks. I push the thought of her homecoming out of my mind and answer Eli's knock.

"Hey," he says, his eyes raking over my white lace top and

floral miniskirt. Then he turns his gaze to my father, who's standing between the living room and kitchen, looking at him looking at me. *Awkward.*

Dad moves forward, hand outstretched and his best car-salesman grin plastered over his face. "Eli," he says, thankfully getting his name right this time. "I've heard a lot about you."

The words make Eli's cheeks go slightly pink. He shakes my dad's hand and says, "I've heard a lot about you too."

They chat for a bit about Rita and the thrift store and I can tell Dad approves, even after the blatant ogling he witnessed in the doorway a few minutes ago. As they're talking, Fergus comes in and rubs against my leg, then Dad's, and finally Eli's, like he's tagging everyone in the room with his scent. Eli bends down to pet him, and I remember him telling me once that he's allergic to cats.

"We should go," I say, afraid he might have some kind of reaction. Also, I'm feeling antsy and just want to get out of here. We leave my father to his slothfulness and head out.

In the elevator, Eli starts rubbing his eyes.

"Just a little itchy, that's all," he explains when I ask what's wrong.

"Great. You'll have to dope yourself up with antihistamines every time you come over."

"Worth it." He grabs my waist and pulls me toward him. "Damn, you're hot."

"I thought you thought I was cute?"

"I do. But today, you're hot."

I reach up and kiss him, weighing the logistics involved in getting us trapped in this elevator for the rest of the day.

Eli's eyes are fine by the time we pull into his driveway. The house looks bigger in the daytime. Brighter and more imposing. Nervousness tickles in my throat. The top I'm wearing is one that I stole a few months ago. Suddenly, it feels scratchy and tight, like it's protesting being on my body. There may as well be a huge red X across the front of it, marking me.

I vow to put it out of my mind as we enter the quiet house.

Eli leads me toward the kitchen and the back deck, where everyone has congregated. On the way, we pass the couch we made out on the last time I was here and my face gets warm. So of course I look like a ripe tomato when we step out onto the deck. His family is sitting around on patio furniture, sipping drinks in the shade. Rita's here, as promised, and she winks at me as Eli does the introductions.

Dr. Randall Jamison is the first to shake my hand. I try to hide my surprise at his appearance. After reading about all the amazing things he's done, I expected him to be almost godlike in person. Intimidating. But he just looks like a regular dad. An older version of Eli, just as tall but without the muscular build.

"It's so nice to meet you, Morgan. I'm Joanna," Eli's mom says warmly. She looks basically the same as she does in the family picture on their end table, but now I can see the resemblance between her and Rita. Eli's mom is about ten years younger and thirty pounds thinner, but they have the same eyes.

Meredith, Eli's sister, is the last to greet me. She looks like her picture too, though the braces have come off since it was taken. And like the rest of the family, she's tall. At least five inches taller than me, but whereas I'm rounded in certain areas, she's lanky and rail thin.

All in all, they're way less daunting than I expected, though I wonder if they're inwardly comparing me to Eli's gorgeous ex, who must have had some good qualities if he stayed with her for two and a half years. I'm the first girl he's dated since she dumped him, and part of me feels the need to prove myself to both him and his family.

Soon, I'm sitting in one of the comfortable patio chairs with a glass of lemonade that tastes like chilled sunshine. The light breeze carries the scent of trees and fresh-cut grass. I could maybe get used to this.

"So, Morgan." Eli's mom crosses her toned legs and looks at me. "Rita was just telling us about you."

My stomach folds in on itself. Oh God. My worst fear come true. Rita has chosen today to spill all my sins to the very people I'm aiming to impress. I glance over at her, trying to read her expression, but half her face is hidden behind extra-large sunglasses. "Really," I say. I take a sip of lemonade, which suddenly tastes like nothing.

"She was talking about what a hard worker you are and how much she enjoys having you around the thrift store," Dr. Jamison says with an affable, Eli-like grin.

Relief whooshes through me.

"I think it's great," he goes on. "I wish more teenagers were willing to give up their time to volunteer."

My body tenses again. His undeserved praise makes me want to slink under my chair. I force myself to return his smile, aware of Rita's gaze on the side of my face. I don't get her. She could have told the truth about me on numerous occasions. She doesn't owe me a thing, so why keep my secret? As grateful to her as I am, I can't help wondering if I'm under some sort of deadline I don't know about. Is she just biding her time, hoping I'll come clean so she doesn't have to do it for me? If that's the case, I hope she's willing to be patient.

Conversation shifts to something else, and I slowly start to relax. I drink another glass of lemonade, which is a mistake. All the liquid instantly rushes to my bladder, and I have to excuse myself to use the bathroom.

When I emerge from the main-floor powder room, the house is empty and still. The icy air-conditioning feels nice on my skin, so I stall for a few moments before heading back outside, detouring through the dining room instead. I know I shouldn't be skulking around the house by myself, but it's not like I'm planning on pocketing the silverware. I just love *things*, and there's a long sideboard in the dining room with several interesting items displayed across its surface.

I move closer, my feet barely making a sound on the hardwood floor. My gaze is immediately drawn to an oval-shaped picture of a small gray bird sitting on a tree branch. At least I think it's a picture. Upon closer inspection, I realize the image is actually made up of thousands of colorful grains of sand, walled between two glass panes. It's beautiful. I run my fingertip over the smooth, cool surface.

"It's a sand painting."

I straighten up, my face igniting in embarrassment when I see Eli's father in the doorway, watching me. I didn't even know he was in the house.

Luckily, he doesn't seem put off by my snooping. "I got it in Vietnam a few years ago," he explains. "The wife of one of the surgeons I worked with gave it to me as a gift. I usually bring back something from wherever I go."

"It's nice," I say. He talks about his trips like they're interesting vacations, not humanitarian missions during which he operates on children for free, just because he cares. He—along with everyone else in the family, including Eli—radiates this fundamental sense of decency that seems to be missing from my nature entirely.

Dr. Jamison heads to the kitchen to gather the food for grilling, while I go back outside to the deck. Shortly after I sit down, Eli goes inside to help his dad with the food, leaving me with his sister, mom, and aunt. His mom is in the middle of telling Meredith a story, something about a trip she took to Mexico when she was in her last year of college.

"I don't remember that," Rita says when the story is over. "Why didn't I go with you?"

"Oh, I think you were pregnant with Bradley then."

The air goes still and everyone freezes. I look at Rita, whose face is rigid behind her sunglasses. *Pregnant?* I remember Eli telling me she didn't have kids.

"Rita, I'm sorry . . . ," Mrs. Jamison starts, but Rita is already on her feet, heading toward the door in a swirl of patterned fabric. Eli's mom watches her leave, then sighs and puts a hand to her forehead. "Shit," she mutters.

I glance at Meredith, but she's looking out into the woods, bottom lip caught between her teeth. What just happened?

"Excuse me," Mrs. Jamison says in my general direction, and then follows her sister inside.

Now it's just me and Meredith, who, for an actress, has seemed pretty reserved so far. I keep my eyes on the door, wishing Eli would hurry up and come back.

"Bradley was her son."

My gaze swings back to Meredith, who's looking right at me. Her eyes are a warm, beautiful hazel, like Eli's.

"Oh," I say.

"He died when he was a baby," she adds. She says the words quietly, like they're too horrifying to be voiced at a normal pitch. And they are.

"That's awful," I say over the tightness in my throat. *Poor Rita.*

"Yeah."

The door flies open again, making me jump a little. It's Eli, finally, carrying a platter of various meats. His dad trails close behind with a dish of aluminum-wrapped objects that I can only assume are vegetables. Mrs. Jamison emerges next, carrying a bottle of barbecue sauce and smiling like everything's normal. Eli catches my eye, and the apologetic expression on his face tells me he's aware of what just happened out here. I give him a brief smile, letting him know it's okay, and he nods at the food as if to say he's busy now, but will explain later. I want to tell him he doesn't need to, that it's none of my business anyway, but I figure it can wait until after dinner.

I assumed Rita had left, so I'm surprised when she reappears at dinnertime and loads up a plate like nothing happened. Everyone else follows suit, laughing and talking and eating like everything is perfectly normal. Maybe Rita storming off and going missing for almost an hour *is* normal for them. I'm beginning to realize that Eli's family has cracks just like anyone else's.

The moment dinner's over, Eli claims he wants to give me a tour of the rest of the house and leads me downstairs to the family room. I have just enough time to glimpse a dark red couch and a cool stone sculpture in the corner before Eli's wide chest blocks my view. He shoots a glance toward the stairs and then starts kissing me.

Okay. I kiss him back in the quiet of the room, my hands on the back of his neck, pulling him lower as I strain to move myself higher. He must get tired of bending after a few minutes, because he puts his hands on the backs of my thighs and lifts me up until our bodies align more evenly. I wrap all four limbs around him and hang on.

"I vote that we kiss like this from now on," he says in my ear as he backs me gently against the wall.

My legs tighten around his waist. "Or I could just buy a step stool."

He laughs and kisses me again, his hand skimming over the lace of my top. After a few minutes, he backs us away from the wall and toward the living room area. When we reach the couch, he sits, bringing me down on top of him.

"I like where this is going," he says, smiling down at my bare legs on either side of his hips.

I give him a shove and slide off his lap, settling onto the couch next to him. His family is still just one floor above us, likely to come down here at any second. I straighten my skirt and try to look innocent.

"That's a cool sculpture." I gesture to the abstract carving in the corner, which is about two feet tall and shaped vaguely like a teardrop.

Eli tips his head back and lets out a breath, like he's struggling to shift tracks. "It's soapstone," he says after a pause. "My dad got it in Brazil."

I try to imagine what it would be like, traveling the world, collecting things from each place to remind you of where you've been. The things I've collected mostly remind me of how badly I messed up. Like the stolen penguin statue, which is currently sitting on my dresser, partially hidden behind a framed picture of Rachel and me.

"About Aunt Rita . . . ," Eli says, drawing my attention back to him. He sounds hesitant, like whatever he's about to say isn't usually discussed.

I shake my head. "Your sister already told me. About Rita's . . . about Bradley."

"The whole story?"

"Well, no. Just that he died." I swallow and run my palm over the smooth, velvety fabric of the couch. "You don't need to tell me anything else. It's not— It's her business, not mine."

"I don't think she'd mind if I told you." He clears his throat. "Her baby was born premature. Like, really premature. He slept in an incubator and needed machines to breathe for him. The doctors told her that if he survived, he'd have all sorts of problems, both physically and intellectually. But Aunt Rita was prepared to face whatever happened. She just wanted to take him home."

My stomach sinks. I know the ending to the story, but I

still have to say it. "But then he died."

He nods. "He stopped breathing one day and the doctors couldn't bring him back. Aunt Rita never really got over losing him. It happened over twenty years ago and she still can't talk about it. And if someone slips up and mentions him . . . well, I guess you saw what happens." He sighs and slouches down, pressing his shoulder to mine. "That's why I said no that time when you asked me if she had any kids. I didn't know you well enough then to tell you the truth."

I spread my hand across his scarred knee, something I've taken to doing since he told me the warmth of it made him hurt less. "She would've been a great mom. It's so unfair."

"I know. I think that's why she raises money for the group home, because she knows her son might have lived there if he'd survived. It's her way of dealing with the unfairness of what happened—by turning it into something positive."

I know this makes sense. What I don't know is *how*. When I think about Eli trading sports for horticulture, and now Rita honoring her son's death by helping others, I long to know how people take their pain and channel it into something good.

Chapter Twenty-One

A WEEK LATER, I DRIVE STRAIGHT TO BEACON Street Diner after work. It was Sophie's idea to introduce Eli to the wonders of our favorite eating spot. But when I arrive, she and the rest of my friends are nowhere to be found.

I check my phone and find a text from Alyssa, saying she'll be late, and another text from Dawson, saying he's not coming. I sigh. He's been withdrawing from us since the night at Zach's house, choosing instead to hang out with work friends on his nights off. I almost dread the thought of school starting in a few weeks. He and Alyssa will have no choice but to see each other then, and if they don't work things out, one of them will probably leave the circle entirely.

Shaking off the thought, I head to the diner's tiny bathroom and exchange my Royal Smoothie T-shirt for a red lace-up tank top. When I come back out, I discover Eli loitering near the entrance.

"Did you notice the *e* is burned out in the sign outside?" he says when he sees me. "How have I never noticed this place before?"

"Maybe because you don't usually hang out in bad neighborhoods."

His eyebrows shoot up, and I realize my tone sounded more contemptuous than joking, which is how I meant it. I think. Since dinner at his house, I've been aware of our differences more than ever. He frequents Starbucks and pristine supermarkets, I frequent run-down diners in a sketchy part of town. His family is strong and whole; my family is messy and fractured. He's wonderful and giving, and I'm . . . me. Sometimes these things are hard to overlook.

Eli lets the comment drop and we go to secure a booth. Sophie and Zach arrive soon after, and my weird mood starts to lift. I'm probably just hungry.

Alyssa doesn't show up until after we all have our food. She squeezes in with Zach and Sophie and swipes a fry off my plate and a slice of pickle off Zach's. Sophie pulls her own plate closer, guarding her chicken strips against roving hands.

"Sorry I took so long," Alyssa says after she swallows. "We had an *incident* at the store today."

I take a sip of Coke. "What kind of incident?"

"An idiot shoplifter."

My glass collides with the edge of my plate, sloshing Coke everywhere. I grab a couple of napkins and start wiping it up, barely aware of what I'm doing.

"Are you okay?" Eli's voice filters through the loud roaring in my ears.

I nod and keep soaking up the mess. When I asked what Alyssa meant, I was expecting her to go into another rant about her mother's incompetence with social media or something. Not *that*.

Everyone's talking at once, asking questions, and it takes everything in me to act normal and focus on the conversation.

"My mother noticed this guy lurking around the necklaces," Alyssa is saying. "She was watching him, but then she had to take care of another customer. By the time she was done, the guy was gone and so was a seventy-dollar necklace."

Sophie's mouth twists in disgust. "How can anyone *do* that? And to a small business?"

Nausea swirls in my stomach. Most shoplifters don't steal from mom-and-pop stores and small businesses—*I* never would—but it's not like I can say that without sounding like I'm defending thievery.

The waitress appears and takes Alyssa's order, then asks if I want another Coke. I shake my head. My appetite—even for liquid—has totally diminished.

"Does the store have security cameras?" Eli asks.

"Yeah, one, but it's not very high-tech. It probably won't give a clear enough image to identify him." She droops in her seat, frowning. "New cameras would be way too expensive. We'll just have to suck it up and take the loss, I guess."

Everyone's quiet for a moment, like they're contemplating the injustice of it all, and then Zach says, "People are assholes."

We all nod in agreement. Even me. There's no disputing it—shoplifters are selfish, dishonorable jerks.

"You're quiet tonight."

I slap a mosquito off my arm and look at Eli, who's barely visible in the dark. After the diner, we all went our separate ways—Alyssa to her house, Sophie and Zach to *his* house, and Eli and me to the small, grassy park near my apartment building. We're sitting on wooden bench facing a swing set, which in the year or so since I moved here, I haven't seen used more than a half dozen times. My neighborhood isn't exactly family-centric.

"Am I?" I say, distracted. My mind is still stuck on what happened earlier, the look of disgust on my friends' faces when Alyssa talked about the shoplifter. I keep imagining them aiming that same disgust at *me*, and how awful and vulnerable it would make me feel. And how much I'd deserve their disappointment.

"You want to talk about it?"

His words wrap around me like fingers, yanking me out of my own head. "No," I reply, and then lean into him, pressing my lips to his. The park is quiet and dark, and aside from some flying insects and maybe a few squirrels, we're completely alone.

At first he kisses me back, but after a minute he pulls away and grabs my hand, stopping its progression across the firm expanse of his chest. "Why do you do that?"

"What?"

"Whenever I try to get you to talk about something personal, you distract me. You've done it a few times now."

I slide my hand out of his. "No, I don't." But even as I deny it, I know he's right. Every time he tries to dig past the surface, I kiss him or make a joke or do whatever else I can think of to get back on the fun-and-simple track. I don't even know why. Maybe because the closer we get, the more I realize the impossibility of keeping secrets from him forever. Someday, I'll have to reveal all the shameful parts of myself, to my friends and to him, but just the thought of it makes my heart race. I'm not ready to ruin everyone's image of me.

"I've told you everything about me," Eli goes on, a trace of hurt in his tone. "Everything about my family too. But I hardly know anything about yours. You never talk about it with me. You haven't even told me where your mother is and why you don't live with her. That's a pretty big thing to keep to yourself, isn't it?"

I look away. How long has this been bothering him? I figured the reason he never pressured me for details about my family life was because he thought it was none of his business. But clearly he thinks that since he told me all about *his* family, I'm expected to return the favor. And maybe I am. I can only stay a closed book for so long.

Something buzzes in my ear. Another mosquito, probably. Annoyed, I brush it away and turn to face Eli again. He wants me to talk about it? Okay, I'll talk about it. "My mother lives about a ninety-minute drive from here, in Sutton. She moved there at the beginning of last summer, a month or so after she was caught cheating with this guy named Gary, who was also married, by the way. Plus, he was one of my dad's best friends. So yeah, when I was asked who I wanted to live with, I chose my father instead of my cheating mom and the man who helped destroy my family. My sister did too, but I guess spending a year away at college gave her a new perspective or something, because now she thinks we need to extend the old olive branch to our mother, who I haven't seen or spoken to in a year. Like it's just that simple."

I pause to take a jagged breath. God, now I'm crying in front of Eli again. But this time, I'm not just some girl he barely knows sniveling in her car for reasons she won't share. Now he knows me, or at least a big part of me. And instead of pulling away, like I half expected him to do when he got his first glimpse past the surface, he wraps me in his arms and holds me while I cry.

The next evening after work, I settle on my bed with my laptop. My deadline to complete the online theft education class is just a few days away, and I still haven't finished it. I started it last week but could only handle an hour before shutting it off and watching a movie instead. There's nothing more boring than a disembodied voice on the computer lecturing you about stealing and its impact on society. Just like I assumed, it's nothing I don't already know.

But tonight I'm going to finish it, finally, so I can get my certificate and send it to the diversion coordinator. Soon, this will all be over and life can return to normal. Obligations complete. No more theft class, no more community service hours.

No more Rita's Reruns.

I ignore the twinge of sadness that comes with the thought of never working at the thrift store again and press play on the third course module: *Why Do People Steal?*

I sigh at the screen. Fergus, who's curled into a ball at the end of the bed, lifts his head and yawns. This makes me yawn, and I think of all the things I *could* be doing right now. Like going to the lake for an evening swim with my friends, or watching a movie, or hanging out with Eli. Or *kissing* Eli. Even better.

But he's off doing something with his friends, so tonight it's just me and the guy from the video, who's droning on about unhealthy thinking and behavior. I'm fiddling with my phone, only half paying attention, when the instructor takes on a deeper, more serious tone.

People who steal often feel like something has been taken from them. They feel deprived somehow, and stealing provides them with a sense of peace or relief. Life—for a moment, at least—is fair again.

The words pierce through my boredom. I look up from my phone.

For some people, shoplifting is a response to what they perceive as an unfair loss—a death in the family, a breakup, the loss of a job. It offers temporary control over a feeling of powerlessness. A person shoplifts for the same reasons someone else might drink, eat, or work too much—because it fills a void.

The hairs on the back of my neck stand up, like someone is watching me. I put down my phone and hit pause on the video, the instructor's words churning in my head. I think about how centered I feel when I take something, the sense of power and control it gives me. Like a wrong is being righted every time I pull it off without detection. Like the video said, it makes life seem fair again, if only for a few moments.

But I've always assumed my compulsion to steal came from some small, damaged part of me. An underlying defect in my nature that surfaced along with the anger I felt toward my mother for ripping our family apart. For hurting my father so deeply that he seemed to shrink overnight. For giving me up so easily, like a bag of old clothes that she no longer had any use for. That amount of anger needs some kind of outlet, and since drinking and overeating never appealed to me, shoplifting was the most viable choice at the time.

Does divorce count as an "unfair loss"? When I remember how we used to be—an average little family, whole and secure—it definitely feels like one. My mother was like anyone else's. Maybe a little distracted at times, and moody more often than not, but she used to at least try. She was there every day. In the audience for Rachel's dance recitals. Wandering around the school gym during my science fairs. Watching TV on the couch, her feet in Dad's lap and a glass of wine in her hand.

But gradually, all of that stopped. She became distant, unable to focus on anything, even Rachel and me. She and Dad started spending evenings—and then entire nights—in separate rooms. It was like she was only sticking around out of obligation, because she had two girls who needed a mother. Eventually, not even that was a good enough reason.

She'd checked out of her marriage—out of her *family*—but at one point, she was in. All in.

So yeah, it's a loss, and an incredibly unfair one. We didn't deserve to be broken and scattered. She shouldn't get to live happily ever after while we're stuck back here, doing whatever it takes to fill the void she left behind.

Chapter Twenty-Two

RACHEL CALLS THE NEXT MORNING JUST AS I'M getting out of the shower.

"Hi, Rach." I pull my bathrobe tighter around me and sit on my bed, wondering if she's going to start in on her upcoming visit with Mom and if I've changed my mind about going with her. It's too early in the morning for that.

But all she says is "Hey, Morgan. I just emailed you my flight itinerary for next week. I'll be getting in at eight twenty p.m. on the nineteenth. You and Dad can pick me up at the airport, right?"

"Uh, sure," I say.

"Great. And I know you guys live off greasy fast food, but

can you maybe stock the fridge with some fruits and vegetables before I come?" She pauses. "Actually, never mind. I'll just go shopping when I get there. Did I tell you I can cook now? Amir taught me. I mean, I don't get as gourmet as Mom did, but I'm pretty good. Remember that chicken Kiev she used to make? Man, that was yummy. I should get her recipe."

I do remember the Kiev, and all the other complex meals she used to create. She always said cooking relaxed her. The kitchen was her turf, and sometimes when I think of her, I see her standing at the counter, dark hair falling in her face as she chops vegetables and hums along with the radio.

"Remember the first time she made it? For Dad's birthday dinner?" Rachel asks, laughter in her voice. "He didn't end up getting off work until, like, eight, so you and I were dying of hunger. We drove her crazy with our whining."

I smile a bit as the memory comes back to me. That must have been about six or seven years ago. "And she finally let us have some crackers so we'd stay out of the kitchen."

"But then we ate the entire box, so when we finally sat down to eat, we were too full to have more than a few bites."

Now I'm laughing too. "And when you cut into your chicken, butter squirted out and hit you in the face."

She gasps. "Oh my God! I almost forgot about that. The butter was *hot* too. It left a big red mark on my chin. I remember you laughing your head off at me. Jerk."

"Can you blame me?"

"No," she says with a sigh. "I guess it *was* pretty funny."

"Yeah." My laughter fades, along with the memory, and I'm overcome with this odd sense of homesickness, even though I'm sitting in my bedroom. Rachel has this way of reminding me of the past, of home and how things used to be. I miss her, miss our unbroken family, in a pervasive, deep-down way that's hard to express in words.

"How are things there?" she asks when I don't say anything else. "Dad mentioned that he met your new boyfriend. Will I get to meet him too? Maybe we can all go out for dinner one night."

I stand up, letting the wet towel fall from my hair, and move over to my dresser to dig out a clean bra. "Maybe," I say, distracted by the sight of the striped bikini that I stole so many weeks ago, still nestled among my underwear. I barely notice it anymore, but sometimes, like now, it's all I can see. I slide one of the string ties between my fingers until I reach the turquoise bead on the end, remembering the way it dug into my skin. "Rach?"

"Yeah?"

I drop the string, tuck it back into the padded cups. "How did you stop?"

"How did I stop what?"

"The drinking and the pot and all that," I say, shutting the drawer without taking anything out. "How did you stop?"

She doesn't answer right away and I squeeze my eyes shut,

instantly regretting the question. Maybe it was different for her. She probably didn't drink to fill a void, or to get relief. A lot of people have vices they're ashamed of, but stealing isn't like smoking or drinking or gambling or any other thing that's vilified but still generally accepted. Stealing is a selfish crime that hurts other people. I know this, but knowing it doesn't seem to matter.

"I told you this already, Morgan," she says, and I can almost see her tilting her head, like she does when she's concerned. "I realized how stupid I was being, so I stopped. That's basically it. Why?"

I sit back down on my bed. "What if you realize how stupid you're being and it's *still* not enough to make you want to stop? What then?"

Another pause. "Why are you asking me this? What's going on?"

The confusion in her voice makes me want to suck the words back in. Not even she understands. "Nothing. Never mind."

"You're not—please tell me you're not still shoplifting. Even after getting caught. Please tell me you learned your lesson and won't ever do that again."

I wind the bedsheet around my finger, unsure how to respond. I haven't stolen from a store since the sunglasses, but that doesn't mean I don't want to, constantly. Every time I'm buying something—milk or tampons or even a pack of gum—I imagine slipping something into my bag. I don't do it, but the urge is always there, in the background, in my fingers, in the part of my brain that craves the rush of release.

The theft education class talked about identifying feelings and behaviors and challenging automatic thoughts and finding alternative emotional outlets, but I have no idea where to even start. For the past year, shoplifting has been my only outlet. If I stop, what will happen when all this anger builds up and has nowhere to go?

I'll implode.

"Morgan," Rachel says when I don't respond. "Exactly how long have you been doing this? When you got caught . . . that wasn't the first time you shoplifted, was it?"

I should have known she'd catch on; she can usually figure out what it is I'm not saying. "I have to go," I tell her, then hang up before she can ask any more questions. Maybe she's not the one I should be talking to about this. I don't know who is, but I do know one thing: I don't want to implode, and I need to start looking for a new method to prevent it. Something that can fill the void for good.

I know the moment I walk in the door after work that Rachel voiced her suspicions to Dad while I was gone. He's sitting on the couch and staring at nothing, just like the day we got the diversion letter.

"Morgan, sit down," he says without looking at me. His face is flushed, his nostrils flared. I haven't seen him this pissed since he picked me up from the mall security office.

"I'm leaving to meet Eli in a half hour. Can it wait?"

"No." He gestures to the chair.

Great. What is wrong with Rachel lately? We never used to tattle on each other to our parents. She kept my secrets, I kept hers. I guess the rules changed without my knowledge.

I sit down. "Dad, I don't know what Rachel told you, but I'm not still shoplifting. I swear." I figure the metal penguin doesn't count as shoplifting, since I didn't steal it from a store. Though in a lot of ways, what I did was even worse. I stole it from someone's house, and I feel more shame over that damn penguin than anything I've taken so far. But admitting that to Dad isn't going to help anything.

"I really hope you're telling me the truth," he says, rubbing a hand over his jaw. "I need to be able to trust you, Morgan. I can't be constantly worrying about you and wondering if you're going to steal something again."

"You don't have to worry about me. Or wonder. I promise, I have not shoplifted since the sunglasses."

"The sunglasses," he echoes, finally looking at me. His piercing gaze makes me want to squirm. "And that's the first thing you ever stole, right? Like you told the police officer? Like you told *me*?"

Shit. My mind scrambles for something to say that won't make him enraged, but there's nothing. "I . . ." At a loss for words, I clamp my mouth shut and swallow.

"The truth," he says when I don't finish my sentence. "You've done enough lying already."

He's right; my first instinct was to lie. Sometimes, with me, lies feel almost automatic. But as the video said, I need to change my automatic thinking, replace my *lie* and *steal* impulses with something else. So for the first time in a long time, I try the complete truth.

"The sunglasses weren't the first time. I've shoplifted before." I address my confession to the floor, unable to look at my father's face as the words sink in.

"How many times?"

I glance up at him. He's gazing at the floor too, his forehead creased with stress and disappointment. I can't believe I keep doing this to him, over and over again. Shame floods through me and my eyes fill with tears.

"I don't know the exact number," I say quietly. "It was a lot."

"A lot," he mutters. He leans back, shaking his head. "So this is what you've been up to while I've been busy trying to keep a roof over our heads. Stealing anything you can get your hands on. Great. What else have you been doing?"

I blink the tears away and meet his eyes. "What?"

"What else have you been doing that I don't know about? Drinking? Drugs?"

"No," I say emphatically. "I don't drink or do drugs." *That was Rachel*, I almost say, but decide against it. There's no need to bring her into this. "There's nothing else. You know every-thing there is to know, I promise."

"And how do you expect me to believe anything you say after this, huh?" He springs off the couch and starts walking away, then pauses at the threshold to the living room. He turns to face me again, his expression stony. "I thought I was doing the right thing, letting you stay here with me," he says in a low voice. "But maybe you would have been better off living with your mother."

His words sting like a slap. He's never said anything like that to me before. Maybe he's thought it, but he's never made me feel like he didn't want me. *You're no better than her*, he seems to be saying. *You two deserve each other.*

Maybe he's right.

I stand up. "Dad—"

"I'm going for a walk."

He turns and heads for the hallway, leaving me to stand there alone. The door closes behind him with a gentle *click*, but I flinch as if he's slammed it shut instead.

I'm not sure if I'm supposed to be grounded, but Dad's not around to tell me one way or the other, so I head out to meet Eli as planned.

I'm fifteen minutes late getting to Donovan Lake, where we agreed to meet up at eight thirty. We intended to go for a walk along the wooded trail that borders the water, but now it's starting to get dark, which will make seeing the path in front of us a little tricky. At this point, it doesn't really matter to me what we do. Honestly, I don't feel like doing much of anything, not even with Eli. But I don't want to be at home either, so here I am.

Eli is waiting in his Jeep in the parking lot. He gets out as I'm pulling into the space next to him.

"Sorry I'm late," I say as I climb out and meet his gaze across the car's roof. I try to keep my voice and expression light, even though my chest feels like something heavy has taken up residence on it. Eli was nice enough to let me cry on him the other night; I don't want to make a habit of it.

"It's fine," he says, frowning slightly as he studies me. I must not be hiding my distress as well as I thought.

Determined to put the past hour behind me, I circle around to where he's standing and take his hand. "Let's go for a walk."

He doesn't budge. "Have you been crying?"

The whole way here. "No," I say; then I remember about the automatic lies and change my mind. "Yes. But I'm good now. Just a fight with my dad."

"What was it about? Your mom?"

I shake my head and look away, toward the lake. The air is turning cooler as the sun sets and the only person left in the water is a kayaker, gliding across the surface.

"You can tell me," Eli says, squeezing my hand. "You can tell me anything."

Can I? I look back at his face, shadowed in the growing darkness. My family drama didn't drive him away, but my secret might. Though if I hadn't shoplifted in the first place, I never would have ended up at Rita's Reruns, and we wouldn't be standing here together right now, hands linked. But knowing this doesn't erase the fact that I've been basically lying to him from the start.

"Thanks," I say, reaching up to kiss him. Maybe I really *can* tell him anything, but right now, that's as much as I'm willing to say.

Chapter Twenty-Three

DAD AND I HAVE BEEN AVOIDING EACH OTHER FOR days, so naturally I'm surprised when I emerge from the back room of the thrift shop and discover him standing by the register, talking to Rita.

"There she is," Rita says triumphantly, like she made me appear just now through magic.

I approach them slowly, wiping my dusty hands off on my jeans. "What are you doing here?" I ask my father. Saturday is the busiest day at the dealership—he doesn't usually leave. And he's never visited me at work before. He seems out of place here in his suit and tie.

"I thought I'd pick you up and take you to lunch," he says

with a buoyancy that must be for Rita's sake, seeing as we've barely spoken all week.

I look down at my filthy self, then at Rita. She smiles and says, "Go ahead. I'll let you out a half hour early. You can make it up next week."

"Thanks, Rita," Dad says.

"You bet." She clasps his hand, her bracelets clinking together with the movement. "You're raising a good girl there, Charles. Bright, hardworking, reliable. The apple sure doesn't fall far."

Dad and I both flush at the compliment, making me glad that Eli's at the store getting replacement bulbs for one of the overhead lights instead of here, witnessing my embarrassment. That's the second time Rita has called me a "good girl." She must have her own unique definition of *good*. Or maybe she's just highlighting my positive qualities for my father's benefit.

Dad takes me to a sit-down, family-style restaurant near the thrift store, where we *both* look out of place. Him because of the suit, and me because I'm covered in dust from unpacking boxes of newspaper-wrapped dishes all morning.

The waitress who takes our drink order doesn't seem to notice or care about our appearance. Once she's gone, Dad clears his throat and looks at me.

"I've had a chance to think and cool off," he says, shifting in his chair. "First, I'm sorry about what I said. About you being better off with your mother. I don't really think that, and I hope I didn't make you feel like I don't want you around, because I do."

My stomach unclenches a bit and I nod. "Okay."

"Also," he continues quickly, like he's been rehearsing this in his head and has to get everything out before he forgets, "I think it would be a really good idea if you talked to someone, a therapist or counselor or some type of professional, about your shoplifting problem. This has gone beyond both of us, Morgan. We need outside help."

My stomach tightens again at the thought of telling a stranger about my personal life, but I know he's right. My issues run too deep to resolve on their own. "Okay," I agree. "I'll talk to someone."

The waitress appears with our drinks then and asks if we're ready to order. We scan our menus quickly and decide to split a large order of nachos.

"One last thing," Dad says when the waitress walks away. "I really think you should you should go with Rachel to visit your mother next weekend."

I sigh. *This again.* "Dad—"

He holds up a hand, cutting me off. "I'm not going to force you. I just want you to seriously consider it. You're never going to get over this animosity you have toward her unless you face it. Face *her*. Go there and talk to her. *Scream* at her, if that's what you need to do. Just get it out and move on. Give her a chance to make things right."

He takes a large gulp of water, like his little speech scorched his throat on its way out. I watch him, doubt swelling inside me. He and Rachel make it sound so simple. Like I can just go see her as if a million things haven't changed. On the other hand, Dad's willingness to mend things with me even after the horrible things I've done makes me think that almost anyone can be forgiven.

"I'll consider it," I tell him.

"Good. Thank you."

A few minutes later, our waitress reappears and plunks a huge plate of nachos and a bowl of salsa in front of us. It's enough food for at least four people. Dad laughs at the sheer magnitude of the pile, and after a moment, I do too.

"So Rita says you're doing really well." More relaxed now, he takes a tortilla chip out of the pile and dunks it into the salsa. "She couldn't stop gushing about you. Have you considered staying on after your community service hours are up? She could probably use the help."

I pull out my own chip, severing the ribbon of cheese with my finger. I *have* considered staying on, but I'm not sure if Rita would want that. A few hours of community service is one thing; a regular job is something else entirely. She'd probably rather hire someone who hasn't been in trouble with the law.

"Once school starts, most of my Royal Smoothie hours will be on the weekends. I don't think I can do two jobs and school." It's the same explanation I gave to Eli when he asked why I was only volunteering for the summer.

"Makes sense," Dad says with a nod. "I'm proud of you, though, for taking the job so seriously. I know you were reluctant at first."

"It turned out to be better than I expected." It's the truth. I think I might actually miss it once I leave. I've gotten used to Rita's outlandishness, and Eli's door slams, and the customers, and the marigolds that greet me on the way in, and the mustiness of the stockroom. I feel more useful there than I do at Royal Smoothie, where my biggest accomplishment is getting the correct ratio of yogurt to coconut milk. At Rita's, I'm contributing to something worthwhile.

Damn my father for being right.

He digs out another chip, so loaded with cheese and peppers and chicken that it sags toward the table. "If only more things in life turned out that way."

Sophie and I both have the next day off work, which rarely happens, so we hop into my car and head to the jewelry store to pick up Alyssa. At first she says she can't get away, but we manage to lure her out with the promise of ice cream.

"I can't stay out long, guys," she says once we're driving again, ice-cream cones in hand.

Sophie twists around to look at her. "You spend way too much time inside that store, Lyss."

the girl you thought i was

"Sorry. I have no choice. It's not like we have the money to hire someone."

I feel a pang of guilt for some reason and change the subject. "Have you heard from Dawson at all?"

"No. Have you?"

I hand Sophie my cone so I can make a left turn. "Barely." He still meets me after work for a drive home sometimes, but otherwise he's been pretty scarce. It sucks.

"He'll come around," Sophie says, giving me back my cone. "Hey, let's hit the mall! I need a dress for my cousin's wedding in September."

"But—" Alyssa starts.

"An hour. That's all. Please? I need you guys to help me find a dress that doesn't make me look twelve."

Alyssa sighs and I head toward the highway, my palms already slick on the wheel. I haven't been back to that mall since I got caught. I want to convince Sophie to go to the smaller downtown mall instead, but I know she'll refuse. All the stores she likes are in the other one. I'll just have to deal with it. I'll stick close to my friends, and it'll be fine.

Or not. My paranoia kicks into overdrive the second we step through the doors. It's Sunday, so the place is crowded. LP officers could be anywhere. I wonder if there's a picture of me posted in the security office, with instructions to arrest me on sight. I feel exposed, like there are cameras on me, tracing my every move.

"You know, Soph, I have tons of dresses," I say as we walk down the mall. "You can borrow one if you want." *Please say yes, so we can leave.*

"Nah," she says, pausing in front of a store. "You actually have boobs and hips. Your clothes would probably be baggy on me."

So much for that. I try to relax as she drags Alyssa and me from store to store, examining and discarding dresses in each one. Finally, about a half hour later, in a trendy little shop with creepy-looking mannequins and dance music blasting overhead, she finds a cute red dress that complements both her blond hair and her petite figure. I'm relieved. Now we can get out of here.

"Now I need shoes," she says as we leave the store. I resist the urge to throttle her.

"Soph, I have to get back soon," Alyssa tells her.

I nod, suddenly grateful for Alyssa's strong work ethic. "Yeah, Soph, you said an hour."

"It'll just take a minute." She makes a beeline for the closest available store that sells shoes. Which just happens to be Nordstrom.

Panic rises in my chest. I can't go into Nordstrom. I'm not allowed. The last thing the woman in the security office told me before I left that day was that I was banned from the store for a year. That if they ever saw me in there before that, I'd immediately be escorted out like the thief I am. Was.

I can't go into Nordstrom.

"One quick look and then we'll go, okay?" Sophie says when I come to a halt, right there outside the doors. She and Alyssa keep walking, unaware that I'm rooted to the floor.

I *could* walk in there with them, take the risk, but being hauled out by security right in front of them and everyone else would be a nightmare come true. So I stay where I am until my friends notice I'm not with them anymore. They both turn to look at me, confusion etched on their faces.

"Morgan, what's wrong?" Alyssa backtracks toward me and touches my arm. Sophie follows a second later.

"I can't." The words come out small and scratchy with shame. With one stupid decision, I ruined my chance to simply walk into a store with my friends like a normal person.

"What do you mean, you can't?" Sophie asks.

Shoppers swarm around us, their presence barely registering in my brain. All I can see are my friends' faces, staring back at me with concern. They love me. They trust me. And unless I can think of a way out of this in the next few seconds, I'm going to ruin that too.

"Morgan?"

"You're freaking us out."

I look over at the store entrance, bright and wide and welcoming. Except if you're me. "I can't," I repeat, this time with resignation. There's no way out of this. And I know, deep down, that a big part of overcoming a problem is admitting, out loud, that you have one in the first place. "I'm not allowed."

They glance at each other, then back at me. "Explain?" Sophie says.

I'm not sure I *can* explain in a way that won't make me look like a horrible person, but I know I have to try. Glancing around me, I take their arms and lead them out of the flow of foot traffic to a vacant spot near a cell phone kiosk.

"Remember the last time we were all here together?" I begin. "At the end of May, when Alyssa was looking for a swimsuit cover?"

Alyssa nods. "You got sick and went home without us."

I lick my lips, which feel as parched as my throat. "I didn't get sick. I got caught."

"Got caught doing *what*? What are you talking about?"

God. They really have no idea. If they even thought for a minute that I was capable of doing something wrong, surely they would have put the pieces together by now. "Shoplifting," I say, finally. "I got caught shoplifting. In Nordstrom. That's why I can't go in there anymore."

Their reactions are immediate—Sophie's face turns blotchy, while Alyssa's goes completely pale. They stare at me, wide-eyed and shocked.

"This is a joke, right?" Sophie shakes her head and laughs. "You? A shoplifter? I mean . . . that doesn't even make sense. You don't *steal*."

"I do. Well, I did. But I want to stop. I'm *trying* to stop." I pause to wet my lips again, wishing for a drink of water. "I've been so angry about my mom, and I didn't know how to deal with it. So I started shoplifting. But then I got caught stealing sunglasses in Nordstrom, and I had the option of doing community service instead of going to court, so that's what I did."

"The thrift shop," Sophie says, the pieces finally clicking together.

"Yeah." I glance at Alyssa, who hasn't spoken a word yet. She's not looking at me anymore; her gaze is focused on the floor, and she's biting her lip and blinking, like she does when she's trying not to cry. *Oh God.* "Lyss?"

Her chest rises and falls as she sucks in a breath. When she looks at me, her brown eyes are glassy and bloodshot. "So that's why," she says, her voice trembling. "The other day at the diner, when I talked about the guy who stole the necklace from my mom's store . . . that's why you were acting so weird. Because you're a thief too."

"Alyssa, I'm really—"

"How can you be so selfish? Do you have any idea how much shoplifting hurts stores? They have to raise their prices. They have to spend extra money on security."

"I know," I say quickly, before she can interrupt me again. "I know all that, Lyss, and I feel horrible about it. Believe me. I regret the moment I ever started stealing."

"Oh." She barks out an incredulous laugh. *"Now* you regret it? Or do you just regret the fact that you got caught?"

Sophie puts a hand on her shoulder, but she shrugs it off, her eyes still burning into mine. I ball my hands into fists to stop them from shaking. I knew they'd be shocked and disappointed, even disgusted, but I wasn't expecting this level of fury. Especially not from Alyssa, who's never lost her temper with me once in all the years we've been friends. Then again, I've never given her any reason to.

"And you try to justify it by saying you're angry at your mom?" she goes on, her face regaining its color. "My father *died* and I don't deal with it by stealing. You know what I do instead? I work. I help my mother. I don't use the shitty things that happened to me as an excuse to rip people off."

Sophie touches her shoulder again, and this time Alyssa lets her. "Come on, Lyss," she says softly. Her eyes flick toward me and then away. She can't even look at me. I'm not the same person I was before. Not to them.

"We'll get the bus home." Alyssa practically spits the words at me, and I feel every syllable. "We know the way."

They turn and walk away together, arm in arm. Again, I'm rooted to the floor, unable to move forward or do anything but stand there, watching them go until they finally round the corner, disappearing completely.

Chapter Twenty-Four

I OVERSLEEP THE NEXT MORNING, MAKING ME late for my shift at Royal Smoothie. Luckily, my boss isn't even there when I stroll in at ten after seven. My coworker Kyle is the only person in the place.

"Man," he says when he sees me. "Rough night last night?"

I know I look like crap. After getting home from the mall yesterday, I climbed into bed and didn't move for the next twelve hours, except to pee and get a glass of water. I told Dad I was sick. When Eli texted me in the evening to ask if I wanted to get together, I told him the same thing. It wasn't a total lie. My stomach felt like something was trying to rip through it from the inside. It still does, kind of. The extra-large coffee I downed on the way here probably isn't helping.

"You could say that," I reply, stationing myself at the register. There's no way I can handle a sharp knife in this state.

Kyle quickly throws a bunch of stuff in a blender and hits the start button. When it's done, he dumps the smoothie in a cup and hands it to me. "Energy booster."

We're not really supposed to drink anything in sight of the customers, but since there are no customers, I take a long sip. It's sweet and delicious, and I immediately feel more awake. "Thanks, Kyle."

He nods and goes back to prepping for the day.

Kyle's concoction gets me through to my half-hour lunch break at eleven. I ask him to make me another one and then take it outside to drink on the office building steps. The weather is beautiful, sunny and not humid for once, but I barely notice the warmth on my skin. I can't stop thinking about yesterday, the shock and hurt in my friends' eyes. They've been my bright spot over the past year, and now they'll probably never talk to me again. I'll be going back to school in a few weeks with no friends at all, and it's my own stupid fault.

My eyes start watering. Shit. I thought I'd gotten all my crying out of the way last night. I sift through my bag for a tissue, but find nothing. Great. I'm contemplating the grossness factor in using the sleeve of my polo when a crumpled white napkin appears in my line of vision. I look up. Dawson is standing three steps below me, wearing his Ace Burger T-shirt and a button inviting me to *Try Our Sizzlin' Sausage and Egg Breakfast Burger!*

"It's clean," he says when I take the napkin. "I think. I was bussing a table earlier and stuffed it in my pocket until I could toss it. Then forgot about it."

I smooth out the napkin, fold it in half, and wipe my nose. I'm not fussy. "Since when does Ace Burger serve breakfast?" I ask as he sits down next to me.

"Since last week. Gotta reach that early-riser demographic."

I nod and take a sip of smoothie. Silence stretches between us. Our friends must not have gotten to him yet. He wouldn't be so nice to me if he knew.

"Aren't you going to ask why I'm crying?"

He brings his feet up a step, aligning them with mine. "I have a pretty good idea."

"You talked to Sophie?"

"No, but I talked to Zach, who talked to Sophie."

"So I guess everyone hates me now."

"No," he says slowly, like I'm silly for thinking such a thing. "No one hates you. Would I be sitting here if I hated you? We're just, uh . . . kind of surprised."

"You didn't see Alyssa's face." I give my nose one more wipe and slide the napkin into my pocket. "She hates me. She thinks I'm a bad person."

"Well, I can't speak for her," he mutters. "But Sophie and

Zach aren't mad or anything. You should text them."

"I will. Soon." We fall silent again. Okay, so most of them don't hate me. That's promising. Still, I can't see how anything will ever be like it was. They'll see me differently now.

"I cheated on a test once," Dawson blurts out.

My head spins toward him. "What?"

"In eighth-grade English. The test was on the elements of a short story and we had to know a bunch of definitions." He smiles with half his mouth. "Well, you know me. I'm a numbers guy. The definitions just did not want to stick in my head, so I wrote them down on a little piece of paper and hid it inside my sweatshirt sleeve."

I gasp. "Dawson. You didn't."

"I did. And I got caught too. I swear, I thought my dad was going to send me to one of those boot camps for delinquent minors."

I shake my head. It's hard to imagine nice, smart Dawson doing anything wrong. "Well, I appreciate you trying to empathize, but cheating on one test in middle school isn't quite in the same league, you know?"

He shrugs. "I'm just saying, sometimes even smart, decent people do stupid things when they're feeling desperate."

I can tell by the flash of misery in his eyes that he isn't just talking about me or the test. "We miss having you around, Dawson," I say, nudging his knee with mine. "All of us. Even Alyssa. She told me about the Lighthouse."

"Yeah, well . . . at least I know exactly where I stand." He rubs a hand over his face like he's trying to wipe off the sting of her rejection and stands up. "I'd better get back."

My break's over too. I stand up and we walk down the steps together.

"Dawson," I say when he turns to leave. He pauses on the sidewalk. "I . . . I don't know how to tell Eli the truth. About my, um, problem. Any advice for me?"

"Wait. He doesn't know?" When I shake my head, his brown eyes go wide for a moment before he composes himself. "Well, he seems like a good dude, and he's obviously into you. I'm sure he can take it."

I wish I were so sure.

Like the coward I am, I play sick that night too. And the next. But when Eli texts me after work on Wednesday evening, asking if he can see me, I know I can't put him off any longer. I'm going to have to talk to him eventually, and the longer I wait, the more pissed off he'll be. I learned that much from experience.

Tonight is Dad's late night at the dealership, so I tell Eli to come over. He shows up forty-five minutes later with a single white flower in his hand.

"It's a zinnia," he says, handing it to me.

I thank him and touch my fingertip to one of the smooth petals. He's not going to make this easy.

"I locked Fergus in my bedroom," I say as I bring the flower to the kitchen. We don't own a vase, so I fill a drinking glass with water and stick it in there. "Hopefully, that'll cut down on the allergens floating around."

"No worries." He follows me into the kitchen and leans his back against the fridge. "I popped some Claritin before I left the house."

When I turn around from placing the flower on the windowsill, I catch Eli gazing at me like I'm something he wants to devour. My pulse thuds.

"Are you feeling better now?" he asks, moving closer.

"Yeah, I feel fine." It's the truth. Living off cereal and smoothies for the past few days has actually helped restore me, at least physically. I'm probably the healthiest I've been in over a year. "Why? Did you miss me?"

He stops in front of me and grips the counter on either side of my waist, fencing me in. "Yes."

It's extremely difficult to focus on anything else when he's standing so close, with his firm, broad chest just inches from my face and his scent filling my nostrils. At the moment, all I can think about is kissing him. Because kissing him would be so much easier than telling him he's been hanging out with a lying thief all summer.

But if I'm going to change and become the person he thinks I am, then he needs to know all the pieces to the story.

"Eli." I press my palm to his chest and push him gently

away. He takes a step back, letting his hands drop from the counter.

"Yeah?" he prompts when I don't say anything.

I stare at him, formulating and then immediately discarding a dozen different explanations. Explanations about my mother, and how her actions affected me, and the stealing, and how sorry I am that I led him to believe that I was someone different, someone who's worth his time and his praise and his family's respect.

But nothing I come up with seems right. Everything sounds like an excuse, because that's what they are. Excuses that don't absolve me or solve a damn thing. And I'm scared that if I tell him the truth, he'll look at me the way Alyssa did, or not be able to look at me at all, like Sophie. I can't stand the thought of either.

I just want one more night of him looking at me like I'm the girl he asked out in the middle of a busy sidewalk. The girl he thinks is smart and funny and obnoxiously cute. One more night of him believing I'm decent person.

"Nothing." I take his hands and pull him toward me again. "I just . . . missed you too."

He leans down to kiss me, and soon we're sitting on the living room couch, my legs straddling his lap, picking up where we left off in his family room. Except this time his family isn't upstairs, and my father won't be home for another two hours.

"I swear the whole *accept this flower as a token of my love* thing I did earlier wasn't some kind of calculated move," Eli says when we pause for a breath. "I mean, I'm totally on board with what's happening right now, but I want you to know I didn't come over here expecting anything."

Love. He said *love.* Not exactly an *I love you,* but in the neighborhood. No guy has ever said that to me before. Just the idea of it, that he might feel that way about me, fills me with a conflicting mix of panic and happiness. But mostly happiness.

Without taking my eyes from his, I grab the bottom of my shirt and slip it over my head.

"Jesus, Morgan," Eli breathes, his throat moving as he looks at me. Luckily, I put on my best bra this morning—the black lacy one with the little silver bow. He's touched it before, but always under my clothes. He's never seen it, or me in it, like this.

"Should I put my shirt back on?" I ask, amused, when he doesn't move or say anything else.

"No." He shakes his head, still dazed. "Please no."

He peels his eyes off me long enough to yank off his own shirt and toss it on the floor next to mine. Then he eases me against his chest, and the high I feel when his bare skin meets mine eclipses all the ones before it.

The next night, I finally take Dawson's advice and text Sophie, asking if she wants to hang out. To my relief, she texts me back a few minutes later. She tells me she's at Zach's and that I can come over if I want. Some of my heaviness lifts. Maybe I won't be a friendless loser, after all.

When I get to Zach's, I let myself in like usual and head to the basement. The two of them are stretched out on the couch, snuggled together and watching TV. They sit up when I walk in.

"Hey there, Sticky Fingers," Zach greets me with a teasing grin.

I stop dead and stare at him.

"*Zach*," Sophie says, whacking him across the head with a pillow. I'm glad. It's far too soon for me to find any humor in my situation.

"Sorry," he says to me.

I nod my forgiveness and sit down on the love seat. "What are you guys doing?"

"Nothing much," Sophie says, yawning. "We were just about to play *Street Fighter*."

Street Fighter. The same game Eli played a few weeks ago when he was here. My face floods with warmth at the thought of him, and suddenly I want to tell Sophie everything about what happened last night. The almost *I love you*. The kissing on the couch that turned into more.

"You want in?" she asks, yanking me back to the present.

"Sure," I say. Maybe we'll get a chance to talk later.

She hands me a controller while Zach sets up the game. For the next hour, the three of us take turns kicking each other's asses like it's any other night. Like I didn't just drop a major bomb a few days ago.

So that's how they want to play this. We're supposed to ignore the elephant in the room and pretend like nothing's changed at all. I guess I can live with that, if they can. At least they're not ignoring me altogether, like Alyssa.

"Damn it," Zach says as Sophie's character uses her high-heeled boot to smash his character in the head. "I'm too hungry for this. I should've brought down some snacks before we started playing."

"I'll get them," I say. I'm between turns right now and my stomach has been growling for the past twenty minutes. "Chips?"

"Yeah. There's a bag in the pantry."

As I'm heading for the stairs, Sophie quickly pauses the game and jumps up to follow me. "Wait. I'll help you."

I look over at her, confused. She was in the middle of a fight, and on the verge of winning. Why stop just to help me get a bag of chips that I can certainly handle myself?

When her eyes slide away from mine, it hits me. She doesn't trust me to go alone. She thinks I'm going to steal something from Zach's house. *Zach.* My friend. Acid rises in my throat.

"Actually," I say, stopping at the bottom of the stairs, "I should probably go. I just remembered I have to do something at home."

Sophie bites her lip. "Morgan . . ."

Tears fill my eyes and I turn away, not wanting her to see them. "Sorry, it's just . . . I need to go. I'll see you guys later."

Not waiting for a response, I spring up the stairs and don't stop moving until I'm outside and in my car. I was wrong. Pretending is impossible. They're always going to be watching me, waiting to see if I slip up. And the sad thing is, I can't even blame them.

Chapter Twenty-Five

FLIGHT 485, THE ONE CARRYING MY SISTER, switches from **On Time** to **Arrived at Gate** on the arrivals board. I walk back to my father, who's sitting in a pastel chair in the waiting area, reading a magazine he picked up at the newspaper stand when we arrived at the airport.

"She's here," I announce.

Dad closes his magazine and stands up. We walk to the baggage claim area and stand by the escalator to wait. My stomach jumps in anticipation. In spite of the tension between us these past couple of months, I'm excited to hang out with my sister for a few days. Since Dad's off work all next week, we made a bunch of plans—dinners, drives, a day trip to the beach. I try not to think about the other day trip Rachel has planned.

"There she is," Dad says, grinning and waving.

I follow his gaze and catch my first glimpse of my sister in eight months. She's walking toward us, smiling, wearing a short white sundress that shows off her tan. Her small pink suitcase trails behind her, the one that goes with the luggage set Mom and Dad gave her two birthdays ago, when they were still together. Like her, the suitcase is still as bright as ever.

Rachel hugs Dad first, then me. We hold each other tight for a few moments before stepping back to examine each other.

"Your hair got long," she says, touching the wavy strands.

"And yours got short." Her light brown hair always reached the middle of her back, but now it just brushes her shoulders. It hits me all over again how much she resembles Mom. Same brown hair and blue eyes, same dimpled smile and long, straight nose. The only thing I got from Mom is her lack of height. Rachel is five five, and I've envied her extra three inches—and the fact that she can tan in the sun instead of frying—for years now.

Rachel tosses her head. "I got sick of having it long. Change is good, right?"

I nod. She looks happy and shining and in love. It's strange. I've never seen my sister in love before. She dated a lot in high school, but none of those boys made her cheeks pink and her eyes sparkly. The look agrees with her. Dad must think so too, because he smiles as he watches her. Or maybe he's just relieved that she didn't come home with an engagement ring or a protruding belly.

We make our way to the parking lot and Dad stuffs the pink suitcase into the trunk of the CR-Z. I climb in back, leaving the passenger seat to Rachel. During the thirty-minute drive to the apartment, she fills us in on her flight and her job and which courses she's taking this fall. Dad listens to her ramble on with a contented expression on his face. I think about this past Christmas, when Rachel's bubbly chattiness filled the normally quiet apartment, and how nice it was to have some life in the place for a change.

It's late by the time we get home. Fergus greets us with a series of panicked meows, like he's spent the past few hours worrying that we'd never come back.

"Fergburger!" Rachel scoops him up and kisses his head. Fergus's purring is audible from here. "Morgan let you get too fat."

"I take full responsibility for my weight gain," Dad says as he flicks on the kitchen light.

"Dad, I was referring to Fergus, not you. You look great."

Dad winks at me, making me laugh. Just like that, all the tension from the past few months slips away and we're a family again. Complete.

We stand around the kitchen and talk for a bit before deciding to call it a night. Dad goes to get sheets for the pull-out bed while I get into my pajamas and brush my teeth. When I'm done, I head back out to the living room to find Dad gone and Rachel sitting on the couch, tapping on her phone. She smiles when she sees me and pats the spot next to her. I flop down and pull a blanket over my legs, settling in for some long-awaited sister bonding. Fergus joins us a few seconds later, curving his plump body against my thigh.

"Amir just sent me this." Rachel tilts her phone toward me, and I lean in to get a closer look at the screen. It's a selfie shot of Amir, leaning back on what I assume is a headboard, shirtless with a crooked smile on his face. The picture only shows him from the shoulders up, but still. I feel like I'm intruding on an intimate moment.

"Oh my God, Rach," I say, pushing her phone away.

She laughs and gazes at the picture again. "He's hot, though, right?"

He definitely has something, an indefinable quality that makes you want to stare at him. "Are you guys serious?"

"Depends on what you mean by *serious*. But if you're asking if I love him, the answer is yes." She places her phone on the coffee table and curls her legs beneath her body. "What about you and Eli?"

"What about me and Eli?"

"Same question. Are you guys an official thing? Are you in love?"

Images flash through my mind—Eli's smile, his easy laugh, the way his eyes go dark when he wants to kiss me. "I don't know," I say. We still haven't said the words. I've never been in love before, so I'm not sure if that's what I'm feeling, or if it's just a very strong fondness. All I know is that I like having him around.

Rachel flashes her dimples. "You're sleeping with him, aren't you?"

I cough, taken aback. "Rach," I hiss, glancing at the hallway to the bedrooms. Now different images are flipping through my head—Eli's mouth on my skin, the sculpted contours of his body, the way his arm muscles swelled as he hovered over me. My face burns as I remember the details of Wednesday night, the two of us together on this couch and then, ultimately, in my bed. "Well, you're sleeping with Amir."

She nudges my leg. "Yeah, and I told you about it, like, the next morning. Unlike you. The detailed text you sent me afterward must not have gone through, I guess."

I nudge her back and we both start laughing. It feels like old times, sisters sharing secrets, our voices low so we won't be overheard. I always miss her, but it didn't hit me exactly how much until right now.

"Dad would kill us both, you know," I say when we finally stop giggling.

"I know. He probably thinks we should stay virgins until

our wedding nights." She lets out a snort. "Like I'm sure he and Mom were, right?"

A cloud passes over the room at the mention of Mom. I was hoping we'd get through at least the first night without her name coming up.

"Morgan," Rachel says, her voice soft.

I realize I've gone quiet. "What?"

"If I ask you something, will you promise to tell me the truth and not shut me out like you did over the phone all summer?"

I tip my head back and meet her eyes. The room is quiet except for Fergus, who's giving himself a bedtime bath. "Yes," I reply finally. I have a feeling I know what her question is going to be.

"Are you still shoplifting?"

Yep, I was right. "I haven't done it in a while, Rach. That's the truth."

"And you want to quit for good." She says it like a statement, as if she doesn't believe I could possibly want anything else.

"Yes, I want to quit for good. And I'm going to get help. Dad's been looking for a therapist for me."

"Good. That's really good." She yawns loudly, her long day of airports and travel catching up with her. "Does everyone know? About the shoplifting, I mean? Your friends?"

I feel a twinge in my chest, remembering Alyssa's and Sophie's faces when I told them. "Yes," I say past the tightness in my throat. I tell her about what happened at the mall last weekend, and the mixed reactions that followed.

"That sucks," she says when I'm finished. "I mean, I understand why they'd be mad or wary or whatever, but it still sucks."

I nod. I understand too.

"Does Eli know?"

The question seems to ring in my ears, tormenting me. "No."

"God, Morgan. How long do you think you can keep it from him? You said it's his aunt who you did the community service work for, right? I mean, eventually the truth is going to—"

"Rachel," I cut in. "Can we not talk about this tonight?"

"Sure. Sorry. Let's talk about something else." She picks up her pillow and holds it in her lap. "So, about Sunday. I'm leaving in the morning for Sutton and coming back later that night. In case you've changed your mind."

God, this topic is even worse. I look away so she can't see my face. "I have to work Sunday, so I couldn't go even if I wanted to."

"You could call in sick."

Annoyance prickles in my stomach, and I cross my legs, jostling Fergus. He hops down and moves to the chair, where it's safe. "I don't care if you go, okay? That's your choice. I just don't see the point."

"The point is she's *family*, Morgan. We have one mom, and she's it. She made a mistake—a huge one—but that doesn't mean we've stopped loving her, right? And loving someone means giving them an opportunity to make up for their mistakes." She taps my leg with the edge of her pillow. "Isn't that what *you* want from your friends? A chance to apologize and be forgiven?"

"Of course, but I also know forgiveness takes time and needs to be earned."

"Mom knows that too. She's doesn't expect everything to be peachy again right away. She's just asking for a chance to try."

I think about lunch with Dad last Saturday, when I told him I'd consider going to see Mom. Well, I *have* considered it, and I just don't see the benefit of looking her in the eye while she tries to reason away all the damage she caused. Maybe I'm just too scared to see the happy new life she's made without me.

"It's okay to miss her, you know," Rachel says when I don't respond. "I do."

"Who says I miss her?" My throat tightens around the words. I swallow hard and quickly untangle myself from the blanket. "I think I'll head to bed now. I'm really tired. Talk more tomorrow?"

She looks at me for a long moment, then she sighs and says, "Sure. Tomorrow. Good night, sis."

"Good night." I get up and leave the room, the in-person version of hanging up the phone before our conversation can veer back into a topic that hurts too much to discuss.

Chapter Twenty-Six

WHEN MY ALARM WAKES ME AT SEVEN THIRTY, I smell the distinct aroma of coffee. Dad doesn't drink coffee and I can take it or leave it, so Rachel must have dusted off the coffee-maker and dug out the can of Folgers from the cupboard above the stove, where it's been since she was home for Christmas.

"Good morning!" Rachel chirps when I shuffle into the kitchen, eyes still half closed.

I look around, trying to make sense of everything. My sister is leaning against the counter, sipping coffee out of the *World's Greatest Dad* mug that we gave Dad one Father's Day when we were little. Dad is sitting at the table, eating scram-bled eggs and reading the newspaper, something he still prefers over getting his news online. They're both fully dressed and ready for the day.

"Morning," I mumble as I open the fridge and pull a carton of orange juice.

Dad finishes with the paper and turns to Rachel. "What's on the agenda for today?"

The cheeriness in his voice hurts my ears. He's clearly enjoying his time with Rachel, the daughter who doesn't cause him any grief. I push down a stab of hurt.

"I'm going food shopping this morning," Rachel says, setting the mug on the counter beside her. "I want to make dinner for you guys tonight."

Dad gives an impressed hum. "Nice change from takeout."

Rachel looks at me. "Want to come shopping with me?"

"I have a shift at the thrift shop."

"Oh, right, you're still doing that. When's your last shift?"

"Next weekend." I drain my glass and put it in the dishwasher. "I'll be back around twelve thirty, though."

"Great. Maybe we'll go for a walk downtown."

I nod and excuse myself to shower. By the time I emerge, my sister has already left and my father is now puttering around in his room. I leave without saying good-bye.

I'm in the stockroom, sorting through a garbage bag of impossibly tiny baby clothes, when Eli slips in and closes the door gently behind him. I had no idea he could shut a door without slamming it.

"Hi," he says with a grin.

"Hi." The tips of my ears start burning. With all the busyness surrounding Rachel's homecoming, we haven't seen each other since he left my apartment Wednesday night, missing my dad's arrival by a mere ten minutes. I blush even harder when I remember dashing into the living room to scoop my discarded shirt off the floor before Dad saw it.

"Aunt Rita's with some customers."

"Oh," I reply stupidly. His presence has turned my brain to gelatin.

He drags over the plastic chair I unearthed to use as a makeshift step stool and sits on it. I immediately drop the baby onesie I'm holding and go to him, perching myself on his lap. His arms circle my waist while mine slide around his neck.

"You're all I can think about," he says, resting his forehead against mine.

He's said as much—and more—during our last two days of texting, but texts can't compare to hearing it in person. "Same here," I tell him.

We kiss until a loud peal of laughter pierces through the closed door, reminding us where we are. I pull back and drop my arms without moving from his lap. Eli loosens his grip on my waist but doesn't let go completely.

"How's your sister's visit going so far?" he asks.

That kills the mood. "Fine," I say, peering down at my hands.

"Are you sure?"

I shrug. As much as I like having Rachel home, for some reason I've been on edge since our conversation last night. Not only has she made our father smile more in the past fourteen hours than he has in the past fourteen months living with me, I feel like at any moment, she and Dad are going to start in on what a fuckup I've become. Like I need the reminder.

Eli smooths a strand of hair off my face. "Does she still plan to visit your mom?"

"Yeah. She's hoping I'll change my mind and go with her."

"Well . . . maybe you *should* go."

I tense on his lap. God, not him too. I thought out of everyone, he was on my side. "Eli," I say, striving to keep my tone light. "I get enough of that from my dad and Rachel. I don't need it from you."

"I just meant . . ." He shakes his head and sighs, then refocuses on me. "Okay," he says, trying again. "What I'm trying to say is, I think seeing her might help bring some closure to everything, you know? I'm not saying you should forgive her, just . . . let her know how you feel."

I slide off his lap and return to sorting baby clothes on the floor. "Telling her how I feel isn't going to fix anything or change what happened, Eli. I might think differently if she'd ever shown even the slightest hint of remorse, but she hasn't."

"Maybe that's why she wants you to visit—so she can tell you she's sorry."

"Well, it's kind of late for that." I pick up a pair of tiny pink overalls. "There's nothing she can say or do to make things like they used to be."

I can feel his gaze on me as I fold the clothes, my movements quick and jerky. Our relationship swerved off the light-and-fun track the moment I first told him about my mother, and I have no idea if I'll ever get it back there. Sometimes I wish I could. It's scary, opening your heart to someone when it's still not fully healed from being crushed by someone else.

"I'm sorry." Eli gets off the chair and sits beside me, wincing on the way down. "Maybe I'm wrong. It's just—I see this anger in you sometimes. You hide it really well, and you try to act like nothing fazes you, but I can see it. Probably because I used to feel the same way."

I stop folding and look at him. I've never seen that past version of him. It's either carefully controlled or gone altogether. I need to find a way to do the same—expel this version of me and start all over again with something new.

"This is good," Dad says, spearing a piece of grilled salmon with his fork. The three of us are sitting around the kitchen table, using knives and forks like civilized people. Aside from the disastrous cooking phase Dad and I went through, we only seem to dine properly when Rachel's around. She used to cook for us sometimes last summer, but nothing as fancy as this.

"Mmm," I agree. It is pretty tasty, though I'm not a fish fan. Neither is Dad, unless it's battered, deep-fried, and comes with tartar sauce.

"Thanks, guys." Rachel says, beaming. "I guess I lucked out and got some of Mom's cooking genes."

"Have you spoken to her since you got here?" Dad asks her.

"Yeah, she called me this morning. She's really excited about tomorrow."

Dad slices off another bite of salmon, his pleasant expression not faltering. "I'm sure she is. It's been a long time since she's seen you."

Rachel smiles and takes a sip of water. "She said they have a dog now," she goes on. "A dachshund. Her name is Sadie."

A snort slips out before I can stop it. Of course she has a dog. She always wanted one, but Dad's not a dog person and always refused to give in. When I was six, he brought home Fergus as a compromise, but Mom never bothered with him. He's always been my cat.

I pop a baby potato into my mouth and look up. They're

both watching me. Heat rushes to my face and I gulp down the half-chewed potato, almost choking. "Sorry," I say, coughing a little. "It's just . . ."

Rachel's eyes meet mine, and whatever derisive comment I was about to make dissolves on my tongue. There's no point. We obviously differ now in our opinions of Mom. Even Dad seems to have come to some sort of peace with her. I drop my gaze back to my salmon. "Never mind."

Everyone's quiet for a minute, the scrape of cutlery the only sound in the room, before Rachel mercifully changes the subject to something innocuous. I'm not really listening. I keep quiet for the rest of dinner, then wordlessly start clearing the table and carrying dishes to the sink. Dad gets up to help, waving Rachel out of the room. She steps outside onto our tiny balcony and closes the sliding glass door behind her.

Dad and I clean in silence for a few moments, him wiping the stovetop and counters and me rinsing dishes for the dishwasher. I'm just starting to wonder if he's going to speak at all when he joins me at the sink.

"You were a little rude at dinner," he says in a casual tone, like he's talking about the weather.

"Sorry," I repeat, but this time it has an edge. "You can't expect me to be happy about Mom's perfect little life with Gary and her dog."

"No one expects anything from you, Morgan." He runs

his cloth under the tap and then wrings it out. "But I do wish you'd go a little easier on her."

"Like *you* went easy on her, Dad?" I shut off the tap and turn toward him. "You asked her for a divorce about a minute after you found out about Gary. Not that I blame you—like, *at all*—but I always find it amusing when *you* lecture *me* about forgiveness."

His eyes go round and he stares at me, red creeping up his neck. "I didn't *ask* your mother for a divorce. In fact, I offered her a chance to stay and work on our marriage. But she didn't want that. She chose to be with the man she loved, which wasn't me and hadn't been me for a long time. *She* wanted the divorce, so I gave it to her. Better than forcing her to stay in a marriage she didn't want."

I stare back at him, dinner churning in my stomach. So instead of choosing him and trying to make things work for her family, she chose another man. Another life. We weren't even worth trying for. Realizing this feels like an extra punch to the gut. "Well, she should have asked for a divorce *before* she hooked up with Gary. She didn't have to cheat."

"You're right, she didn't. But life doesn't always work that way. Sometimes people are selfish. Sometimes we do things without thinking about the consequences."

I lean back against the counter and cross my arms. "I still don't know how you can defend her after what she did to you."

"It's not all about her," he says, his voice rising. "It's about me too. I'm through wasting time feeling sorry for myself. At some point I need to accept the way things are and move on with my life. And yes, part of that is making an effort to forgive your mother." He sighs and tosses the dish cloth in the sink. "That's why I wish you'd go see her, Morgan. Not just for her sake, but for yours. She hurt you horribly—I get that. But I promise you, cutting her out of your life isn't the answer."

I think about what happened after I got caught shoplifting. The disappointment on my father's face. The shock in my friends' eyes. The empathy in Rachel's voice. Then I wonder how I'd feel if they all tried to erase me from their lives forever over one bad mistake. And how desperate I'd be for a chance to make it up to them.

I look at my father, standing there in the faded red Budweiser T-shirt that he likes to wear on his days off. His stares back at me, his expression sad but hopeful. He wants so much for me to resolve this bitterness inside me, before it takes over and swallows me whole. I let out a long, resigned breath and close my eyes.

"Okay," I say, opening them again. "I still don't think seeing her will change anything, but if it means that much to you . . . okay."

He smiles and lifts his arms toward me, but my body feels too rigid for a hug. Instead, I walk over to the balcony door, yank it open, and stick my head out. Rachel looks at me, expectant.

"Change of plans." I swallow, feeling my pulse thump in my neck. "I'm going with you tomorrow."

Chapter Twenty-Seven

"ARE YOU OKAY?"

I tear my gaze from the house—a cozy white split-level with grayish-blue shutters and a tidy, bright green lawn—and look at Rachel. She's sitting in the driver's seat of my car, her upper body turned toward me. I was much too distracted to drive here, and now that we're parked in my mother's driveway, my focus has only deteriorated further.

"I'm fine," I say firmly. She asked me the same question two hours ago, before we left for Sutton. She asked me again when we stopped halfway at a gas station so I could pee, my nervousness constricting my bladder. And each time, I tell her I'm fine, even though I feel like throwing up.

Get it together, I tell myself. All I have to do is get through the next hour or so, two at the most. I don't even have to talk if I don't want to. I'll just sit there, mute, until it's time to leave. Just the fact that I'm here is enough. Dad and Rachel can't say I didn't try.

My phone chirps, and I slide it out of my purse.

How you doing?

A text from Eli. At least he didn't ask me if I was okay.

Just arrived, I type back, even though it wasn't what he asked. But I'm sick of lying about being fine. Text you later.

Did I mention I'm proud of you?

Only about a half dozen times since last night, when I told him I planned to call in sick to work so I could visit my mother. I tuck my phone away without answering him. I appreciate the sentiment, but I can't deal with his praise when I haven't done anything to earn it. Not yet. I'm still sitting in my damn car.

"Ready?" Rachel asks, taking off her sunglasses. She looks nervous too, which only succeeds in making me *more* nervous.

I nod and we get out of the car. My legs feel wobbly as we walk up the stone path to the front door. A giant leafy tree towers overhead, draping us in shade. Everything about this place matches my mother's taste perfectly. When I was little, she wanted a big yard with trees almost as much as she wanted a dog. Now she has both.

The door swings open as we approach, and before I can prepare myself, I get my first look at my mother in over a year. She's smiling wide, her eyes noticeably shiny even from a few feet away. She looks the same, like an older copy of Rachel, only her brown hair is a shade darker than Rachel's and she's three inches shorter, like me. In her arms is a small, floppy-eared black dog with patches of brown on her face and legs. The dog watches us warily, like the strangers we are.

I feel Rachel's hand on my arm and realize I've stopped moving. She basically tugs me the rest of the way.

"Hi, Mom," Rachel says when we reach her. Up close, her face looks pale and puffy, like she's spent the morning crying. Fine wrinkles bracket her eyes and mouth.

"Hello, girls," Mom says, her smile quivering.

She ushers us into the entryway and closes the door behind us before putting the dog on the floor. When she straightens back up, she reaches for Rachel, drawing her in for a hug. I turn away, feeling the dog's wet nose on my calf as she inspects me. I want to lean over and pet her, but my body feels like the soapstone carving in Eli's family room, cold and hard and unmoving.

My mother stops hugging Rachel and turns to me, her expression almost shy. "Morgan," she says softly as she leans in, wrapping her thin arms around me. The scent of vanilla—ten times stronger than what I'm used to smelling in my car—rises up and surrounds us, filling my head and releasing a surge of memories. Suddenly, I'm six again, drawing comfort from that sweet, reliable scent.

But I'm seventeen now, and I know my mother can hurt me just as well as she can comfort me.

I stiffen and back out of her arms, just like I did the last time I saw her. If she notices, she doesn't let it show on her face.

"I'm so happy to see you both," she says, swiping a finger under each eye. "I missed you more than I can say."

"Where's Gary?" Rachel asks as our mother leads us through the house to the kitchen. Everything feels familiar; my mother's decorating tastes haven't changed much since we lived in our old house downtown. The living room is all neutral colors, plump pillows, and lush green plants. Framed photos rest on an accent table near the window. One shows Rachel in her graduation cap and gown, and there's also one of me—a school picture from last year. Dad must have either mailed it to her or given it to her during one of their lawyer meetings.

"Oh, he went out for a bit, to give the three of us a chance to catch up," Mom replies, opening the stainless steel fridge. The kitchen is bright, with white cupboards and sunny yellow walls. "Iced tea? Water?"

We all choose iced tea and take our glasses to the cozy-looking living room. Rachel and I sit on the couch while our mother settles into the patterned wingback chair diagonal to us. The dog—Sadie—stations herself by Mom's feet.

"You both look so grown-up and beautiful." She places her glass on the coffee table, on top of one of the coasters laid out across the shiny wood surface.

I think of my apartment, where we don't even *own* a coaster, and feel a stab of guilt. I'm here because my father wanted me to come, but I still feel disloyal for fraternizing with the enemy, so to speak. When Rachel and I said good-bye to Dad before we left this morning, he looked at me with a trace of apprehension in his eyes, like he was afraid I wouldn't want to come back. I would have assured him that he has nothing to worry about, but I was too busy assuring myself that I'd made the right decision by agreeing to go. However, even now, sitting here a few feet away from my mother, I'm still not sure that I did.

We make some stilted small talk and Mom asks us questions about school and our jobs. Rachel carries most of the conversation, occasionally prompting me to take over. But I don't. I *can't*. My voice seems trapped in my throat, and I can only utter a brief answer here and there, leaving out details unless I'm asked. It's so excruciating, I'm almost relieved when the front door opens and Gary Ellsworth appears.

He looks exactly the same as I remember—tall, sturdy, with a thick head of dark hair and dark brown eyes that crinkle at the corners when he smiles. I saw that smile so often growing up—at the dealership, at company parties, even at my own dinner table when my parents were still together and good friends with Gary and his ex-wife, a tiny blonde named Pam who he's currently divorcing. Unlike my parents, they never had kids. Sometimes I feel jealous of those nonexistent kids who didn't have their nonexistent lives torn apart by their parents' lies.

"Hello," Gary says, hovering at the edge of the room. Sadie glances up at him dispassionately, like she's thinking, *Oh, it's you again.* I think I'm beginning to like her.

"Hi . . . Gary," Rachel says haltingly, and I suddenly remember that we used to call him *Uncle Gary* when we were little. It makes me slightly nauseated to think about it now, and I take a fortifying gulp of iced tea.

Gary's gaze slides from Rachel to me and then settles on Mom. "Should I start setting up lunch?" he asks her.

Mom jumps up. "Right. I guess we should get that started." She looks at Rachel and me. "You girls finish your iced tea. We'll be right back."

They go into the kitchen, Sadie trotting after them. The second they disappear, Rachel turns to me and whispers, "Are you okay?"

God, I wish she'd stop asking me that. "Yeah, why?"

"You just, like, *glared* at Gary instead of saying hello to him. Morgan, I know this is weird, but you really need to—"

"How long are we staying here?" I don't want to hear what I need to do or how I need to act. We're two different people, with two different approaches, and just because she's trying to play nice doesn't mean I have to do the same.

"Morgan—" she starts to say, but she's interrupted by the reappearance of our mother in the entrance to the living room.

"Lunch is on the dining room table," she announces with a wide smile. It's a touch *too* wide, like she's forcing it. What, is she worried we won't like her cooking anymore?

Rachel and I file into the dining room, where we discover a spread of food usually reserved for all-you-can-eat buffets. There's chicken and rolls and various kinds of salads, all beautifully displayed like we're the kind of people who need to be impressed.

"Wow, this looks great," Rachel says enthusiastically.

I glance at her, wondering how she can be so . . . *normal*. Like visiting our cheating mother and her lover is a perfectly ordinary occurrence. Doesn't she harbor even the tiniest grudge? Why does this seem so easy for her? Being here is even more awkward than I imagined. I don't know what I was expecting, exactly. Maybe a house that looks less like the one I grew up in? A mother who's distraught and remorseful instead of smiling and prattling on about what she puts in her pasta salad? This whole thing feels surreal.

I take small portions of everything, knowing I won't be able to eat much. My throat feels tight and my stomach is like an empty washing machine, the liquid inside churning and spinning around nothing. Maybe putting some food in there isn't the worst idea.

A white tablecloth covers the table, so I don't realize until I pull out a chair that it's *ours*—the same six-chair oak table that once sat in our dining room at the old house. The same table we ate countless meals on, from takeout pizza to Thanksgiving dinner. The same table I accidentally colored on with a black Sharpie when I was four, leaving an irremovable streak. I know, if I were to lift up the tablecloth in front of the chair on the far end, I'd still be able to see it.

Our table, where Dad once sat, is now in the house Mom shares with the ex–best friend who betrayed him in the worst possible way. My stomach seizes even more, and it takes everything in me to sit down and not sprint for my car. I can do this. I can be just as fake as she is.

Somehow, we make it to dessert without any issues. Then, as my mother sets my apple tart in front of me, I catch a glimpse of a ring I've never seen before on her left hand. A diamond ring. An engagement ring.

My breath catches. She and Gary are engaged. They're getting married. Their relationship isn't just some fling that'll fizzle out once the novelty wears off. She's in—all in.

I glance at Rachel to see if she's noticed too, but she's digging into her tart with a single-minded focus. I want to say something, maybe ask Mom why her engagement never came up once in the past forty-five minutes, but suddenly I'm too angry to form words. Gary Ellsworth. Dad's old friend. My *stepfather.*

My nausea intensifies, and I'm just about to escape to the bathroom when my mother reaches over and rubs the sleeve of my dark blue V-neck between her fingers. "I like your shirt," she says with that same too-wide smile. "This shade of blue really suits you."

Her touch aggravates the thorny ball of rage growing inside me, and I completely forget about my plan to stay silent. "Thanks," I say, returning her smile with an icy one of my own. "I stole it from Old Navy last spring."

Mom leans back and blinks in confusion. "What?"

Rachel kicks me lightly under the table, but it barely registers.

"I stole it," I repeat, then hastily bite into my apple tart. It tastes like sawdust. "That's what I've been doing since you left. Shoplifting. I've done it dozens of times in a dozen different stores. Every chance I get."

Mom looks at Rachel, who's resting her head in her hands like she can't bear to watch, and then back at me. "What . . . what is going on? Does Charles know about this?"

My rage ball expands at her mention of my father's name. "Of course," I say, dropping the remnants of the apple tart on my napkin. "He's the one the police called a few months ago when I got caught stealing a pair of designer sunglasses."

Her face drains of color. I feel a twinge of satisfaction,

knowing I've disrupted the perfect little life she's set up for herself here. Did she really believe that starting over with a new house and a new man would absolve her from all the damage she left behind? Well, I'm here to remind her that it doesn't.

Mom's gaze shifts to Rachel again. "Did you know about this?"

Rachel looks up from her hands and nods.

"Why didn't you tell me?" Mom demands, eyeing my stolen shirt like she's waiting for it to burst into flames. "Why didn't any of you tell me? Don't you think this is something I should have been made aware of?"

I bark out a laugh. "That's ironic, coming from someone who didn't tell us she was engaged."

Rachel's jaw drops and she looks at Mom, then Gary. Okay, so clearly this is news to her too. Gary's face goes pink while my mother's turns even whiter. She rises stiffly to her feet and looks down at me. "I'd like to speak to you alone," she says, her voice strained.

I shrug and stand up too, eager to get this over with so we can leave and never return. As Mom leads me out of the dining room, I glance back at the table. Rachel is watching us with a frown and Gary just looks bewildered, as if he'd been expecting a nice, peaceful lunch with the daughters of the man he screwed over. Right.

My mother steers me into her bedroom and shuts the door

behind us. Before I get a chance to look around, she steps in front of me and grips my arm. I attempt to pull away, but she holds on tight.

"What's going on with you?" she hisses. "*Shoplifting*, Morgan? That doesn't sound like the daughter I raised."

I give my arm a good yank, finally breaking free. "Makes sense," I fire back, "considering you're no longer the mother who raised me."

She flinches like I hit her, then backs up like she's going to hit *me*, though she never has. I almost want her to. A slap across the cheek would end it all—this visit, our relationship, Dad and Rachel's insistence that I give her a chance. But she doesn't touch me. She keeps backing away until she reaches the king-sized bed, then sinks down on the edge of the fluffy taupe comforter. She's all over this room too—neutral colors, bright pillows, green plants. Maybe prettying up her new house distracts her from remembering the old one.

"I knew you were mad," Mom says, her fingers pressed to her temples. "I knew you hated me for what happened. I was terrified that I'd say or do something to make it worse, so I tried to give you space to deal with it on your own. That's why I didn't want to tell you about the engagement right away. But I'm done giving you space, Morgan. I'm done being the only bad guy here. It takes two people to end a marriage, and it's time you understood that."

I cross my arms. My heart is thumping in my ears, so loud and so fast that it's making me dizzy. "Sure," I bite out. "Dad's not the one who cheated. *You're* the one who screwed around behind his back for two years and then left."

She drops her hands from her temples and looks at me, her expression sad. "I'm not proud of what I did. But, Morgan, you have to understand how unhappy I must have been to get to that point."

I scoff and shake my head. "Yeah, poor you, stuck in a marriage with a great man who doesn't cheat on you or abuse you. It must have been horrible."

"Cheating and abuse aren't the only ways to break a marriage," she says, her voice rising a few octaves. "I felt invisible, okay? Like I didn't matter. Like my opinions didn't matter. Your father stopped *seeing* me. I was just existing, as the mother of his children and the person who paid half the mortgage."

I shake my head again, unwilling to accept her words. Yes, Dad has his flaws, but he didn't deserve the nightmare she put him through. Put us all through.

"But Gary," she goes on, her eyes filling with tears. "He saw me. He listened. He made me feel valued and appreciated, something your father hadn't done in a very long time. Charles is a good father—he's *always* been a good father—but he wasn't a good husband. At least not for me."

"But he fought for you." My voice comes out strangled,

and I turn away, willing myself not to cry. I refuse to be vulnerable in front of her. "He asked you to come back and work on your marriage. He told me that."

"He did, but it was far too late by then. I was happy with Gary. I still am, which is why I said yes last month when he asked me to marry him." She stands up and creeps toward me like I'm a frightened animal about to bolt. "I hope someday you'll be able to accept it and find a way to forgive me. I miss you, Morgan. I miss you to the moon."

I take a step back. "Don't."

She pauses and lets out a sigh. "You're so much like I used to be. I saw everything in black and white. Good and bad. It took me a while to realize there's a lot of gray in between. You'll realize it too, eventually."

I meet her eyes. They're wet with tears, unlike mine, which are still bone-dry. "I'm nothing like you," I say. "I actually feel regret for *my* mistakes." Then I walk away, leaving her behind in her perfectly coordinated bedroom. I keep walking, past the kitchen and dining room, out the front door, down the stone path, not stopping until I reach my car.

My car, not a castoff of Mom's. Mine. I sit in the driver's seat and breathe in the vanilla, which is even more subtle after smelling it firsthand, and wait for Rachel. She emerges ten minutes later and climbs in the passenger side, her features heavy with worry and regret.

"Please don't ask me if I'm okay," I tell her as I start the engine.

She opens her mouth, shuts it, and then stares straight ahead, not saying a word. We drive like that, quiet and facing straight ahead, for the next several miles. Then, as we're flying down the highway with the windows down and the stereo on low, my sister squeezes my knee and says, "I'm sorry."

I turn to look at her, feeling the wind lift my hair. "I'm not."

Chapter Twenty-Eight

THE REST OF RACHEL'S STAY IS UNEVENTFUL, AT least compared to the trip to Sutton. She cooks healthy meals for us. We spend a day at the beach, and Dad and I come home with sunburns. We go out to dinner twice, once just the three of us and once with Eli, who Rachel immediately takes to. We play board games and watch movies and laugh.

We don't talk about Mom or what happened during our visit. At least I don't. Any time Rachel or Dad or even Eli brings it up, I change the subject. I just want to forget it ever happened.

After dinner on Friday, Dad takes Rachel to the airport to

catch her eight thirty flight, and I have the apartment to myself
for the first time all week. I immediately text Eli.

> I'm alone for the next two hours. Want to come
> over?

My phone dings almost instantly. Hell yes.

We head straight to my bedroom when he arrives, not
wanting to waste any time. After, I set my phone alarm to go
off at eight—a half hour before my father is due home—and
snuggle against Eli for a few extra moments of warmth.

"Are you sure he's not going to come home unexpect-
edly?" Eli asks, lifting his head off my pillow and peering at
my closed bedroom door. "Do you have a fire escape?"

I laugh and pull the sheet over us. "He was going to hang
out with Rachel until she had to go to her gate, and the airport
is a thirty-minute drive from here. So I think we're good."

He relaxes a bit and drops his head back down on the pillow. "Why didn't you go? To the airport?"

"There was no need. Rachel and I said our good-byes
here." I think about how tightly she hugged me, the words she
whispered in my ear as she pulled away. Three words phrased
like a promise: *You'll be okay.* The certainty in her voice ignited
a tiny spark of hope in my chest. Out of everyone in my life,
Rachel's opinion of me seems to carry the most weight.

Eli and I lounge in bed until my alarm goes off, then get

dressed and head out to the living room to watch TV. That's what we're doing when Dad arrives home at twenty to nine. He doesn't even blink when he walks in and sees us. As far as he knows, we've been sitting here all evening, a foot of space between us as we watch a sitcom rerun. Dad usually sees what he wants to see when it comes to his daughters' love lives.

Later, when there's nothing left to watch on TV and Dad has gone to bed, I walk Eli down to his Jeep. Before he gets in, he holds me against him and rests his chin on the top of my head.

"Your phone has been awfully quiet lately."

"Huh?" I say into his chest. Those aren't the words I was expecting.

"Usually, when we're together, you're getting texts and messages from your friends the whole time, but that hasn't happened for like two weeks now. And we haven't done anything with them for a while either." He pulls back to look at me. "Did you guys have a fight or something?"

Damn it. I was hoping he wouldn't notice, but how could he not? Things have been awkward with Sophie and Zach since the night I walked out of his basement, and we haven't hung out or texted much since. Dawson's around, but lately our schedules have been conflicting, so I haven't seen much of him either. As for Alyssa, she's still not talking to me, even though I've sent her several messages, begging for a chance to explain.

"Kind of," I say vaguely.

There are times, like right now, when I want to tell him so badly. When the truth scratches against my tongue, just waiting for me to open my mouth and let it spill. I think of how liberating it would feel, even if he ended up hating me. At least I'd be free.

I press my face into his T-shirt again. "Eli . . ."

"Yeah?"

His heartbeat echoes in my ear just like it did earlier, when I rested my head against his chest as we lay together in my bed, savoring our last few minutes. Thinking of it makes my throat ache. I'm not ready to let go of that. I'm not ready to let go of *him*. The truth would probably be easier if our relationship were just a light summer romance, like I intended it to be at the start. But at some point over the past few weeks, we'd become something else. Something I don't want to risk losing.

So rather than tell him about the shoplifting, as I know I should, I confess a different kind of truth instead.

"I love you."

His arms tighten around me. "I love you too," he says, and I can hear the smile in his voice. "I've wanted to tell you a million times, but . . . I don't know. I think my last relationship affected me more than I thought."

I wish I could promise him that I'll be different, that I'll never hurt him like she did, but I can't. At least not yet. All

I can do is press my lips to his and hope it'll be good enough for now.

"Last day, huh?"

I glance up from my oatmeal and look at my father, who's leaning against the counter and holding a glass of pineapple juice. "What?"

"At the thrift shop," he says, smoothing down his tie. "Today's your last shift."

"Oh. Yeah."

He puts his glass in the sink. "Do you have plans tonight? Now that Rachel's gone, I think you and I should have a talk."

I stand up and grab my car keys. "I'm probably going out with Eli. Maybe tomorrow." I know exactly what he wants to talk about. Rachel obviously told him her version of what happened at Mom's, and now he wants mine.

"Okay. Well, have a good day."

"You too."

As I drive into the city, I try to figure out why I've been feeling slightly uneasy around my father since my visit with Mom. All week, certain things she said kept popping into my head, triggering bursts of memories I didn't even know were there. Quiet arguments between my parents, their tones carefully controlled. Dismissive remarks. Loaded silences. They never really yelled—at least not in front of Rachel and me—but

rebecca phillips

sometimes there was this undercurrent of tension that even I, as a child, could sense.

My mother said she was unhappy. Looking back, there *were* signs. A few times I walked in on her sniffling as she did the dishes. Or I'd hear her muffled crying through the bathroom door. Or I'd hear the frustration in her voice when she was talking to my father and he didn't want to see her point of view. But he was my father. He might not have been the perfect husband, but he also wasn't the one who had the affair, so I've always taken his side.

So why do I feel mildly pissed off whenever I'm in the same room with him?

Rita's Reruns is looming on my right, so I vow to put it out of my mind for now. Maybe I *will* take Dad up on his offer to talk later. Before I tell him my version of events, maybe I'll ask him to tell me his.

"Morgan!" Rita trills when I enter the thrift shop. "I'm glad you're here a few minutes early, because today is going to be *wild*."

I look around. The store is liberally plastered with handmade signs, each one spelling out *Fill a Bag for $10!* Beside the entrance is a towering stack of large paper bags. I've never seen this before.

"Fill a bag for ten dollars?" I ask, peering at the sign closest to me. The letters are ornate and curly—clearly Rita's work.

296

"That's right." She strides around the store, bracelets jangling. "Customers pay a flat ten dollars for as much as they can stuff in one of those bags. Clothes, books, toys, dishes . . . anything that fits without falling out or ripping the bag open. Fun, right? I do this a few times a year, and it's always a smash."

"Fun," I agree, picturing swarms of people grabbing anything they can get their hands on, like Walmart on Black Friday. "Where's Eli?"

"Oh, he had to drive his sister somewhere this morning. He'll be in a little later."

I nod and move behind the register, where I assume she'll need me today. And I'm right. As soon as the doors open at nine, the customers start piling in. For the next three hours we're flat-out busy, me on cash and Rita on the floor, trying to prevent the place from getting ransacked. When an older lady comes in with a shopping cart and tries to fill five different bags (the limit is two), I start feeling less sentimental about today being my last day. By the time noon and the end of my shift rolls around, I'm completely exhausted. I wish I could lean against Eli's sturdy body and go to sleep for a while, but he never did show up. He must have known it's *Fill a Bag for $10* day and decided to stay away. Smart.

"Well, I guess this is it," Rita says when I approach her at the back of the store during a lull in customers. The place is empty save for a guy flipping through what's left of the men's outerwear rack.

"Yeah." Pushing down a twinge of sadness, I hold out my hand. "Thank you for the opportunity. It was great working with you."

She waves my hand away and folds me into a long, rib-crushing hug instead. "Remember what I told you," she says as she releases me. "You're a good girl, Morgan, and someday you're going to believe it. Don't let those bad decisions define you, because they don't. Okay?"

"Okay," I say, feeling suddenly awkward. "Thanks for, um, keeping things between us. You didn't have to, and I appreciate it."

She shrugs lightly. "Not my story to tell."

"Oh, that reminds me." I reach into my back pocket and bring out a folded sheet of paper, which lists all the hours I worked. "You need to sign this time sheet for the diversion coordinator so they can give it to the judge. It just shows that I completed all thirty of my community service hours."

"Of course." She takes the paper and carries it up to the counter. I follow her and watch as she signs it with a flourish. "Here you go," she says, handing it back to me.

I fold the paper back up and return it to my pocket. "Thanks. I'll come back and visit soon. And I'll probably see you around Eli's house too, I guess."

Rita smiles. "You bet."

I wave at her and leave, holding the door open for a couple pushing twins in a double stroller as I go. When I get in my car, I put the signed paper in my glove compartment and send a text to Eli.

Where are you?

Five minutes pass without a response, which isn't like him. He's probably still chauffeuring his sister around. I still have a six-hour shift at Royal Smoothie ahead of me, so it's not like I'll be able to spend any time with him anyway. I drive away from Rita's Reruns for possibly the last time and head home to change.

Chapter Twenty-Nine

THE MINUTE SCOTT SENDS ME OFF ON MY HALF-
hour break, I dig out my phone and turn it on. My body lightens when I see a text from Eli.

> Can you meet me after work?

> Where? Your house? Starbucks?

His response comes quickly: **Somewhere more private so
we can talk. Crawford Park? By the maple trees?**

Crawford Park is a huge grassy square in the middle of the
city with playgrounds, basketball courts, a skate park, and lots

of open spaces. We've never gone there together, and I'm not sure why he wants to start now. And what does he want to talk privately about?

I text him back a *yes* and put away my phone. There's no point in asking for details now. I'll find out soon enough.

After work, I drive straight to Crawford Park. Eli texted a few minutes ago to tell me he's already there, waiting. I park as close as I can and head in through the South Street entrance, my palms already sweaty even though I have no idea what to expect. As I get closer, I spot Eli, standing under one of the massive maple trees that line one edge of the park. He's not smiling. My stomach lurches, and I have to push myself the rest of the way.

"What's going on?" I ask once I've joined him in his secluded spot under the tree. The park is still crawling with people, even though it's starting to get dark and the air smells like rain, but they're all a good distance away.

"I wanted to ask you the same question." He looks at me, his expression a mix of hurt and confusion.

It hits me then. *He knows. He knows about me.*

"What do you mean?" I ask anyway, my mouth going dry. A summer's worth of stress and worry and paranoia are about to come to a head, and all I can do is stand here and let it happen.

"I was there this morning," he says. "At the thrift shop."

"What?" His words make zero sense. "No, you weren't."

"Yes, I was. I came in late. You and Aunt Rita were both

busy with customers and didn't see me." He crosses his arms over his chest. "I was in the stockroom, trying to make some space for the donations that came in yesterday. I heard you talking. You and Aunt Rita. A few minutes before you left."

My body goes from warm to cold as his meaning sinks in. He was there. He heard us. I replay that moment in my head, Rita and I saying good-bye. Her telling me I'm good, and that my past decisions don't define me. Me asking her to sign the paper, verifying my completion of thirty hours of community service.

Community service. I spoke the words out loud, completely unaware that Eli was in earshot. Unaware that he was even there at all.

This is bad.

"Rita told you, then."

"No," he says, surprising me. "I wanted her to, but she kept telling me to ask you. So I'm asking you. What the *hell* is going on?"

"Eli . . ." I trail off helplessly and look away, across the expanse of grass to the busy streets beyond. I wish I could take off running, past the soccer field and skate park, past the food stands and benches, until this spot under the tree—and Eli—are just dots in the distance. But I won't. It's my fault he's looking at me right now like he's not sure who I am, and I have to stay and make it right.

"You told me you were volunteering so you could use it on your college applications," he reminds me in an accusing tone. "Or at least that's what you let me think. Either way, it was a lie, right? You were never a volunteer, were you?"

"No," I say, forcing myself to meet his eyes. "I wasn't volunteering at Rita's Reruns. I was doing community service for shoplifting."

My confession lands like a brick between us, and I watch as his expression shifts from confused to shocked. I have no clue what he'd *thought* I'd done to get community service, but it clearly wasn't this.

"Shoplifting," he repeats, like he's not entirely sure I'm being serious. "You shoplift."

"I did," I correct. "Not anymore."

He unfolds his arms and rakes both hands through his hair, looking up at the graying sky. After a moment, he drops his gaze to mine again. "Why?"

"Why shoplifting?" I nudge my shoe into a patch of dirt at my feet and shrug. "I'm still in the process of trying to figure that out."

A muscle twitches in his jaw. "Were you ever going to tell me about this? Or did you plan on keeping it from me forever and hope I never found out?"

I take a step closer to him, and he immediately retreats, crossing his arms again. Defensive posture. I'd seen him do the same thing with his ex at Zander's party. The same ex who'd pulled the rug out from underneath him, the same way I just did. I'm no better than her. No, I'm *worse* than her.

"I was going to tell you," I say. My arms ache to reach out and touch him, but I know he won't let me, so I cross them instead, mirroring his stance. "I wanted to tell you so many times, but I just . . . I couldn't. I was ashamed. My friends—they look at me differently now because of this. You're—you were one of the only people I had left, and I didn't want to—"

"Stop. Just stop." He turns and paces a few steps away from me, then switches direction and returns to the same spot. "I feel like such an idiot. You let me think— God, I thought you were amazing. You were the first girl I met in a long time who I could actually see myself falling in love with, and then I did, and now it turns out you're not who I thought you were at all. Now you're just this girl who's lied to me all summer."

I've never really seen Eli angry before. I've seen him annoyed, I've seen him moody, I've seen him bitter and trying to hide it like at Zander's party, when he found about Colton Latimer playing for the team he wanted, but I've never seen him truly angry. And he's certainly never been angry at *me*. One of my biggest fears before we got together was that I'd wind up hurting him, and now here we are. The reality of it is even worse than I imagined.

"Eli, I'm so sorry." My voice breaks on the last word as the significance of what I've done crashes into me all at once. I misled him in the worst way. Distorted my real self and let him believe I was a different kind of person. A better kind of person. And even if I *am* better now, it's too late. The damage is done. He'll only ever see me as the girl who lies, steals, and deceives.

He turns away again, and this time I'm sure he's going to keep walking, leaving me alone under the canopy of branches. But again, he changes his mind and walks back to me, this time stopping just a foot from where I'm standing. His face is flushed and his eyes blaze as he looks down at me.

"Did you take it?"

I blink at him, confused. "What?"

"The little ceramic pot my father got when he went to Tunisia a few years ago. It was always on the shelf next to the TV in the main floor family room, but it's been missing for the past month or so." His jaw twitches again. "Did you take it?"

Goose bumps rise on my skin, even though the evening air is still warm. I know I deserve this. I deserve accusations and mistrust and blame, but that doesn't make it any less painful, especially coming from him. "No," I manage to say. "Of course I didn't take it."

"And I'm supposed to believe you?"

I remember my father saying basically the same thing, in basically the same tone, a few weeks ago. Maybe it'll be the automatic response to everything I say now. Established liars and thieves don't get the benefit of the doubt.

"I get why you'd be suspicious of me after everything I just told you," I say, trying to sound calm and even, though I feel the opposite. "But I didn't take the ceramic pot or anything else in your house. I swear. I like your family, Eli. I'd never steal from them."

He lets out a humorless laugh. "So if we were assholes, then stealing from us would be justified? What kind of fucked-up logic is that?"

"No. That came out wrong. I just meant—"

He holds up his hands and backs away again. "You know what? Never mind. I'm done."

I start to follow him. "Eli—"

"I'm done," he says again, louder this time, so I'm sure to get it.

I do get it. He's done—with this conversation and with me. And I don't really blame him for walking away from both, so I stay where I am and let him go.

Dad's sitting on the couch, a takeout pizza box open on the coffee table in front of him, when I enter the apartment a half hour later. The smell of sausage makes my stomach roll.

"Hey," he says when I walk past the living room, ignoring both him and the pizza. "Aren't you hungry?"

"No."

I go to my room and close the door behind me, startling Fergus, who's balled up against my pillows. I sit on my bed and stroke his head until he settles again, then dig my phone out of my purse. No messages. Not that I expected a change-of-heart text from Eli after what he said, but it never hurts to check.

My thumb hovers over a different name. *Alyssa*. I miss talking to her so much. I wish I could talk to her right now. I wish I could pour out everything that happened in the park and then listen to her calm, reasonable voice telling me that life will work itself out eventually. Alyssa believes everything works itself out eventually. Except for our friendship, apparently, and that makes me sad.

We've never gone this long without speaking. We used to tell each other all our secrets, even the most embarrassing ones. I know about ninth-grade gym, when she got her period while doing yoga and ruined both her pants and her yoga mat. She knows about last summer, when my then-boyfriend Nathanial and I lost our virginity to each other in the woods near his parents' lake house and I got bug bites where no one should ever get bug bites.

Alyssa has always been there. Before this year, she knew everything about me, good and bad. She never judged, never turned her back on me . . . until she discovered something about me that she just couldn't forgive.

I turn off my phone and set it facedown on my nightstand, then flop back on my pillows next to Fergus. Maybe tomorrow I'll be able to handle rejection, but not tonight.

"Morgan?" Dad knocks on my door, three sharp raps. When I don't answer, he slowly opens it and pokes his head in my room. "Are you sure you don't want some pizza?"

"I'm sure," I say, not taking my eyes off the ceiling.

"Okay, well . . ." He goes quiet for a moment, and I turn my head to check if he's still there. He's leaning against the doorframe and peering at my floor. "Maybe we can have that talk now?" he says, glancing at me.

God. That's all I need tonight. "Not now, Dad."

He sighs. "Morgan, honey, you haven't been yourself since you went to see your mother. Rachel told me about the engagement. I really think we should—"

"I said no, okay?" I turn back to the ceiling. "Mom said you never listened. I think I get what she means now."

The second the words are out of my mouth, I regret them. I'm being unfair. Dad has never treated me the way my mother says he treated her. He always listens to me. He cares about my opinions. He sees me. I don't even know why I said that.

Maybe because I need to release all this anger and sadness somehow, and better here—on him—than in the blind spots of a store. Or maybe I simply want to hurt him enough that he'll finally leave me alone.

Whatever the reason, it works. Before I get the chance to apologize, he backs out of my room and quietly shuts the door.

Chapter Thirty

ONE OF THE THINGS THAT STUCK WITH ME FROM my theft education class was *Have a relapse prevention plan.* Avoid triggers, learn to control impulses, and find alternatives to stealing. Something distracting that keeps your mind and hands busy and fills the void in your life.

For most of the summer, spending time with my friends or Eli seemed to keep me on track, for the most part. But now that avenue is closed, so I've resorted to something else to help me stay grounded.

Yesterday, when I opened the cupboard where we keep the storage containers and half of them rained down on my head, something in me snapped. I cleared out the rest of the

containers and piled them in neat stacks, then did the same
with the lids. After that, I decided to clean out the junk drawer,
which still had Target receipts from the week Dad moved in.
Once that was done, I moved on to the fridge, throwing out
expired jars and cheese with green dots and a single blueberry
yogurt several months past its best-before date.

During my hours of frenzied organizing, my father only
spoke to me once, to ask me what on earth I was doing.

"Cleaning," I told him. He took one look at me, elbows-
deep in the cereal cupboard with my hair in a messy bun and
a *don't mess with me* look on my face, and scurried off to watch
TV for the rest of the afternoon.

I went to bed last night exhausted and sore but calm, then
woke up this morning to start all over again. Today's project is
my bedroom, which I admit hasn't seen a dust cloth in weeks.
Everything goes fine until I start tackling the closet and notice
something I haven't paid attention to all summer.

"I need new clothes," I mumble to myself as I survey the
sizable gaps in my wardrobe. Not only do I need clothes for
fall, but school starts in five days and I haven't bought a single
school supply in preparation.

It's inevitable. I'm going to have to go shopping.

I've been steering clear of stores as much as humanly possible for most of the summer. When I do have to go, to pick
up shampoo or a box of tampons or something, I get in and
out as fast as I can. I haven't risked shopping for cloth in a

rebecca phillips

while, simply because I know I'd be tempted to do my changing room trick, which I haven't done since the bikini.

But I can't avoid stores forever. Eventually, I'm going to have to test myself.

Once my bedroom is organized, I force myself to take a shower and get ready to go out. What I want to do is crawl into bed and forget shopping and wear my summer wardrobe right into February, but I refuse to let myself mope. Or cry. Or spend the rest of the day staring at my phone, waiting for Eli to text me back. I've sent him six messages in the past three days and he's ignored every one of them. His silence—*everyone's* silence—makes me feel like I barely exist.

A little voice in my head tells me I'm being dumb, exposing myself to temptation when I'm feeling this low, but another part of me feels like it'll be good. Maybe learning how to shop like a normal person will make me feel less like a freak.

On the way down to the lobby, I open the zippered pocket inside my purse and reach in. It's still there—the curved hook I used to pop off countless security tags. Taking this into a store with me is just asking for trouble, so I fold my fingers around it and carry it outside, pausing near the trash bins at the back of the building. They smell like death in this heat, but I hold my breath and lift the lid, dropping the hook inside with my other hand. *There.*

Feeling a bit more confident, I drive to the next town over, where there's a huge outdoor mall with every kind of

312

store imaginable. I try not to list off each one I've stolen from, because I know the total will make me want to turn around and go back home.

I start with the safest items—school supplies. It helps that every aisle is packed with people, and I fill my basket without any issues at all. Once everything's paid for, I bring the bags of supplies out to my car so I won't have to carry them around while I shop. I've done *that* trick too—putting unpaid-for items in bags I brought in from other stores. Risky but doable.

I push the thought away as I head down the sidewalk to Rampage, one of my favorite clothing stores. Their security cameras are top-of-the-line, so it's a little too risky to lift from, even though I've managed once or twice. But not today. Today I'm being good. I can do this.

"Hey, how's it going?" one of the salesgirls says when I walk in. She looks right at me and smiles, letting me know I've been seen. A tactic, I've learned. If you've been noticed, you'll be less likely to try anything funny.

I smile back at her and start browsing, paranoia already crawling up the back of my neck. It's like a reflex, popping up even when there's no reason for it. Am I ever going to be able to shop without being constantly on guard? Am I ever going to be one of those people who stroll through a store, perfectly relaxed, the notion of shoplifting never even crossing their minds? I wish I remembered what that felt like.

After ten minutes, I've gathered a half dozen items to try

on. The same salesgirl who greeted me shows me to a change room, then takes my pile of clothes, and hangs everything up herself. Another tactic—she sees exactly what I came in here with. Which is fine. Good, even. This way, I won't be tempted.

But when I try on the white scoop-neck top that laces up in the back and clings to my torso like a second skin, it doesn't seem to matter who saw me come in with it. I look at the price tag for the first time. It's fifty dollars—way above what I'd spend on one shirt—but all I can think about is how much I want it, and how Eli's eyes would light up in approval if he saw me wearing it.

Eli. Saturday evening in the park slams into me all over again. His eyes, burning with accusation. The shock and betrayal on his face when he learned that the honest, selfless girl he'd fallen for wasn't honest or selfless at all. In fact, she was the complete opposite.

I examine myself in the mirror, carefully avoiding my own gaze. It would be so easy to slip the shirt I wore in here over the white one I'm wearing now. I can picture just how it would feel: The surge of adrenaline that somehow balances out the chaos inside me. The calm as it drains away. Then the shame, hot and prickly, settling into my bones when the high wears off. This last stage is the one I always seem to forget, and forgetting the bad parts is probably why my craving never stops.

But maybe the key to quitting isn't about killing the urge.

Maybe it's about making the choice, every single day, not to act on it.

I take off the white top and put it back on its hanger, itching to get out of this tiny room. *Screw it.* I'll wear last year's clothes, even though they're all a little tight. Maybe if I eat a vegetable once in a while, I'll fit into them again by Christmas.

"No luck?" the salesgirl asks as I hand her everything I went in with, each item present and accounted for.

"Nothing fits," I tell her. Before she can offer to find me some different sizes, I turn and walk away.

I don't feel like going home yet, and the failed shopping trip has made me hungry for something greasy, so I head downtown to Ace Burger. Maybe Dawson's working today. He's the only one in my friend group who still treats me exactly the same as before.

My mood lifts when I walk in and see him behind the register, ringing up some customers. Then it plummets again when I realize those customers are Sophie and Zach. Speaking of awkward.

Dawson sees me first and lifts his chin in greeting. Sophie turns to check out who he's looking at and several emotions cross her face when she sees me—happiness, fear, embarrassment, sadness. She finally settles on resigned and raises her hand in a wave. Zach glances over too, smiling at the sight of me.

I contemplate leaving, running away like a coward so I

don't have to talk to them, but I will myself to stay put. I'm so sick of running. Sick of avoiding. Leaving right now would make me no better than my mother. The last thing I want is to be like her, giving up after a couple of failed tries. Staying away in fear of making things worse, only to end up doing nothing at all.

No. Unlike my mother, I'm not going to stop trying to fix what I ruined.

I wait until they finish ordering and then move forward, my legs shaking slightly. "Hi, guys," I say, trying to smile.

"Hey," Sophie says, still looking slightly uncomfortable. Dawson clears his throat, and I realize I'm holding up the small line that's formed behind me. I order the first thing I see on the menu board—a Chompin' Chipotle burger—and dig a twenty out of my purse. Dawson gives me my change and my order number and I step aside, joining Sophie and Zach by the drink machine.

"Do you think . . . ," I begin, my voice fading out. I take a breath and try again. "Do you think I could sit with you guys? We need to talk about this."

Sophie looks at me for a moment and then nods. "Yeah, we do."

Once the orders are ready, we bring our trays over to a small table in the corner. I don't look over, but I can sense Dawson watching us from the cash register, probably hoping that the three of us can figure out a way to be normal again. If normal is even possible anymore.

"First, I want to apologize," I say as soon as we sit down. "I never wanted you to find out the way you did. I should have told you guys long ago, and I'm sorry for keeping it from you."

Sophie slowly lifts a fry to her mouth and takes a bite. "Why did you?"

I look down at my still-wrapped burger. Coming in here, I was starving, but now the thought of swallowing food seems impossible. "I don't know. I was ashamed. And I was scared of . . . this. What's happening right now. I knew you guys wouldn't trust me anymore if you found out what I did."

They exchange a quick glance; then Zach looks at me. "I still trust you," he says. "And yeah, of course the whole shop-lifting thing was a shock, but that's not what surprised us the most, honestly."

Confused, I shift my gaze from his face to Sophie's. "What do you mean?"

Sophie swallows the bite of burger in her mouth and says, "The lying, Morgan. You, like, lied to us for *months*, just because you had this idea in your head that we'd hate you and turn our backs on you if we knew the truth. I mean, yeah, things have been awkward since we found out, but if you'd told us earlier, we might have been able to *help* you. Instead, you hid it from us because you automatically assumed we wouldn't understand. And maybe we don't, but it would have been nice if you'd at least given us the chance to try."

My face warms and I drop my gaze to the table. She's right. I did assume they wouldn't understand; how could they? None of them would ever do what I did. We steer clear of the kids at school who drink every weekend or do drugs or cause trouble, because it's not our scene. But stealing is just as bad as or worse than all of that, so of course I was worried they'd lump me in with the kind of people they didn't have any use for.

But maybe I was the one who was judging. Maybe I shouldn't have assumed I had to censor myself around them just so I could feel worthy of their friendship.

"I'm sorry," I say, meeting Sophie's eyes, then Zach's. "Friends should tell friends the truth, and if you . . . if it's not too late and if you still want to be my friend, I'll never lie to you again. I promise."

I don't look away, or even blink. I need them to know I mean it. Zach breaks eye contact first and dips a fry into his little paper cup of ketchup. Sophie stares at me for a moment, the straw of her cup between her lips. I still haven't touched anything on my tray.

"Okay," she says, setting her cup down. "Are you still doing it?"

"Am I . . . ?"

"You said you won't lie, so I'm asking. Are you still shop-lifting?"

I think of earlier, in the Rampage change room, the smooth fabric of the shirt against my skin. I think of the compulsion that still lingered, even as I walked out empty-handed. "I wanted to, earlier," I tell her. They want the whole, uncensored truth, so that's what I'll give them, even if it's hard to say. "When I was in Rampage today, I found a shirt I really liked and I thought about stealing it."

They both watch me, eyes wide and food forgotten.

"But I didn't," I go on, leaning forward a bit. "I wanted to, but I didn't. I walked away instead, which I guess is something I should've done from the beginning. But I'm starting to do it now."

Relief flickers across both their faces. It feels good to know they care one way or another about my issues and struggles, even if they don't fully understand them. I hope Alyssa feels the same, when I finally gather the nerve to approach her. With her it'll be harder, since we've known each other for so long and been through so much. But if I want to distinguish myself from my mother, then I'm not going to waste time being afraid.

"Well, that's something," Sophie says after several moments of silence. She lifts her burger to her mouth, then puts it down again without taking a bite. "I think I owe you an apology too. I'm sorry I acted suspicious of you that night at Zach's house. Friends should also give friends the benefit of the doubt, and I promise to do that from now on."

"And I promise not to call you Sticky Fingers or ask if you paid for that gravy on your tray," Zach adds with a crooked grin.

This time, my smile comes easily. "Thanks, guys."

They both go back to eating. I wait for them to say more, to grill me about details or give me conditions that I'm not sure I can keep, but they don't. I consider telling them about my visit with Mom and about Eli dumping me and the various other ways my dirty little habit has screwed everything up, but I don't. Instead, I unwrap my Chompin' Chipotle and take a huge bite, because right now, all I want to do is eat lunch with my friends.

Chapter Thirty-One

MY PHONE RINGS THE NEXT DAY AS I'M WALKING through the rain to my car after work. I dig it out and check the screen, hope blooming in my chest. It disappears as quickly as it arrived when I see my sister's name.

"Hey, Rach."

"I know you don't want to talk about Mom," she says, diving right in as usual. "But she called me last night, upset. She wanted my advice."

I slow my pace, even though it's now pouring and my clothes are almost soaked through. Rachel hasn't mentioned our mother since the disastrous visit ten days ago. On the way back from Sutton, I told her everything Mom said, everything

I said, and exactly how fed up I was over the entire situation. Rachel wasn't exactly thrilled about Mom and Gary's engagement news either, and she even agreed that maybe going there was a mistake. So I'm not sure why she's telling me this now.

Still, I'm curious. "About what?" I ask as I finally reach my car. I unlock it and get in, shivering in the cool, dry air.

"About you," she says. "And what to do about you. She said you're ignoring her calls."

What to do about you. Like I'm some sort of problem to be resolved. And it's true—she's called me three times since I stormed out of her house, and I've ignored every call. I know if I answer, all I'll get is another earful of excuses.

"You're right," I say, dabbing at my dripping arms with a napkin. "I *don't* want to talk about Mom, and I also don't want the two of you plotting about me behind my back. Forget it, okay? Now can we talk about something else?"

She lets out a sigh. "Fine. I'm just saying, I don't think she's planning on backing off this time. She's pretty determined to talk things through with you and—"

"Rachel."

"—I've been thinking about it and maybe her and Gary getting married isn't the *worst* idea. I mean, we used to really like him when we were kids, and she obviously loves him if she agreed to—"

"Rachel."

322

"Okay, okay, sorry." She's silent for a moment, like she's trying to come up with a topic that won't set me off. "How's that cutie boyfriend of yours?"

Bad choice. I haven't had a chance to tell Rachel about the breakup. "Not my boyfriend anymore."

"What? Why?"

"Take a guess."

"Oh, Morgan," she says, and the sympathy in her voice makes my eyes well up. "He found out about the shoplifting? Was he really mad?"

I blink and focus on the windshield, following the networks of raindrops as they stream down the glass. "He told me he was done, and I can't really blame him. He also accused me of stealing something from his house."

Another pause. "Did you?"

"*No,*" I say a little too forcefully. But I can't blame her for asking any more than I can blame my friends and Eli for being suspicious. I've done bad things, so of course people are going to assume the worst of me until I manage to prove myself again.

"I believe you," Rachel says, and I know she means it. Lying to her is nearly impossible. She could always see through me, and vice versa, even over the phone. "And Eli will too, when he cools down and thinks about it."

I shake my head, even though she can't see me. "He'll

never trust me again, Rach. Neither will my friends. They might say they do, but deep down they'll always wonder if I'm being straight with them."

"It'll take some time, but keep working on them. Eventually, they'll stop wondering and start focusing on the amazing person you are outside of all this. You had a bad year, that's all. It happens. You'll find your way back."

"I hope so." I start the car and flick the wipers on full blast. "Listen, Rach, I gotta go. Can we talk more about this later?"

"Of course," she says. "I'll be here. Bye, Morgan."

"Bye, Rach. And thanks."

We hang up and I drive home slowly through the rain, feeling comforted by my sister's support. We're hundreds of miles away from each other, but in some ways, it's like we're still huddled on the couch, a few short inches between us as we share our secrets and lives.

I smell the smoke as soon as I step off the elevator, and somehow I know it's coming from our apartment.

Panic flares in my chest and I rush down the hall and push open the door. I'm greeted by a cloud of white smoke, the acrid smell of burning, and the blaring smoke alarm. Dad's in the kitchen, waving a dish towel toward the open window. Dirty dishes cover the counter, and there's a whole chicken sitting in a roasting pan on the stovetop, smoke still rising from its very crispy-looking skin.

Without saying anything, I grab the broom and use the tip of the handle to turn off the hallway smoke alarm. My ears ring in the sudden quiet. Poor Fergus must be hiding under my bed, but I don't have time to worry about him right now. I go back to my father, who's now glaring at the chicken like he wants to stab it with a steak knife.

"Dad, what the hell?" I cough and wave my hand in front of my face. I thought he was done with trying to cook. It's safer for everyone that he doesn't. Clearly.

"I got home early and thought I'd roast a chicken," he says, still scowling at the bird in question. "I must have turned the oven up too high, because grease splattered everywhere and then it started smoking. It got worse when I opened the oven door." He picks up the towel again and whips it around, but it does nothing to diffuse the murky layer of smoke. "I wanted us to sit down to a nice dinner together and finally have that talk, but I should've known better, I guess. Everything I touch these days turns to shit."

He tosses the towel on the counter, sending an empty can rolling into the sink. I gape at him, surprised. He rarely talks like that, so self-critical and defeated. And he certainly never throws things around.

Slowly, like I'm sneaking up on a ticking bomb, I move over to the stove and peer down at the chicken. It's overly crispy, for sure, but the juices on the bottom are running clear and the meat seems tender enough when I poke it.

"Let's carve this thing," I say.

Dad lets out a breath, and after a lengthy pause, he nods. I point to the chicken, indicating he should take care of it, while I drain and mash the potatoes. We work together silently, the range hood fan the only sound in the apartment. Well, that and Fergus's hungry meow. He's decided that leaving his hiding spot was worth a few scraps of chicken, which—surprisingly—turned out better than expected.

"I'm sorry," Dad says a few minutes later, when we're sitting at the table with our plates. "I had a bad day at work. A bad *month*, actually. My boss has been on me lately about my sales numbers, and business has been slower in general because of the damn construction that never stops on that street. And then the chicken . . ." He sighs deeply. "I guess it was the last straw."

I press my fork into my potatoes. "Dad, you know you don't have to cook for me."

"I know. It's just . . ." His fork drops to his plate with a loud *clank*, making me jump. "Damn it," he mumbles, turning his head to the side, facing away from me.

My heart stutters. His behavior is freaking me out. "Dad?"

"Sorry," he repeats. He turns back to me, his expression agonized. "It's just that I've been worried ever since you got back from your mother's. You don't want to talk to me, and you look at me like . . ." He shakes his head and leans back. "Anyway, Rachel told me what happened, what your mother said to you about me, and I thought . . . well, I was worried you might be thinking about leaving."

I have no clue what he's talking about. "Leaving?"

"Yeah," he says, blowing out another breath. "I thought after hearing about what a crappy husband I was to your mother, you'd decide to move out and go live with her and Gary. I mean, of course I'll support you if that's what you decide to do, but . . . well, I'd miss you around here."

I'm starting to think there's some kind of hallucinogen floating around with the smoke, because this conversation is far too bizarre to be real. "Why on earth would you think I'd want to live with Mom and Gary?" I ask, laughing at the absurdity of it. "I'd never do that, no matter how much Mom bad-mouths you. Besides, most of what she said probably isn't even true. She's just trying to paint herself as the victim."

"No." He rests his elbows on either side of his plate and rubs his hands over his face. "I'm sure it was all true. I wasn't a very good husband to her. I took her for granted. Didn't give her the attention she deserved. I shouldn't have let you place so much of the blame on your mother. It was my fault too. Jesus, I practically drove her into Gary's arms myself."

"Dad, come on." I don't want to hear him blame himself for their marriage ending. Okay, so it takes two, like Mom said, but she didn't have to dull her misery by cheating.

I put down my fork, my throat suddenly tight. *Isn't that what I did too, but with shoplifting? Am I really any better than her?*

Something Rachel said a while ago pops into my head: *She did an awful thing, but she's not an awful person.* Okay, so maybe she's right. Maybe Rita was right too, when she told me my bad decisions didn't define me. If I'm more than my mistakes, if I can learn from them and start fresh, then the same is true for everyone. Even my mother.

"I wouldn't blame you if you wanted to leave." Dad glances up at me, the creases around his mouth deepening as he frowns. "I wouldn't like it, but I'd understand. I mean, look at me. I can't even cook a goddamn chicken."

"I don't care about the goddamn chicken," I snap, shoving my plate away. "And I don't want to live with Mom. My life is here. My friends, my job, school, you . . . This is where I choose to be. Okay, so you weren't a good husband. I get it. I haven't exactly been a good daughter either, but you still want me around, right?"

Dad looks at me for a long moment, and I'm almost afraid he's about to say no, that I've made his life hell all summer and he *does* wish he could get rid of me for good. But then the worry lines in his face disappear and his lips form the barest hint of a smile. "Yeah, I still want you around. You and Garfield over there." He gestures with his chin to Fergus, who's sitting a few feet away, his huge green eyes taking in our every move. "I'll always want you around."

"Good. Then it's settled." I pull my plate toward me again

and spear a piece of chicken. "Nobody's perfect, and I'm not going anywhere."

Dad nods and picks up his fork again, his shoulders finally loosening. Even with the leftover smoke still hovering, the air between us feels clearer than it's been in a while.

Chapter Thirty-Two

IT'S FRIDAY AFTERNOON, AND I'M SITTING IN MY parked car outside Karalis Custom Jewelry, trying to work up the nerve to go inside and face Alyssa. Out of everyone, it's her forgiveness I crave the most, and not just because I miss her. She's my best friend, and she deserves the same honesty that she's always given me.

I glance at the store's sign, simple and familiar, and breathe in deep through my nose. I can do this.

My fingers find the door handle, and just as I'm about to pull, a face appears in the half-open window and scares the hell out of me.

"Morgan?" Alyssa's brows shoot up as she looks in at me,

sitting there with my hand pressed over my heart. "What are you doing?"

I press the button to lower the window, then realize the car isn't running. I open the door and step out onto the sidewalk instead, stopping in front of Alyssa. Her dark hair is smoothed back from her face in a ponytail, and she's carrying three white paper bags.

"Um," I say, my bravado fading now that I'm face-to-face with her. She's not smiling, and she's got this wary look in her eyes, like she's waiting for me to spring another shocking revelation on her. "I came to talk to you. What—what are you doing?"

She holds up the bags, which give off a subtle spicy scent. "I was getting lunch. Why are you here? I mean, why come talk to me while I'm working instead of, I don't know, some other time?"

I look past her to the store. "Because you're always here, Lyss."

She watches me for a moment, quiet and serious. I don't look away. Finally, her expression softens a bit and she sighs. "Fine. Since you're here, you may as well come in."

Her tone isn't exactly welcoming, but I gratefully follow her into the store. Nothing has changed since I was last in here. The cluttered display cases still gleam with gold and silver and gemstones. The oil paintings of Greek landscapes and architecture still hang on the walls. Mrs. Karalis still stands behind the counter, a pen tucked behind her ear. She smiles when she sees me.

"Morgan," she says, and I know just by the way she says my name that Alyssa hasn't told her about me. "Long time no see."

Alyssa hands her one of the white bags and brings the other one back to Louis, the guy who does the custom work and engraving. Mr. Karalis's job until he died.

Being in here makes me think of him. Alyssa and I used to spend quite a bit of time here when we were younger, and Mr. Karalis would put us to work dusting or wiping fingerprint smudges off the glass cases. Sometimes he let us make displays. We'd carefully arrange rings or watches or necklaces, maybe trying a piece on when no one was looking.

"I'll be right back, Ma." Alyssa puts her own bag of lunch on the counter and heads for the door, gesturing for me to follow. We step out onto the hot sidewalk, then wordlessly decide to turn left, away from the loud construction at the other end the street.

We're both quiet for a couple of blocks. I came here to talk, but everything I think of to say sounds inadequate in my head. Finally, I just start at the beginning. "A few days after my mother moved out, I stole a lip gloss from Walmart. That was the first time. I was so angry, but I wanted to keep it together for my dad, so I tried to hold a lot of it in. But I had to find a release somehow, and I just thought . . . God, I don't even know how to explain it. I'd been so *good* all my life. Quiet, well behaved, straight As . . . I thought doing something bad would make me feel like I was getting back at her somehow, even if she never found out. It made me feel *better*, like I had control over myself again. I know it was stupid, and selfish, but shoplifting was the only thing that kept me from sinking." I shake my head. "I know it probably doesn't make any sense to you."

We reach the edge of the street and stop, waiting for the *walk* signal. "No, it does," she says. "Surprisingly."

I glance at her. Sunglasses cover her eyes, but the frown she's had since I first showed up here is starting to fade. "Really?"

"Really." The walk light blinks on, and we cross the narrow street. "I just wish you would've told me, Morgan. Friends aren't supposed to keep huge secrets from each other. It really hurt that you didn't trust me enough to tell me what you were going through. If you'd been honest from the start, I wouldn't have gotten so mad. None of us would have. We would've stood by you and helped you through it."

I nod. "Sophie said the same thing. I guess I should've given you guys more credit. It's just you're all so . . . I don't know. *Decent*. And I didn't feel like I measured up. I thought you guys would look at me differently if you knew."

"Well, we do," she says in her usual blunt way. "But that doesn't mean we've given up on you. I know I haven't. Even after all this, you're still the best friend I've ever had."

Tears spring to my eyes and I squint, pretending to be

bothered by the sun. But Alyssa notices and reaches for my hand, squeezing for a second before letting go. My eyes well up even more. I had no idea how much I needed to hear what she just said.

"I've been reading a bit about shoplifting," she says, leading us around a corner to a shady section of sidewalk. "It's like an addiction. You know when alcoholics are in recovery and they have a sponsor to help keep them on track? Well, maybe I could be that for you."

I slow my pace and raise my eyebrows at her. "You want to be my shoplifting sponsor?"

She shrugs. "Sure."

"So if I'm in a store and I get the urge, I'll call you instead?" The idea seems so bizarre that it makes me laugh. "I think that's the nicest—and strangest—offer I've ever received."

"What are friends for?"

We smile at each other, and all the anxiety and dread I felt on the drive here melts away. "I really am sorry, Lyss."

"I know." We turn another corner and start heading back to her mom's store. "Just do me a favor and don't ever lie to me or keep things from me again, okay?"

"Deal."

She nods and lets out a relieved breath, like she's accomplished something difficult and can finally move on. "We're all meeting at the diner on Sunday so we can mourn the end of summer, if you wanted to come. Six o'clock."

I don't think I've ever wanted anything more. "I'll be there."

On the short walk back, Alyssa updates me on everything I missed since we stopped speaking, including another fraught social media tutorial with her mother and her tentative reconnection with Dawson, who she's been texting again. He hasn't mentioned it to me, and I'm glad to hear it. Maybe senior year won't be so awkward after all.

When she's done filling me in, it's my turn. I spill everything—the visit with Mom, the confrontation with Eli, the therapy I'm due to start in two weeks. With each chunk of truth, I feel myself getting lighter. And sadder too, when I think about how much time I spent shouldering the weight of secrets when I could have shared the burden all along, if only I'd been brave enough.

By the time we've finished talking, we're back at the jewelry store. Just as Alyssa pushes open the door, I glance down the street and notice a woman standing by my car. Her back is to us, and at first I think she's trying to break into it. I start walking toward her, my brain scrambling for the correct way to confront a car thief in action and wondering if this is some sort of karma. Then, just as I close in on her, the woman turns her head and I catch a glimpse of her profile.

"Mom?"

She spins around, her expression lightening with relief when she sees me. "Oh, there you are."

I stare at her. My mind can't accept the sight of her here, on this street, standing between me and my car. "What are you doing here? And how did you know where I'd be?"

Alyssa approaches before she can answer. She stops beside me and touches my arm. "You okay?" she mumbles. When I nod, she turns to my mother and says, "Hi, Mrs. Kemper." Then she winces, remembering she's no longer a Mrs. And once the divorce is final and she marries Gary, she'll no longer be a Kemper either.

"Hello, Alyssa," Mom says, ignoring the slip. "How are you? And how's your mother?"

"We're both fine, thanks." She catches my eye and starts backing away. "Well, I should probably go eat my sandwich while it's still fresh. Talk to you later, Morgan." She gives my mother a stilted wave and disappears into the store.

"I won't keep you long," Mom says when I turn back to her.

"How did you know where to find me?" I ask again. Does she have a spy? A tracking device in my phone?

"I didn't." She tucks her hair behind her ear. "I went by your apartment building first and no one answered. Rachel told me a while ago that you worked at Royal Smoothie, so I was heading there when I turned onto this street and spotted my car."

My car, I think, but I don't correct her.

"Anyway," she goes on. "I thought I'd wait here until you got back."

A woman passing by accidentally bumps me with her purse. Realizing I'm blocking foot traffic, I move closer to my mother. She looks better than she did the last time I saw her. Well rested and somehow stronger, like she's better equipped to face me this time. I realize with a shock that I am too. The last time we spoke, I started off nervous and then progressed into enormously pissed. Now I'm just confused and vaguely numb.

"Why are you here?" I ask her.

"I wanted to talk to you, and you wouldn't answer my calls or texts. So here I am." She fans her face with her hand. "Do you think we could find a place with air-conditioning? It's hot as Hades out here."

I don't want to have this discussion—whatever it's about— in a public place, so I motion toward my car. We get in, and I immediately start the engine, trying to ignore the fresh waft of vanilla filling the air and mixing with the faded scent from before.

"Car still runs well?" she asks over the noise of the vents, which are working overtime to crank out cool air.

"You didn't drive an hour and a half to ask me about the car."

She looks at me for a moment, then drops her gaze to her

lap. "You're right. I didn't. I came here to say some things, and I need you to let me say them without interruption. Okay?"

I lift my hand in a *go ahead* motion. She can talk all she wants; it doesn't mean I have to listen.

She takes a deep breath and nervously adjusts her vent, pointing it toward her face. "I meant it when I said I was done giving you space. That was my first mistake, I think. No, my first mistake was cheating on your father, obviously, but I shouldn't have let you avoid me for so long. I should've made more of an effort to reach you. I shouldn't have given up when you kept shutting me down. I handled things poorly, and I apologize for that. I apologize for everything. There's no excuse."

Her words seep in despite my resolve to let them skim over me. She's never said these things to me before. Never expressed regret over the affair and our fractured relationship. I'm not sure how to feel.

"The shoplifting thing threw me for a loop," she goes on. "It seemed so unlike you. I knew my actions affected you, but I'll admit I didn't realize how much. To think your anger at me drove you to be the kind of person who would—" She clamps her lips shut, probably realizing she has no room to judge. "Anyway. I'm sure I threw you and Rachel for a loop too. I was selfish, Morgan. I—"

Her voice breaks and she presses a hand to her mouth, like I've seen her do so many times when she was trying not to cry in front of us. Something in me unravels, just a tiny bit. It always hurt me to see her cry, and I'm not immune to it now. Still, I'm not ready to touch her or give her words of comfort. Or maybe I've just forgotten how. Either way, I keep silent and wait for her to collect herself.

"I know I'm not the person you thought I was," she pushes on, her voice thick with tears. "I hurt you and disappointed you, and you have every right to be upset with me. But you're my daughter, Morgan, and we've already wasted so much time. I want to watch you graduate from high school and go to college and grow into an amazing woman. You said I'm not the same mother who raised you, and I can accept that. Maybe I'm different now, but I'm still your mother. I still love you more than anything in the world."

A tear rolls down my cheek and I quickly swipe it away. I want all those things too. I want a mother who's there for milestones and occasions and for no special reason at all. I want to see her in the audience, her face lit up with pride. More than anything, though, I want the mother I thought she was before all this.

"I'm asking for a chance," she says, resting her fingers on my forearm. Somehow I don't flinch away. "We can start slow, if you want. A phone call once in a while. Even texts, if that's easier for you. I know it'll take time. But we just have to start, okay? Baby steps."

A bus passes by, shaking the car. I think about Alyssa,

accepting my apology when she realized I was ready to change, to be better. I think about Rachel, and how easy it seemed for her to forgive. But it probably wasn't easy at all. It takes courage, opening your heart to someone who hurt you once and might do it again. The kind of courage I'm still not sure exists in me. But I can't expect people to forgive my mistakes if I'm not open to forgiving others for theirs.

"Okay," I say softly.

"What?"

I clear my throat and speak louder. "Okay. Baby steps."

She smiles, her eyes still glassy with tears. Then, without another word, she lets go of my arm and leaves the car.

Chapter Thirty-Three

MY EYES POP OPEN AT SEVEN THIRTY THE NEXT morning out of habit, even though I barely slept all night. Seeing my mother evoked a mess of conflicting emotions in me, and my brain wouldn't shut up long enough to let me sleep. Normally, when I feel overwhelmed like this, I deal with it by stealing or, lately, by organizing. But since I don't steal anymore, and I've already organized the entire apartment, I don't know what else to do besides lie here and wait for it to pass.

In the meantime, I check my phone. Nothing. My heart sinks, even though I should be used to it by now. It's been a week since I've seen or spoken to Eli, and missing him is a persistent ache that doesn't fade. It's worse than usual this morning, probably because this is the first Saturday since June that I don't have to go to Rita's Reruns. I thought I'd feel relieved to be done with my community service, to have the slate wiped clean, but it doesn't feel that way at all.

Nothing will erase what I've done. The effects of my bad decisions are everywhere. In the lines on my father's face. In my friends' eyes as they look at me. In the silence coming from my phone. When I think about shoplifting now, I don't see it as an escape from the hostility that eats at me. Not anymore. Now I see it for what it is. Now, when I think of everything I've lost because of it, how much it's destroyed, a different kind of anger burns through me. The determined, all-consuming kind that won't let up until I figure out a way to somehow make it right.

An idea breaks though the flurry of thoughts in my head. I jump out of bed and go the kitchen. Fergus watches me from his perch on top of the fridge as I grab a garbage bag out of the box in the cupboard, then bring it back to my room. I start in my closet, pulling out tops and belts and shoes, stuffing each item—even the things that still have price tags attached—into the trash bag. Then I go through the rest of my room, grabbing clothes and books and trinkets, until the garbage bag is almost full and the fire in my stomach has dampened to a flickering ember. Satisfied, I close the bag with a tight knot and drop it on my floor.

Inside is everything I've ever stolen. All the things I thought I couldn't live without. Unopened makeup. Jewelry. The striped bikini with the turquoise beads, meant for Jasmine Tully's pool party but never worn. Even that damn penguin statue is in there, buried among the clothes.

None of these things are really mine, so they shouldn't be in my room. But since I obviously can't return anything to the stores, and I refuse to throw away perfectly good things, there's only one place left for them to go.

I knew, seeing as it's Saturday morning, that Eli would probably be around. But I wasn't expecting him to be the first thing I see when I pull up to the thrift shop an hour later.

He's kneeling in front of the garden, like I've seen him do countless times over the summer. The marigolds are brighter than ever, thriving under the late-summer sunshine and Eli's meticulous care. I remember how distracting they were when I drove in here for the first time, so distracting that I accidentally ran over a box of breakables with my car. Today, though, I barely see anything but Eli.

At the sound of my car, he glances over his shoulder in my direction. We lock eyes, and he straightens up, his arms falling to his sides. He's wearing his dark gray T-shirt with the rip in the neck, the same one he wore the first time we kissed. My breath hitches in my throat. Everything in me wants to jump

343

out of my car and run to him, but the rigid set of his jaw warns me against it. I slowly get out of the car and walk toward him instead.

"Hey," I say, stopping at the edge of the garden.

He looks at me for a moment, his expression guarded, then turns back to the marigolds and continues to dig out the weeds sprouting up from the soil. "Hey," he replies after a long pause.

His voice is toneless, empty, not at all like I'm used to hearing from him. Shame washes over me again, hot and swift. I did this. I made him sound that way. I put that wariness in his eyes. It's my fault, and only I can make it go away.

Hesitantly, I move closer and kneel down beside him on the warm grass. He keeps on weeding like I'm not there. I watch him for a minute as he loosens each weed at the root before yanking it free, then I copy his movements on the one closest to me. The scents of flowers and fresh dirt fill my nostrils, and surprisingly, my anxiety starts to recede. Eli told me gardening was calming, and now I see what he means. There's something about the warmth of the sun on my back and the coolness of the soil between my fingers that makes me feel almost peaceful.

"I just want to say a few things," I tell him, my eyes on my hands. "And then I'll leave you alone if that's what you want. Okay?"

He raises his arm and rubs it across his forehead, his shoulders lifting slightly in a shrug. I decide to take that as a yes.

"I regret a lot of things," I begin haltingly. This is probably my only chance to do this, and I have to get it right. "I regret that I ever started stealing, of course. And not being open with my father and asking for help. I definitely regret keeping it a secret from everyone, and lying to my friends—and you—all summer. What I did was shitty, and I'd understand if you were done with me forever. But I hope you're not."

He's completely quiet beside me, but I don't want to look at him. I'm afraid that if I do, the sobs building in my chest will rise up and break free. And I can't cry now. Not until he hears every single word that I've been writing and rewriting in my head for the past week.

I swallow and keep going. "The one thing I *don't* regret is getting caught. Because if I hadn't gotten caught, I never would've ended up here, and I never would've met you."

His body goes still for a second, a weed gripped between his fingers, and I hold my breath. But then he rethinks whatever he was about to do or say and tosses the dead weed on the grass like it personally offended him.

"I know that doesn't cancel out what I did or make it okay," I say quickly, in case he thinks I'm trying to make excuses. "I'm just saying there are some things I'd never want to take back." I lay my hands on my lap, not caring that they're coated in dirt and I'm wearing white shorts. "I don't know what else to say, other than I'm sorry. And I still want to be with you, if you'd be willing to give me a second chance."

My mother's words from yesterday echo in my head. *I'm just asking for a chance.*

"One more thing," I say, turning to face him. He doesn't look at me, but it doesn't matter. I need to see his face when I say this next thing, so I can be sure he hears me and understands. "I didn't steal the ceramic pot from your house."

He stops what he's doing and leans back, wincing as his knee flexes with the movement. "I know."

They're the first words he's spoken since *hey*, so it takes me a moment to respond. "You know?"

"It wasn't stolen," he says, finally meeting my eyes. "It was broken. Meredith accidentally knocked it off the shelf weeks ago. She knew it was valuable, so she didn't want to admit she broke it, but she finally came clean the other day. So that's what happened to it. I apologize for falsely accusing you."

I shrug. "It was a logical conclusion, after the bomb I'd just dropped on you."

"Still." He shifts his weight and turns until he's seated on the grass, his legs stretched out in front of him. "I'm sorry. I shouldn't have been so quick to assume the worst. It's just, when you feel so sure about someone and then you find out they've been lying to you since the day you met them . . . it's a lot to take in."

"I know." I turn around and sit cross-legged beside him. "But not everything about me was a lie. Yes, there were things

I should've told you, but everything I felt for you was real. *Is* real," I correct, glancing over at him. He's gazing out into the parking lot, his brow furrowed, and I try to remember the last time he smiled at me. Probably the night he came over when Dad was gone, taking Rachel to the airport. The night I told him I loved him, and he told me he loved me too.

Maybe he hasn't stopped. Maybe there's still time to show him that the girl he thought I was is exactly the girl I'm hoping to become.

Or maybe not. He doesn't respond to what I've said. He doesn't even look at me. Clearly, he's not interested in working things out. Embarrassed, I stand up and start walking toward my car, hoping I can make it there before bursting into tears.

"Morgan."

I stop and turn around. Eli is standing a few feet away, a conflicted look on his face. He opens his mouth, then shuts it again.

"What?" I ask in a shaky voice. If he's about to tell me to screw off, I'm not sure I can take it.

"Where are you going?"

Without taking my eyes off his, I answer, "To get something out of my car."

He stuffs his hands in his pockets and looks away, like he's trying to decide something. After a few agonizingly long seconds, he looks at me again. "Do you need any help?"

Everything falls away, except for the two of us and the tiny spark of hope blooming inside me. Without even thinking about it, I nod. "Yes."

We walk to my car and I open the trunk, where I stowed my garbage bag full of stolen treasures. Eli lifts it out easily and swings it over his shoulder.

"What's in here?" he asks.

"Just some things I don't need anymore."

I walk with him to the donation bins and watch as he tosses the bag inside. Just knowing those things are in there, waiting to be sorted and tagged and put on display for someone else to find and take home, balances me more than stealing them ever did.

"Well, I'd better get back to weeding," Eli says. He brushes past me and starts walking away, then stops after a few steps and turns around. "Did you . . . want to help me?"

I smile. I can't help it. Helping him in the garden is such a small thing, but it feels like the start of something more. Baby steps.

"Maybe later," I tell him. "I have to do something first."

He nods and keeps walking, leaving me by the donation bins. Where we first met. I smile again at the memory as I push open the side door and step inside the thrift shop. Rita's behind the register, chattering away to a woman with a toddler on her hip. I hang back until the woman leaves, then walk up to the counter.

"Hey there, Morgan," Rita says when she sees me, like she was expecting me to show up all along. "What can I do for you this morning?"

"I was wondering if you still needed help."

She laughs and pushes her glasses up on her head. "Look around you, my dear. I *always* need help."

"Good," I say. "Because I'd like to volunteer."

Chapter Thirty-Four

ALL FOUR ES IN THE BEACON STREET DINER SIGN are working again. Alyssa and I make our way inside and immediately spot Sophie and Zach, sitting side by side in our usual booth by the kitchen.

"Hey," they say as we slide into the opposite seat. Sophie adds, "Didn't we say six? It's quarter after. The waitress keeps giving us the stink eye."

"Sorry," Alyssa says, glancing at me. "Morgan wanted to wait outside for a few minutes before coming in."

"Why?"

In response, I take out my phone and show them the text I sent Eli a few hours ago:

I'll be at the diner at six, if you wanted to drop by.

I'd planned to ask him in person yesterday, after I finished pricing another box of paperbacks for Rita. But when I got back outside, he wasn't at the garden anymore, and his Jeep was gone from the parking lot. I wasn't entirely sure how we'd left things, if I still had a shot or if he wanted to stay done with me after all, so I figured sending this text would give me my answer. But he never answered and, as of now, he's still nowhere to be seen.

"He'll show," Alyssa assures me.

Sophie nods in agreement, and Zach says, "Yeah. I mean, who'd want to miss all this?" He waves a hand to indicate the sticky booths and peeling wallpaper and the subtle yet persistent aroma of stale grease. I laugh, even though my heart aches. I really missed hanging out with my friends.

The door opens then, and the three of us look over. But it's just Dawson, unusually late. Or maybe I shouldn't say *just Dawson*, because there's a girl with him. A tall, pretty girl with short, blue-streaked hair and multiple piercings in each ear. She looks vaguely familiar, and then it hits me that I've seen her once or twice at Ace Burger. She works there too.

"Hey, guys," Dawson says, leading the girl to our table. "This is Peyton."

We all greet one another, and Alyssa moves over to Zach and Sophie's side of the booth to make room for the new girl.

I watch Alyssa's face as Dawson squeezes in next to Peyton, searching for signs of jealousy or regret, but there's nothing. She just looks happy. Maybe even a little relieved to see that he's moving on.

"Should we order?" Sophie asks, directing the question to all of us but looking at me.

I check my phone. It's six thirty and still no answer. Still no Eli. Maybe I need to consider moving on too, even though the thought of it kills me. But I've done all I can do. Said all I can say. What happens next is up to him.

"Sure," I say. "Let's order."

Sophie gets the waitress's attention. As she's heading over, order pad at the ready, the door swings open again, this time with a little too much force behind it. At the last second, a large hand shoots out and grabs the corner of the door just before it slams against the wall. My breath stops. There's only one person I know who makes entrances like that.

"Eli," I say as he steps inside and glances around. Our eyes meet and he smiles, setting off a million tiny explosions inside my stomach. *He showed up.*

"Sorry I'm late," he says when he reaches the booth. His eyes lock onto mine again. "My phone died earlier, so I just got your text about an hour ago."

Before I can answer, the waitress sidles up next to him and raises her eyebrows like she's wondering if he's going to leave or sit down.

"I think we're going to need a bigger table," Zach says, glancing around at the cramped quarters of our booth.

Everyone agrees and starts to file out of the booth, much to the waitress's annoyance. We find two four-person tables and push them together, making one big one. The chairs aren't as comfortable as the booth, but that's okay. I have Alyssa on one side of me and Eli on the other, and nothing can bother me tonight.

Everyone is talking and laughing and complaining about school starting tomorrow, but I'm having trouble following the different conversations. I'm almost entirely focused on Eli's presence beside me, and I think he feels the same. Our knees brush under the table and he looks at me, his eyes darkening like they do when he wants to kiss me. I hold his gaze, hoping my own eyes convey exactly how grateful I am that he's here, giving me the chance I asked for but wasn't sure I deserved. He must get what I'm trying to tell him, because he nods slightly and reaches for my hand.

As Eli's fingers close over mine, I start thinking that maybe it really is possible to turn pain and loss into something good. Because right now it feels like *he's* my something good, and all I have to do is hold on.

Acknowledgments

TRYING TO TURN A PETTY CRIMINAL INTO SOME-
one worth rooting for wasn't easy. Thank you to my editor,
Catherine Wallace, for helping me do just that. Again, your
sharp eye and insightful suggestions have transformed a messy
draft into something I'm proud to share with the world. Thank
you to the rest of the amazing HarperTeen team, namely Janet
Robbins Rosenberg and Renée Cafiero, for adding and delet-
ing all those dashes and commas and fixing my many grammar
mistakes (I'll get the *farther/further* thing one of these days),
Michelle Taormina and Marta Bevacqua for the gorgeous
cover, and everyone else who had a hand in this book.

Words cannot express how grateful I am to my extraordinary

agent, Eric Smith. Thank you for dropping everything to read the first draft so quickly, and for loving it so much that you couldn't think of anything to criticize. You continually go above and beyond, and I don't know where I'd be without your hard work and encouragement. I'm the luckiest author in the universe to have you on my team.

Speaking of teams, a million thanks to TeamRocks, for putting up with my venting, anxiety, and bad jokes. I love you guys in all your waterfall glory. Another big thanks to P.S. Literary, for the past six wonderful years.

As always, thank you to my Number #1 fan, Shannon Steele. I know that as long as I keep writing, you'll keep reading and then ask for more. Thank you to the rest of my fabulous friends, for the support, kindness, and countless hours of fun and laughter. I'm so fortunate to be surrounded by such a wonderful group of people.

Thank you to the amazing YA community, on Twitter and beyond. It helps to know that no matter where we all are in the publishing process, we're all walking the same long and twisty road. And a special thanks to YA bloggers, BookTubers, and bookstagramers, for their commitment to getting the word out and helping little authors like me succeed.

Thank you to my family, extended family, and in-law family. You guys make me feel like a rock star, and your pride in me means everything.

Thank you to my beautiful children. Though neither of

you are readers (how did that happen?), you understand how important books and writing are to me. Thank you for putting up with my crankiness—and all those frozen pizzas—as I pounded away on this book.

Lastly, thank you to my loving and patient husband. Writing this book was stressful and often felt impossible, but you were always there to assure me that it would all work out in the end. And you were right.